I0760593

THE HIDDEN WARRIOR

DRAGON REBELLION

M. LYNN

Dragon Rebellion © 2020 M. Lynn
Cover by Covers by Combs
Editing by Melissa A. Craven
Proofreading by Caitlin Haines

For the rebellious.
Change the world.

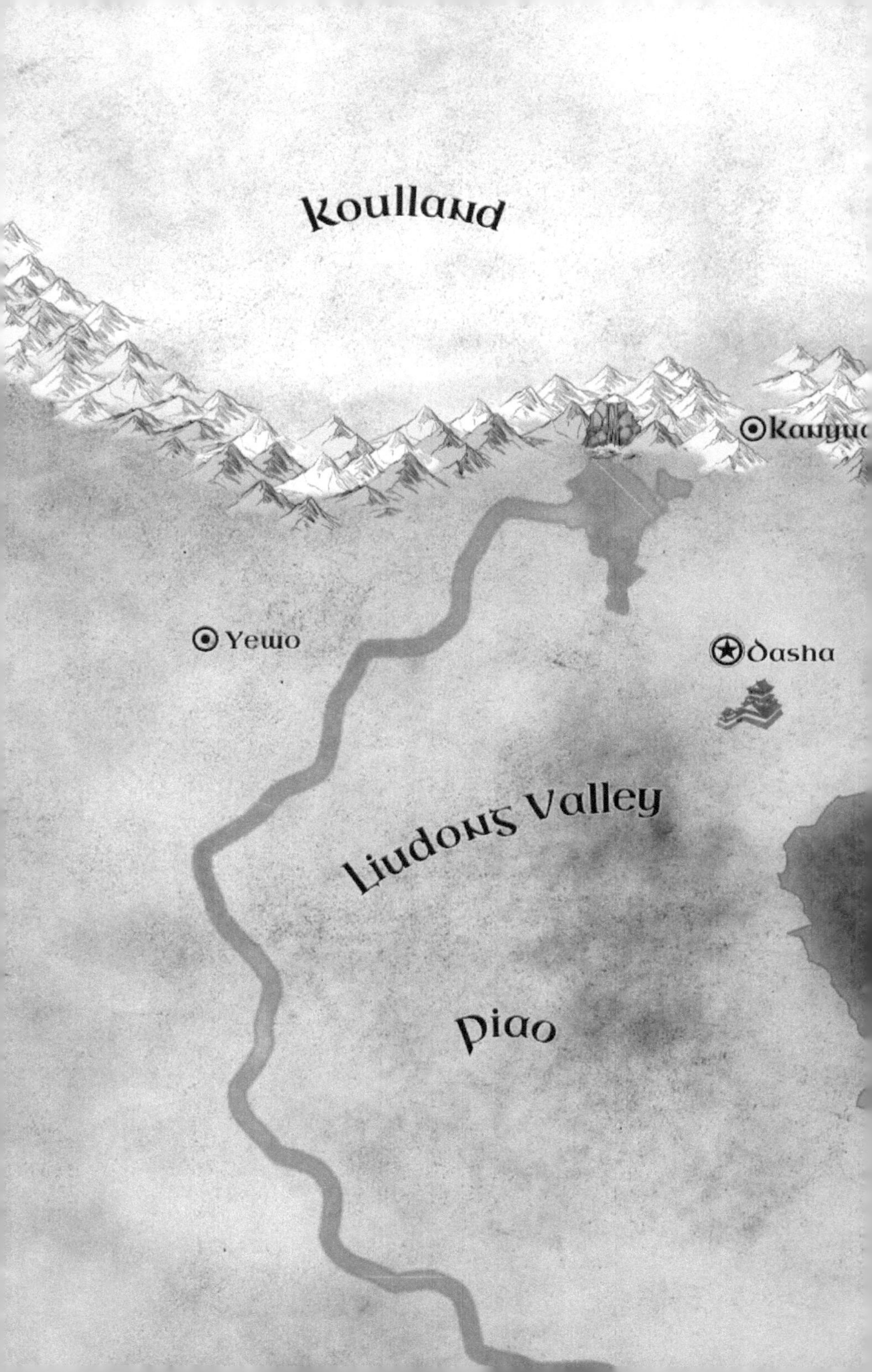

Koulland

Kanyu

Yewo

Dasha

Liudong Valley

Piao

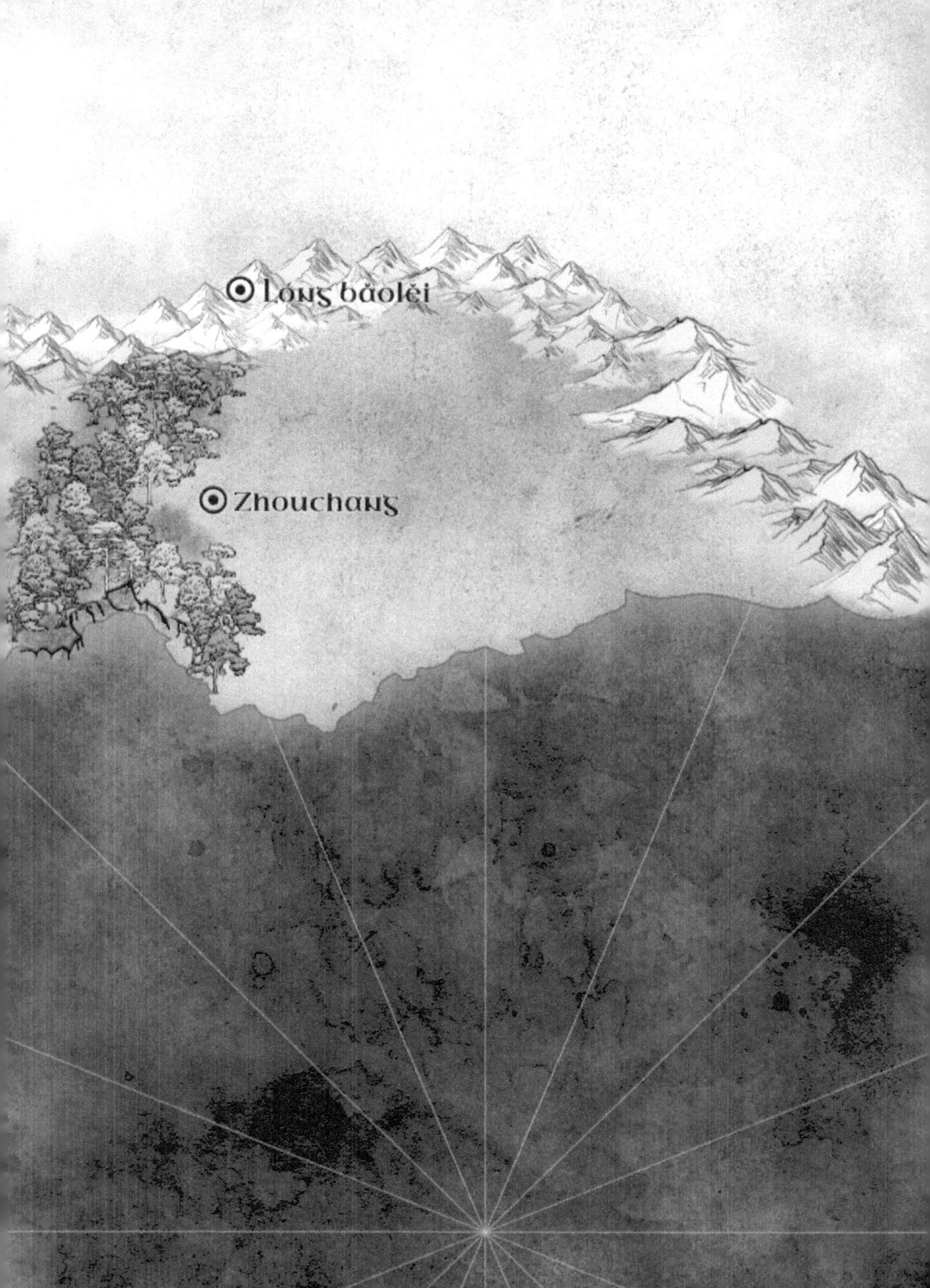
Lóng bǎolěi
Zhouchang

CHAPTER 1

Hua

Fire. Blood. Death.

Hua Minglan saw nothing else in her mind as her eyes twitched beneath closed lids.

A battle.

A town destroyed by a winged beast.

Her.

A scream tried to escape her throat, but it never made it past her lips as flames consumed her surroundings, lighting up the darkness and sending plumes of smoke stretching to the burnt sky.

Hua thrashed, wanting to break free of the dragon. Its hold over her tightened. The Nagi were supposed to be creatures of the past, those spoken of in hushed tones by the ones carrying their bloodline.

This wasn't real

Only it was. Hua shrank in on herself, the flames dancing in her dark eyes. For a moment, she wondered if it was the last thing she'd ever see.

For a moment, she wished it was.

CHAPTER 2

Jian

"Run!" Gen Minglan's word struck Jian Li with the full force of its meaning.

He dropped the shovel he'd been using to clear out the now-empty horse stall and leaped over the low wall of the gate.

The sound of horses coming up the dirt road reached him as Ru came running into the barn, his eyes wide.

"Soldiers are coming." Ru ran on short legs to the side door, thrusting it open and motioning for Jian.

There could only be one reason soldiers would come to a

small farm outside Zhouchang. They were looking for the dragon. Jian had to get back to the house, he had to protect her. Darting out the door, he didn't look back. He sprinted into the trees behind the barn. In the three weeks he'd been a guest of the Minglans, he'd learned every corner of their property.

The fields stretched far and wide with the woods separating their farm from the village. He stopped when he reached the tree cover and tried to get a view of the soldiers. They'd halted in front of the barn and dismounted to speak to Gen.

The Minglans thought Jian had brought their daughter back to them. He hadn't had the heart to tell them the truth of the battle of Kanyuan. News traveled slowly around Piao and hadn't yet reached the rural farms, giving him time to come to terms with the bloodshed and destruction wrought by a dragon he'd never imagined existed.

Weeks ago, he woke in a strange place surrounded by people he didn't know. And the girl he'd arrived with? She never opened her eyes.

As soon as the soldiers disappeared into the barn, Jian ran across the open ground between the woods and the small three-bedroom house belonging to Hua's family. He burst through the cracked wooden door and skidded to a halt, his chest heaving. He'd recovered from his injuries but was still regaining his stamina.

Fa Minglan appeared from one of the bedrooms at the back, her face drawn as it always was when she sat with her unconscious daughter. "What is it?"

He looked from Fa to Hua's grandmother—who insisted he called her Nainai as if she were his own. "Soldiers."

They mirrored each other's alarm. "They can't find her." Fa rushed back into her room where they'd kept Hua. Jian followed, taking in the pale face of the girl who once seemed the strongest among his men.

"We need to get her into the loft." Nainai moved to the other side of the bed.

Jian nodded. It was the only way. He slid his arms under Hua's limp frame, freezing when mumbled words pushed past her lips. Were the words hers or the dragons? He cradled her against his chest and hurried to the ladder. Shifting her body over his shoulder, he gripped the rail with his free hand and climbed slowly, careful not to smack Hua's head into the opening.

Once he made it through, he laid her down on the floor and looked through the opening at the two women and their tired expressions. It had been a hard few weeks for all of them.

"We'll call to you when the soldiers have left." Nainai attempted a smile.

Jian nodded and pulled the ladder up before swinging the door in the floor shut, closing them up from the world beyond the small loft.

He sat back on his heels and released a breath. With so little news coming from the front, they didn't know what the army knew of Hua. Jian wasn't even sure what he knew of her. Three weeks ago, she'd transformed before his eyes. A couple days before that, she'd turned from Huan to Hua in his mind. He hadn't had time to process everything. All he knew was he had to protect her, even if it meant shielding her from his own brother, the emperor.

Getting to his feet, he ducked his head to avoid hitting it

on the low ceiling. A bed took up the back half of the small room next to a window that let out onto a flat roof.

He bent to lift Hua and set her on the bed. Summer heat stifled the room, but he didn't dare open the window for fear of being seen.

Hua's lips parted, letting a moan pass them. Sweat dampened her brow, and Jian wiped sticky hair out of her face. If anyone told him she'd pretended to be a man, he'd never have believed it. But he saw Huan. He thought of him as just another soldier to get battle ready, one who tested Jian every step of the way.

He should have known she wasn't an ordinary man.

But it seemed she wasn't an ordinary woman either.

Footsteps echoed through the house, and the walls shook as voices sounded in the courtyard below, many voices belonging to people Jian didn't know.

Until one man spoke.

"Thank you for your hospitality, General Minglan." Jian would recognize that timbre anywhere. General Yu, the man who'd wish nothing more than to punish Jian for what he saw as his sins, his relationship to the emperor.

"My son," Gen said. "Huan Minglan. Do you bring news of him?"

It was all an act, of course. Jian looked down into Hua's serene face. Huan was just another side of her.

"I'm sorry, Gen. I have no news of the boy. The army is still regrouping after the fight. We do not have a full count of the living or the dead." He said it so matter-of-factly, that there were too many dead to count in such a short time. Jian sighed. What of his remaining men? What of Chen, Yan, and Zhao?

Or Luca. He'd tried so hard not to think of his friend or if he lived or died. It took every ounce of willpower not to find a messenger to send to one of the garrisons in search of him. There'd come a time when he would have to face those he'd left behind. What did they think of him now?

He shook those thoughts from his mind to focus on the voices below. "What brings you to Zhouchang, General?" Fa's voice was tight.

"That is a matter for the army, Taitai Minglan."

Jian shook his head. He'd only known the Minglans for a few short weeks, but he'd already learned Fa Minglan was not someone to be trifled with. She had more bite than her husband.

"Well, General, then the refreshments in this house are a matter for friends."

Jian's lips curved up at that. He'd give anything to see General Yu's response. Fa wasn't a warrior like her daughter, but she was definitely the source of Hua's stubbornness.

A beat of silence stretched out before General Yu responded. "Gen, handle your wife."

"My wife can handle herself." Jian pictured Gen straightening to his full height, his face stern. "Tell me why you and your men have come onto my land."

General Yu was the first to relent. "We're traveling from Zhouchang to Yewo in search of deserters."

"Deserters?" Gen dropped his voice.

"I forget how slowly news travels in the... countryside." He said the last word with a hint of distaste. "The imperial army has recovered Kanyuan."

Jian had already told them this, but he'd withheld just

how that battle unfolded. Only Hua's grandmother knew why she hadn't yet opened her eyes.

"I didn't realize the army lost Kanyuan." Gen was testing him, goading him.

"We didn't," General Yu snapped. "Jian Li was given command due to his relationship with the emperor. He lost the border village. The rest of us had to step in to recover it. The battle was bloody, and the town now lies in ruins. In the weeks since, men have deserted the army in droves, in search of safety from the Kou warriors."

Hua's grandmother spoke next. "The Kou… is that all they fear?"

"It doesn't matter what they fear," General Yu growled. "They pledged themselves to this war, and by running, have named themselves traitors. It is my duty to bring them to justice."

"So, you're hunting down boys?" Jian imagined disgust on Nainai's face. "Our home is not open to your kind, General."

"General Minglan, you would have one of the emperor's generals disrespected in your home? He signed the order to hunt deserters. It is an imperial decree."

Jian wanted to believe his brother would do no such thing, but he didn't know to what lengths Bo would go to end this war, especially if he knew a dragon had returned to Piao. Dragons represented a power the emperor could never hope to wield. It was why emperors of the past hunted all those descended from the last Nagi.

He brushed a finger over Hua's cheek. Not all families were destroyed by that hunt, some went into hiding and changed their family names.

The Minglans were not his family, they didn't belong to him, but Jian wanted to be here with them, he wanted to work the farm with Gen or sit at night playing games with Ru.

He wanted Chichi to run to him whenever he entered the yard.

He got so distracted by his own thoughts, he didn't hear Gen's response. Instead, the slamming of the front door jolted him back.

A knock sounded moments later on the door in the floor. Jian crouched down and pulled it open to look down into the worried eyes of Gen Minglan, a man whose history in the army was so storied even Jian heard about it while growing up in Dasha.

"They will not enter the house again." He rubbed his eyes. "But they're making camp on our land, so you two should stay up there until they're gone."

Jian nodded. "I agree."

Hua's grandmother appeared, the line between her brows deepening. "Don't use the lantern in the room." She slid a plate through the door toward him. "Your supper. Good-night, Jian. Thank you for taking care of our Hua."

He shut the door and looked back over his shoulder to Hua. When they'd first arrived, her family thought it was important to try to force sustenance into her, massaging her throat until she swallowed. As time went on, she didn't seem to need it. He didn't understand, but there was so much about her that confused him.

The biggest question he had was had she known? Was that why she left her family to pose as a man and join the fight?

Or was she just as much a victim in this as the children of Kanyuan?

He settled back onto the bed beside her and put the plate on the tiny table near the window. Focusing on the full moon hanging in the starry sky, he thought back on the night he'd sat with Hua atop a tower at Prince Dequan's fortress.

No, the girl who'd spoken with such honesty, the one who'd melted into his arms before pulling back, he couldn't believe she knew of the enemy within her.

But now that he did, what could he do? The beast inside her held a danger unlike any they'd ever seen. The girl, though, she only posed a danger to Jian, because he'd give up his life to keep her safe.

Sometime in the night, Jian woke to a crash down below. He jolted up in bed, shaking the frame. Hua's arm rolled off her chest and brushed his thigh, the contact shocking after a tense night of trying to keep his distance.

If only Luca could see him now. His friend would probably make some joke about Jian sharing a bed with Luca's betrothed, but the joke would only be a cover for the worry he felt. Hua Minglan walked constantly on the edge of shame. If anyone learned of her time as a soldier, or that she spent the night with Jian—conscious or not—it would change the way the world saw her.

It wasn't the first night Jian spent with her. For the past three weeks, he sat by her bed, sometimes sleeping right in the chair, as if leaving his vigil meant giving up on her.

He'd have given anything to see the stubborn eyes of the soldier he trained, the friend he'd reluctantly made.

Glass shattered somewhere in the house, and Jian jumped from the bed. He looked back over his shoulder, studying Hua for a moment as he listened for other sounds. It wasn't until he heard a child's cry that he slid the door open.

General Yu stood below with his men at his back. He held an arm around Ru's chest and a knife to his throat.

Gen and Fa pleaded with him to release their son.

More glass broke as a projectile flew through the front window, landing with a thud on the wooden floor before bursting into flames.

Hua's grandmother stumbled from her room, clutching her sleeping robes, her gray hair askew. "General, what is the meaning of this?"

Smoke curled through the room and still, the family stood frozen, their youngest child in the grips of Yu. Jian surveyed the room, noting the placement of each soldier. Jian's possessions were bundled in the corner of the sitting room near the pallet Fa had made up for him. His dao was tucked into a pile of clothing the Minglans had given him. The weapon was an old one of Gen's but still serviceable. The problem? It was across the room.

He scanned the loft for any kind of weapon, knowing the room belonged to Hua before she left for the war. The one thing he knew about her for sure was that she was a fighter. "What did you keep up here, Hua?" he whispered.

He dug his hand under the mattress, sighing in relief when he hit the cool steel of a small blade. It wasn't much, but it was better than he had before.

With a final glance at Hua, Jian drop through the door,

not bothering with the ladder. His feet hit the floor, and he twisted to face the soldiers, snapping his wrist as he did.

The knife sailed end over end, and it was like everyone in the room watched it, frozen in anticipation.

Ru screamed as the blade missed him, lodging into the arm of his attacker.

General Yu reared back, yanking the blade from his arm. Ru scurried away from him, collapsing into his mother's arms.

As smoke swirled around his feet, Jian pictured another time, another place. General Altan trapped him in a tent with Luca and the others. He'd been so sure he was going to die until a savior walked through the flames. Hua.

But she wasn't coming to save them this time. Now, they had to save her.

General Yu shouted orders to his men to capture Jian, but despite what some said, he'd earned the title of commander because he was the best.

Jian slammed his shoulder into one of the attackers, knocking him back. He didn't give the men a chance to explain why they'd barged into the Minglan home in the middle of the night, or why flames spread along the wooden floor.

They didn't need to tell Jian what he already knew. He took in the ragged clothing of the men. Only General Yu wore a uniform, but even he looked disheveled, so unlike the uptight general Jian had known.

These men weren't hunting deserters.

They were deserters.

The man pinned beneath Jian no longer moved so he

jumped to his feet and ran for another, yelling back over his shoulder. "Go. Get out of here."

Fa scooped up Ru and ran to the back door, but Gen and Nainai didn't follow. Gen jumped into the fight, using his cane as his only weapon.

Jian retrieved a dao from the man he'd knocked unconscious, feeling like himself for the first time since the dragon flew him away from Kanyuan. He'd never wanted to be a fighter but had no other choice in life. Now, it was all he was.

He coughed through the smoke and twisted, slicing the sharp edge of the dao through a thick-necked man. Gen fought alongside him, disarming his opponent with an unnatural skill and retrieving the weapon.

They were outnumbered, but that had never mattered to Jian. He'd survived the mountain battle despite the enormous odds against them. He was still standing after the Kou attacked his camp. And Kanyuan... he shouldn't have survived that one. But he had.

His eyes flashed as they met General Yu's.

"Jian Li," the general yelled, his entire body going rigid. "You're supposed to be dead." Shock colored his voice.

"And you're supposed to be pledged to the emperor."

Jian yanked his dao free of another man, letting him crumple to the ground before approaching the general. No, not general. He gave up that title the moment he walked away from the army. Just as Jian had.

Yu's lip curled and his eyes narrowed. "I should have known you fled after the battle. They all think you died a hero, but Jian Li is no hero."

"You're right." He stepped over a dead man. "I'm not a hero. I did not run, but I did not stay either."

Gen dispatched the last of Yu's men and joined Jian.

Yu held out his dao. "Go ahead. Try to kill me. I have nothing left."

Jian stepped closer as a cough wracked his body. His lungs cried out for air, but all they got was smoke. "These are good people, Yu. I should cut you down where you stand."

"Érzi." Gen put a hand on his arm. Jian froze at the term. Son. "Let him go. Sometimes mercy is the greatest strength."

It was something Bo would have said. Still, Jian's grip on his dao tightened.

"The entire house is going to go up in flames." Yu looked from Jian to Gen. "Do you have time to fight me?"

The house… Hua.

Yu walked backward toward the door, and Jian didn't follow. He couldn't. Not with the house burning around him.

"Jian!" Gen gripped his shoulder. "Get to Hua."

Fear ripped through him. He'd left her in the loft while smoke rose toward the ceiling.

There was no time for vendettas, not anymore. He ran to the ladder and climbed the rungs, covering his mouth with his arm as he pulled himself into the loft. A thick blanket of smoke cloaked the room, hiding Hua from view.

He stumbled across the room, his shins slamming into the table next to the bed as his legs weakened. His lungs begged for air, but there was none to be found. As darkness crept along the edges of his vision, he saw her. Hua's pale skin shone, a glow emanating from the inside out.

His knees hit the wooden floor next to the bed, and as his head lolled forward onto the feather mattress, her eyes snapped open.

CHAPTER 3

Hua

Fire had a smell. Smoke and ashes. Burned bodies that could have passed for cooking meat over the stove.

The scent invaded Hua's every pore, sinking into her.

Fire had a feel. Heat and peeling skin.

It slithered along Hua's arms, hitting her every nerve ending until her body buzzed with the energy.

Destroy.

The dragon's voice thundered through her mind, reveling in the destruction fire caused. She'd never heard it as clearly as she had while she was asleep.

Avenge.

Avenge what?

She inhaled, her body reveling in the smoke filling her lungs. A smile curved her lips, one that was not her own, one that yearned to see the flames. Hua tried to claw her way to the front of her mind, but she slammed into a wall time and time again.

She'd spent weeks fighting this very battle, preventing the beast inside her from opening its eyes—her eyes. If she couldn't gain control, she didn't want the Nagi to have control either.

But the smoke breathed new life into the dragon, infusing her with a strength she hadn't yet encountered.

Hua shrank further into the back of her mind until she hardly felt anything at all.

When the dragon opened her eyes, there was nothing more she could do to stop it.

Hua Minglan had lost her final battle.

CHAPTER 4

The Nagi

A Nagi had no name pronounceable to humans, nothing to speak of who they were. Instead, they took on the identity of those they possessed. The curious female's hold on the Nagi lessened until she forced her eyes open.

The Nagi became Hua Minglan. Her eyes searched the room, seeing through the smoke to the door in the floor.

A man's voice yelled up to her, calling for someone else. The Nagi sat up, gazing down at the unconscious man and searching Hua's mind for a name. Jian. The army commander she'd wanted to save in the battle. It seemed he'd have been dead many times over if it wasn't for her.

She sighed. It wasn't the Nagi's nature to save men she should want to kill, but she owed it to Hua if they were to share the same body.

Crawling from the bed, she pulled Jian's body over her shoulder and stood, his weight nothing to the strength coursing through her veins. The Nagi descended the ladder, wishing she could transform and use her wings to travel instead. But if she were truly going to take her revenge on the people of Piao, she must become one of them, not the dragon they feared. At least, that was what she told herself when she tried to shift into a dragon and failed.

Down below, flames covered every surface and an older man gripped the wall as he tried to stay on his feet. Relief washed over his face once he saw them, and he stumbled forward.

"We need to get out of here. Let me take Jian." The Nagi didn't protest as the man she remembered as Hua's father took Jian from her shoulders and started dragging him toward the door.

A gray-haired woman ran to the Nagi. She gripped Hua's shoulders—the Nagi's shoulders—and warmth spread through her, coming from the girl trapped inside. "Come." She pulled on Hua's arm, but the Nagi yanked it back and pushed Hua's nainai away.

Turning to the flames licking up the wall, she reached out, needing to touch them, to feel their energy. The Nagi called to the dancing fire as her hand disappeared into the glow. It snaked up her arm, infusing its power into her.

"Hua!" Nainai screamed. "We have to go."

The Nagi curled her fingers into her palm and stared at the unblemished skin. With one final glance at the flames, she followed Nainai into the sitting room where charred bodies were scattered along the floor. A battle took place here. The Nagi cocked her head. Interesting.

The metallic scent of blood mixed with the smoke, making the Nagi feel at home.

But it couldn't last because they had to leave it behind. Destroying Piao and Koulland was more important than the draw of the flames. It was why she had returned generations after the Nagi disappeared from the empire.

Out in the yard, Hua's family huddled together. Her mother held Ru close to her chest and her father's arms wound around them both. Jian knelt beside them, his body wracked with coughs. Nainai's arm wrapped around the Nagi.

"We're all okay. We're alive."

The Nagi only nodded as she turned back to look at the flames engulfing the Minglans' home. A tinge of sadness entered her mind, a leftover feeling from the girl who once owned this body.

"Hua." Jian lifted his face to her. "You saved me. Again."

Pride filled her, and she lifted her chin, her voice coming out smooth and calm. "Yes, I did. You seem to need that quite a lot." She turned away, having no time for the weak.

"Dear girl." Nainai cupped her cheek. "It is good to see those eyes again."

She pushed the hand away as Ru ran to her. "You're awake. I didn't think they'd ever get you out of there."

"They didn't get me out." The Nagi scrunched her brow. "I got myself out." Without another word, she walked away from them to avoid the tears pricking her eyes for the first time in her life.

"Stop trying to make me feel guilty, girl." She pressed a palm to the side of her head as foreign feelings of sadness swirled inside her. "This body doesn't belong to you anymore."

Pain pounded at the Nagi's temples, a fist hammering against the walls of her mind. "None of this is yours."

The girl's words broke through the Nagi's thoughts. *"If you hurt them, I will kill you."*

The Nagi growled. "I'd be careful if I were you. Your family is now at my mercy." She slammed the wall back in place, cutting off her response.

The smoke from the burning house obscured the stars above, but staring at the heavens was a fanciful pursuit. Nagi had no use for such practices, not when there were wrongs to right.

She didn't take her eyes from the flames as she stood apart from her host's family, her family for the time being. Even if she wasn't the true Hua, the Minglans were Nagi descendants, and that made them her people.

The people she had come to avenge.

Once upon a time Nagi protected Piao from their enemies, but that was before cruel rulers hunted their descendants, destroying any chance of their return.

The emperor of Piao considered the Kou his greatest enemy.

He was wrong.

Ru's little legs sprinted across the lawn. "Hua, it's all gone, they destroyed everything."

Without understanding her actions, the Nagi kneeled in

the dry grass and pulled Hua's brother into her arms. "We're going to be okay, Ru. I'll make sure of it." The Nagi didn't need to wonder where that promise had come from. She would have to fight off Hua's inane sympathies.

A sob shook his body. "I didn't think you'd ever return to us, and when you did, I didn't think you'd wake."

The rest of the family joined them, forming a morose circle around them. Everything they had was gone, leaving them with only each other to hang on to.

The Nagi released Ru and stood. "How long have I been here?"

"Three weeks," Jian answered.

Three weeks. She stared at him, not sure what to make of it. She had battled Hua for control for twenty-one days after succeeding in the first step of her revenge. Destroying Kanyuan, a border town essential to both the Piao people and the Kou.

All she'd had to do was light the match, and the people of Piao would burn their own country down.

"Who were they?" Hua's mama asked.

"Deserters." Her husband snorted in disgust. "On the run from the army."

She sniffled. "We can't stay here."

He nodded. "The barn. At least for tonight. We will figure something else out in the morning." His voice held no emotion, only resignation. Gen Minglan sounded like a broken man as he looked toward their house with smoke spiraling toward the sky.

Jian wiped soot and blood from his face as he turned and led the way across the expansive sea of grass and up the dark hill. Exhaustion weighed them all down, but the Nagi felt more energy than she had in a long time.

They reached the barn and Hua's father stopped. "Hua, my girl." He choked back emotion. "You've returned to us." He pulled the Nagi into a hug, and she let him because of the girl inside her begging for his comfort.

No matter what, she couldn't reveal what she was, that she had stolen their daughter from them, their sister and granddaughter, but something inside the Nagi couldn't fathom hurting this family. Something pulled at the back of her mind making her feel uncomfortable things for them. Warmth? Worry?

She pushed that away and entered the barn, taking note of the hay bales along one wall and the empty horse stall as she tried to recall the horse's name who should be there… Heima. Lost to the battle of Kanyuan.

It was better that way. There was only room for one beast in this barn. Barking sounded at the door before a large dog barreled toward her, knocking her to the ground. It pinned the Nagi down and pulled its lips back into a snarl.

"Chichi," Ru chastised. "It's Hua. Let her go."

The dog didn't back down as he snapped his teeth.

Enough of this. The Nagi pushed the dog from her, sending it slamming into the wall of the stall. Chichi whimpered as he got to his feet and hid behind Ru.

The rest of the family only stared as the Nagi lifted a heavy hay bale to pull it to the ground. She ripped into it, ignoring the looks, as she spread the hay before lowering herself onto it and curling onto her side.

The strength from the fire seeped out of the Nagi as she drifted back into the world of dreams where she would once again face off against the girl in her mind, knowing one thing.

The Nagi had to win. Every night as she fought for control, she kept her mission in the forefront of her mind.

And if the real Hua knew the Nagi's mission, she might even understand.

Chapter 5

Jian

Sleep was hard to come by in the barn that night. Jian's body ached from the fight, and pain wound through him with every breath he took, every cough. He almost hadn't made it out.

It seemed he was destined to die in flames.

He sat with his knees bent and his back pressed against the door of the stall he'd cleaned out hours before—in what seemed like another life. For the Minglans, there would forever be two parts to their lives. Before they lost everything and after.

Few of their belongings were stored in the barn. Old armor hung along the back wall with a couple of rusted daos and halberds. Horse tack draped over the stall wall, a hook holding it in place. Bales of hay took up half the limited floor space, placed there to keep them out of the elements.

Tilting his head back, he rested it against the cracked wood. He needed water, they all did, but the pump for the well was on the other side of the house, and he had no more energy in his bones.

How could Hua fall back asleep so easily? She'd been awake for less than an hour, only long enough to save him from the flames that would never leave him. No matter the enemy—General Altan, General Yu, the dragon—they all doused him in smoke and flame.

When would it ever end?

He'd joined the army during a time of peace, when all there was for a soldier to do was train or accept missions into foreign lands. When the war began, he jumped into it, ready to make a difference.

But now… now he wasn't sure what they were fighting. An enemy within Piao could do as much damage as the one across the border.

Hua's nainai slid down to sit beside him. "I envy that girl, able to turn her mind off on a night like this."

Jian nodded in agreement. He'd give anything to forget cutting his way through Yu's scared men. They'd barely put up a fight. They weren't warriors, only men who feared what they'd seen in Kanyuan. The truth was, Jian couldn't fault them for running after that, for leaving the army behind.

He studied Hua's sleeping form, noticing how restless she

appeared, so different from the three weeks she'd been unconscious.

"Hua is back." He whispered the words to himself, but her nainai's lips tipped up.

"Our girl has returned to us."

Maybe it was the shock of waking in the middle of the fire or seeing her childhood home crumble to the ground, but Hua hadn't fallen into her parents' arms. She hadn't offered them any part of her. Jian couldn't imagine what it was like for Gen and Fa after their last remaining daughter left to fight. They deserved some kind of reunion. Instead, what they got were ashes and pain.

As if reading his mind, Nainai rested a hand on his arm. "This family is strong, Jian."

He blew out a breath before sucking in another and half expected it to be filled with smoke. The fresh air was a balm to the rawness of his lungs. He didn't even mind the musty smell of the barn.

A soft patter sounded from outside. Jian got to his feet and walked to where Gen stood at the doorway looking toward their still smoldering house.

"The rain will put out the flames." Gen's voice sounded distant.

"Any sign of Yu?" Jian rested his arm on the door frame.

Gen shook his head. "He's long gone by now. A horse ran across the fields a bit ago, probably belonging to one of the men we..."

He didn't finish his sentence. He didn't need to. Jian had killed a lot of men in his life, but it never hurt any less.

"No sign of the rest of them?"

Gen sighed. "No. But those were quality beasts. If some of

them got loose and they're roaming the village, people will ask questions." He rubbed his eyes. "This farm has been part of Zhouchang for many years."

"Gen, your home is gone, but you still have your land. You can rebuild."

He looked like he wanted to disagree but stayed quiet, his eyes once again focusing on the pounding rain turning the dirt outside the barn to mud.

Chichi's yip had Jian turning. The dog stood near Hua, a growl rumbling in his throat. She didn't stir.

"Chichi," Ru called. "No. It's Hua. We love her."

The dog didn't listen. Nainai scooted toward Chichi on her knees and swatted his nose. "You're going to wake her. Heaven knows we all wish we could be asleep right now." She sat back and yanked the dog into her lap. His large frame collapsed onto her, and he quieted.

Jian turned back to Gen. "I'm going to need to send a letter to the commander. Yu is probably not their only officer who broke rank and now terrorizes the countryside, stealing what they need." They all knew what that meant. Commander Yang wouldn't take an anonymous message seriously. Sending him a letter meant fixing Jian's name to it and letting others know he still lived.

He glanced over his shoulder at the sleeping Hua. He could still protect her. They didn't have to know she was alive. If anyone suspected Hua Minglan of being of the dragon blood, of harboring an ancient beast inside her, they wouldn't know she was still a danger if they thought her dead.

Gen's voice pulled his thoughts away. "She carried you down that ladder. I don't know how she managed that, but my daughter saved your life."

"A habit of hers." He had his suspicions for how she'd carried him. The dragon must have given her strength.

"She wasn't burned by the flames."

"Luck." Jian hid the lie in his eyes. Knowledge of the dragon was too dangerous. Hua's nainai seemed to know, but she hadn't told anyone for a reason Jian didn't understand. Yet, he respected it. He knew the risks involved in knowing Hua's power.

It was the same reason he hadn't contacted Bo since the battle. He'd have to lie to him.

Qara was right, it seemed. The seer he'd once loved had foretold this. Well, maybe not this exactly, only that Hua would need him, that she had a role to play, and Jian had to stand by her.

"I never thought I'd see her again." Gen's voice was barely above a whisper. "When she left, I thought I'd lost my last daughter."

"Why didn't you come after her? You could have forced her home."

He sighed. "Because, Jian, I respect my daughter and her decisions."

"She did it to protect you."

He shook his head. "No, she cut her hair and donned a man's armor, she lied and left her family for more personal reasons than that. I have trained Hua her entire life, always hoping she'd never have to use the lessons I bestowed upon her. It seems I prepared her only for vengeance." His shoulders dropped. "Tell me, Jian, did she find what she was searching for?"

No, but she found so much more. He wanted to tell Gen

that Hua would have found her way into the fight one way or another with that dragon inside her, but he didn't. Instead, he put a hand on the older man's shoulder. "She once told me she didn't need me to promise she'd return home, because she'd already promised herself. Your daughter was one of the best warriors I had. She challenged my authority at every turn, but my men were in awe of her."

"That sounds like my Hua." He bowed his head. "Thank you for taking care of her."

He'd done nothing of the sort. Hua had been one of his more capable men. Even after he knew her true identity, she proved herself to be more than anyone thought. A stubborn girl. A grieving sister.

A warrior.

He turned away from Gen and passed a sleeping Fa and Ru, curled together on a pad of horse blankets. Nainai sat in the same place he'd left her watching Hua sleep.

"I can't take my eyes off her." She smiled.

Jian hadn't been able to take his eyes off her since the first day they met, but now it was different.

Nainai went on. "We just lost our home, the house my husband built, and yet all I feel is gratitude. I would set fire to that house a thousand times if it meant bringing Hua back to us."

"Do you think it was the fire?" He crouched down next to Hua and looked back at her nainai. "The flames, did they wake her?"

She dropped her voice so they weren't overheard. "She harbors a Nagi, Jian. The flames will always call to them. I know a little about the beast inside her. Our entire family has the dragon blood."

"What does that mean?" Everyone in Piao knew the basics of the blooded from the stories of emperors hunting them down. Bo's father once rounded up many suspected blooded families and executed them at the dragon festival.

Nainai sighed. "It is a long and winding tale."

He stood and walked over to sit beside her once more. "I don't know about you, but I won't be sleeping tonight."

She closed her eyes for a moment, her entire body stilling as if preparing to release its secrets. When she opened her eyes, there was a hint of resignation in their depths. "Our family is descended from the last Nagi who roamed the earth more than one hundred years ago. The humans they lived within passed on that ability. The blood only refers to our ancestry. It has little to do with the actual Nagi. It is not our blood that allows them to enter us, it is our minds.

When Hua was a young girl, I recognized in her a spirit unlike that of most girls in Piao. She had no interest in fancy robes or crushed pearl face paint. I knew there'd be no musical skills in her future or love of embroidery. That was her sister, but never Hua. Instead, she followed the farm hands on their daily chores and played in the woods. She'd come home streaked with dirt and give her mama a fright."

Jian's lips curved up. "Sounds like quite the child." He remembered his boyhood days running through Dasha with Bo and Luca. There were moments he could forget he was the unwanted child at court, and moments it was the only thing he saw.

Nainai smoothed her robe over her legs. "She was something. My husband was executed at a dragon festival when Gen was young. The family went into hiding after that. We changed our name and moved to an out of the way farm.

Those events made Gen into a wary man who only ever wanted his family to be safe. That was why we started training Hua. Once we saw her desire to be something other than a typical Piao woman, everything changed. Our family never wanted to lose another person to the dragon festivals. Hua became more skilled than we ever imagined." She met Jian's eyes. "The morning my son woke to find his daughter gone, he was both proud and terrified."

"The first time I met you, you told me you're the reason the Nagi chose her."

She sighed. "That is a story for another time." Her eyes slid shut. "Rest, for tomorrow we will have to deal with the events of tonight."

Jian didn't fall asleep until the sun rose on the horizon, sending streams of light to chase away the shadows in the barn.

He didn't know how long he'd been asleep when Gen's voice woke him. "Riders!"

That word sent a jolt through Jian, and he shot to his feet. Nainai stood next to Gen and Fa at the door, peering out at the horses coming down the muddy road.

"Soldiers." Jian cursed, thinking back to the day before when he'd been standing in that very barn as General Yu and his men descended on them.

That hadn't turned out so well.

Gen turned to him. "Go into the stall with Hua. They cannot see you."

Jian didn't want to leave Gen in case these were more

soldiers—or ex-soldiers—with bad intentions. But if they weren't, if they truly represented the Piao army, he couldn't be seen.

Nainai put a hand on his arm. "We will yell if we need your help. Take Ru with you." Jian nodded and walked to the far wall where two rusty daos hung. He handed one to Gen and took the other with him into the stall. Ru shut the door, shielding them from view.

Hua rolled over, her eyes fluttering open. Confusion flashed across her face, and Jian held a finger to his lips as he crouched down below the half wall.

The sound of hooves drumming against the road drew nearer. The rain from the night before turned everything outside into a muddy mess, muffling the sound.

Jian calmed his breathing as his heart pounded against his ribs. Hua knelt beside him. "What's happening?" she whispered.

"Soldiers."

Her eyes widened. "Then we must get out there, fight them." There was something off in her voice, some tone he'd come to associate with Hua missing. He shook his head, reminding him she was probably just exhausted and scared like the rest of them.

"We have no way of knowing if they're deserters like the men yesterday or true warriors of Piao just traveling the country."

"Does it matter?"

Jian shrank away from the darkness in her words. Of course, it mattered. Yes, he wanted to protect Hua if any of his brother's men came for her, but that didn't mean he was now an enemy of the Piao army, the same men he'd commanded less than two months ago.

They were Piao's shield against Batukhan Altan and the hordes of Kou at the border.

"You don't mean that." He looked away from her, not recognizing the venom in her gaze.

"Weak." She said the word under her breath as if she hadn't meant for him to hear it.

She'd only woken from her unconscious state less than a day ago. Jian should have known something wouldn't be right within her. Did she remember the battle? They hadn't had a chance to talk about it. Part of him hoped she didn't. How was she supposed to live with what she'd done?

The horses drew near, and armor jangled as someone jumped down from his warhorse.

Silence stretched for too long as Jian held his breath.

Gen's voice snapped the tension in the air. "General! I didn't expect to see you around these parts."

"I'm following the trail of a group of deserters who've been terrorizing the land between Yewo and Zhouchang for the last two weeks." There was something familiar about the man's voice, but it was too quiet for Jian to be certain. "We rode past your home, Gen. What happened?"

"The men you're chasing, they came here. We did not extend our hospitality, so they extended theirs."

The soldier cursed, the sound so familiar to Jian he couldn't help but smile. He'd heard the same exasperation in his best friend more times than he could count. He stood, revealing himself. Gen and his companion didn't see him, but Nainai tried to wave him away, to tell him to stay hidden.

If anyone knew Jian still lived, they could connect the dragon to Hua since they'd both gone missing from the battle together. He didn't know what they'd seen or what stories now wound through the army. But in that moment, he didn't care. His best friend was alive, and that was all that mattered.

Pushing open the stall door, he stepped through and couldn't keep the smile from spreading across his face.

"About time you did something in this war."

At Jian's words, Luca froze. His eyes searched the barn until they locked on Jian. He recovered from his shock. "It wasn't easy when my commander had me training new recruits instead of on the front lines."

"Sounds like a terrible commander."

One corner of Luca's mouth tipped up. "No. He was the best man I've ever fought beside." His smile dropped. "But he died in Kanyuan. I mourned him for weeks."

Jian shook his head. "I'm here. I've been right here since the battle."

Luca rushed toward him, no longer caring about their audience. He threw his arms around Jian. Jian stumbled back with the force and gripped his friend. "I worried you were dead." He'd tried to keep himself from worrying about the soldiers he'd left behind. Most of the men who'd entered Kanyuan either died by a Kou dao or by fire.

"You've been missing, Jian. We said words of goodbye to you." He pulled back. "I can't…" Tears shone in his eyes. "I can't believe you're here." As if realizing they were not the hugging type of friends, he stepped back. A tear slid down his cheek, and he didn't bother to wipe it away.

Jian took in everything about his friend. The dirt-stained

uniform that said he'd been on the road for a while. The exhaustion in his eyes and the strain of his smile.

Luca's eyes widened further as he glanced behind Jian. Jian turned to find Hua standing in the middle of the barn, her eyes narrowed.

"Hua." Luca said the word on a breath. "You're..." Jian waited for him to say the word 'dragon,' for him to reveal everything to Hua's parents. But he didn't. "Back at camp they're saying the dragon killed you before taking off with Jian."

Jian released a breath. They didn't know. Anyone who saw her transformation must have died in the village.

Hua didn't move, she didn't run to her betrothed or make any sign of acknowledgement. Luca crossed the distance between them and pulled her into his arms. Jian looked away, focusing on the men on horseback waiting for Luca's command.

A moment passed before Luca and Hua both joined him. "We have so much to catch up on. Our horses could use the rest. We'll stay here for the day and leave tomorrow." He clapped Jian on the back. "This is... everything, friend. Have you sent a messenger to your brother?"

Jian shook his head. "No. He can't find out I'm alive. Not yet."

Luca stared at him for a long moment as if he didn't know him at all, as if his words betrayed a man they both loved. He shook himself out of it when a horse snorted behind him.

"Heima?" Gen approached the horse, one hand held out in caution.

Jian could see it then. The white streaking down the horse's nose. The massive flanks and mischievous eyes.

Hua's horse.

He expected Hua to run to her old friend, the horse Jian overheard her speaking to in the dark. Instead, Hua only watched, no sign of recognition in her eyes.

Luca smiled when he looked back to watch Gen rub the horse's nose. "I found her after the battle. She was unharmed, yet she still ran from me. I thought if I caught her, if I took care of her, it would be like having Hua or Jian back with me." He met Jian's eyes once more. "I was wrong. Nothing quelled the pain of losing you."

Jian gripped Luca's shoulder. "I'm glad you're here."

His eyes flicked from Hua to Jian and back again. "Me too, brother. Me too."

CHAPTER 6

Hua

Hua needed to see Luca, to speak with him, but she couldn't navigate her way to the forefront of her mind. When he'd wrapped his arms around her body, she hadn't felt it. When he'd looked into her eyes, there'd been no sign of suspicion, nothing to tell her someone knew of her plight.

Tears of joy gathered in the corners of his eyes every time he looked at her. His men set up camp outside the barn, and Luca hadn't wanted to leave either her or Jian. He shared his food with the family, his smile pulling Hua almost to the surface of the Nagi's mind as she fought for every moment.

What if she never broke free? What if this was her life? As a passenger while the Nagi controlled her every move. She hadn't been able to hug Luca back, but he hadn't seemed to notice how her arms hung loose at her sides. She'd felt the Nagi recoil at the soldier's touch.

"Let me talk to him," she'd begged, knowing only the beast in her mind could hear her. *"Please."*

The Nagi wiped at her eyes—Hua's eyes—agitation making her jaw clench. *"Forget the soldier, Hua. He does not matter. None of them do."* She turned back to the empty horse stall. *"For soon they'll all be dead."*

CHAPTER 7

Jian

The fire crackled, sending sparks into the night. Jian stared into the flames, remembering the heat from the night before. Fighting Yu's men in the Minglans' home seemed like another life. In one moment, everything could change.

They made camp with Luca and his men that night after spending all day sorting through the wreckage of their lives. After a simple soldier's supper, they sat around the fire, needed more for light than warmth on the summer night.

Jian and Luca hadn't yet finished their earlier conversation, but maybe it didn't matter. Maybe none of this did.

Watching Hua's every movement, Jian couldn't help but wonder what would happen the next time the dragon let itself be known.

She'd barely spoken a word to anyone all day, opting to stay apart from her family, a family she should have been overjoyed to see.

Something was off, but he didn't want to imagine what it could be. Was the dragon fighting to transform again?

He didn't look up as Luca sat beside him. "You were right."

Jian only grunted his agreement.

"Hua deserves more than I can give her."

Scanning the faces around the fire, he made sure no one listened to a conversation that shouldn't be had. Even if Hua did deserve more, that wasn't how it worked in Piao. Only the lucky few fell in love and married. Most had their lives chosen for them by elders who thought they knew better.

Tradition was a powerful thing.

Jian removed a knife from a sheathe at his waist. He'd found the blade in the barn, abandoned and ill-cared for, just as he'd once been. The rusted steel felt good in his hand, like holding it gave Jian back some of the power he'd lost as his life spiraled out of control with the flap of a dragon's wings.

Luca eyed the blade and dropped his voice. "I have a secret, Jian. One I never told you or Bo. If I reveal it, I'm not only putting myself in danger."

He didn't know what Luca's secrets could have to do with Hua. Sliding the tip of the dull blade along his palm—not pressing hard enough to cut skin—he ran through everything he knew of his friend in his mind. Luca's father and Gen were old friends from their days in the military. "You never told me of the betrothal. That means one of two things. You didn't want Bo to know, or there's a deeper reason you've tied yourself to Hua."

"To be honest, it was a bit of both. Bo knows where we stand. The moment his father chose him as heir, our future was written. But that's not the reason I agreed to a marriage."

It wasn't the first time Jian thought of how hard life must have been for Luca. He was in love with a man who could never allow himself to give in to the feelings he had for Luca. Not only that, but Bo's harem was constantly at his side. And he loved them, he did. Maybe not in the usual way, but he cared for each of them, a fact Jian knew Luca had come to terms with.

The anger Jian felt toward Luca earlier in the day faded away, leaving only a deep sadness behind. "Then why did you accept Hua as your betrothed?"

Luca looked to his men. They lay on their bedrolls fast asleep along with the Minglan family. Only Jian and Luca remained awake at such an hour. "I… Jian, my family is blooded."

The words didn't register. It couldn't be true. He'd known Luca since they were boys running around the city. How was it possible that someone who felt like family wasn't who he'd thought at all? "Does Bo know?"

"Of course not. Emperors throughout history have hunted those descended from the dragon lines as if we pose a threat to their power. All we've ever wanted was to be left alone. My grandfather was executed at a dragon festival along with Hua's."

It made so much sense now. Luca and Hua both knew what it was to hold life-altering secrets. It tied them together for what… "So, you and Hua are meant to be allies against the emperor?" Against Bo. Jian's jaw clenched. The blooded families weren't only trying to live normal lives, they were forming alliances. There had to be some purpose in that.

Luca gripped his arm. "No. We don't want power. We only want to protect each other." He froze. "You're not surprised." A breath hissed through his teeth. "You knew about Hua, that she has the blood."

Jian released a long sigh.

"I'm here. We used to never keep anything from each other."

"Except the fact that you're descended from the last Nagi."

"I couldn't tell you."

What would Luca say if he knew Hua was the dragon who'd destroyed Kanyuan? "I know. And like then, I can't tell you how I know about Hua. I just… take care of her, please."

Luca met his gaze through the darkness. "If I could end the betrothal, I would. I need you to know that. It is not up to me, and my family can protect her."

Jian did know. Luca was the best friend he could ever ask for, and he'd somehow seen behind the questions from Jian to his true feelings, feelings Jian didn't yet understand. He'd been drawn to Hua since she first set foot in camp, back when he believed her to be a man. But now… after watching her sleep for weeks, he'd begun thinking she would never again fix those stubborn eyes on him. And that, he couldn't take. "I know, Luca. I do."

Hua needed the protection of other dragon-blooded families now more than ever. Luca couldn't back out of the betrothal for that very reason. With a dragon now known to be in Piao, the blooded had to remain united, leaving Jian on the outside of their alliance. He wasn't one of them. His brother was the emperor.

Yet, he had nowhere else to go. If he returned to the army, he'd have to leave Hua, something he refused to do when he was the only person other than her grandmother who knew of the beast inside her.

"Will you do me a favor?" Luca nudged him.

"You know I will."

"Keep her safe. I can't return to my post tomorrow unless I know you won't leave her. Take her family to my father's place. They shouldn't stay here."

Jian nodded, knowing his friend was right. "You know I could never leave her."

With a nod, Luca pushed himself to his feet and looked down on Jian. "You'll always be my commander, Jian, no matter if you think you earned it or not. Until now, it was you and me. I'm going to miss fighting at your side."

"Something tells me we'll fight together again someday."

Luca spared him one final look before walking around the fire to find his bedroll. Jian stayed where he was a while longer, the flames flickering in his dark eyes. They'd see a lot more fire before this was all through.

He just didn't know how much.

CHAPTER 8

The Nagi

Sleep was for the weary, and the Nagi had slept enough.

She lay with her head on a rolled-up fur blanket, staring at the stars above. The dragon shone the brightest in the sky, a beacon in the night. This was where the Nagi was supposed to be, the people she was supposed to observe.

But observation wasn't enough.

The conversation she overheard hours ago rolled through her mind. The soldier who always looked at her in apprehension knew of Hua's dragon blood. Interesting. Even more interesting was the newcomer, the one Hua remembered as Luca, he too had the dragon blood.

The Nagi turned her voice inward, speaking only to the girl in the back of her mind. *"Hua, how do you live in such a place?"*

There was no response, but she hadn't really expected one. The only time she heard from the persistent girl was when Hua tried to force herself to the front of her mind. Hua desperately wanted to be free.

One day, she would again.

Once the Nagi finished what she'd come to accomplish.

The emperors of old feared the blooded would challenge their power. They had no idea how right they were.

No one else stirred in the camp, and the flames dwindled to glowing embers. Reaching into the scorching hot remnants of the fire, Hua—or the Nagi inside—wrapped her fingers around a still glowing log and covered her hand in ash. Hua's skin bubbled where it burned, but no pain came. Instead, heat seared through the Nagi, forcing all weariness from her mind.

She needed to be clearheaded to complete her tasks. It was while she slept the girl inside fought hardest for release, taking advantage of the Nagi's weakened state.

The cure for that? Do not sleep.

Half a dozen soldiers slept nearby. The Nagi did not know their names, only what they represented. On the other side of Hua lay her family, along with Luca and Jian, the two men the girl felt great affection for.

Standing out of her crouch, she walked back to the furs she had rested on and slipped a hand underneath, feeling for the knife hidden underneath. Her fingers closed around the hilt and pulled it free before stepping toward the sleeping soldiers.

She wasn't evil. The Nagi had protected Piao a long time ago. But that time was before Piao hunted their descendants, destroying their legacy.

What happened next was not her fault, only her duty.

She crouched down next to a sleeping man with thick ebony hair falling over his forehead. A beard coated his young face. Soldiers of Piao were her enemy, and one destroyed their enemies. Holding the knife tightly, she sliced it across the man's throat, not waiting for the gurgling of blood to stop before moving on to the next.

None of the sleeping men were able to put up a fight, and she knew this would be much easier than the battles to come. Bloody tasks like this were necessary if the Nagi was ever going to bring Piao to its knees.

The Nagi killed with soundless efficiency, an emotionless drive. Her head ached as Hua became aware of her actions and screamed for her to stop.

She couldn't. Not now.

One day, girl, you will understand. We do what we must.

As she reached the final man, his eyes sprang open, and a scream built in his throat. The Nagi ran for him, pinning his mouth shut and slitting his throat. His arms fell limp at his sides as blood bubbled from the wound.

The Nagi wiped her blade on the grass before standing.

"Hua," a choked voice said behind her.

The Nagi froze for only a moment before turning to find Ru staring at her in horror, tears dancing in his eyes. He opened his mouth to scream, and the Nagi lunged for him, clamping a bloody hand over his mouth. He struggled against her, bucking and kicking.

The Nagi didn't want to kill the kid. He was dragon blooded and loved by the girl in her mind. The pain in her head intensified, and her hand slipped from the boy's mouth.

He released a scream.

Both Jian and Luca scrambled from the ground, sleep long forgotten.

"Hua." Jian peered through the darkness as if he didn't believe it was her holding a knife to the kid's throat. "What are you doing?"

The rest of the girl's family stirred as the scene played out before them.

The Nagi—Hua—backed away, dragging Ru with her. He whimpered as the knife nicked his flesh.

"Hua," her father called, confusion and horror mixing in that one word. "Talk to us."

Luca glanced behind the Nagi to the dead men at her back. "You killed them." He choked on the words. "My men… Hua…"

Jian stepped forward.

"Stay back," the Nagi yelled.

Jian's wide eyes studied her.

They all tried to speak at once, tried to yell for Hua.

"Quiet!" she yelled, unable to think. She glanced behind her to where the horses were tied. They'd even kept Heima close rather than putting her in the barn. A plan formed in the Nagi's mind.

She kept walking backward. "Don't move!" She had to be free of them to pursue her own mission. Hua's family would only hinder her. The real Hua wouldn't stop fighting in her mind as long as the Nagi posed a danger to them.

The pain in her skull nearly blinded her now as Hua hammered against the mental wall of her mind.

When the Nagi reached the horses, she used one hand to untie Heima as she met Jian's eyes in challenge. He wanted to save her, to bring the girl he cared about back. That much was evident on his face.

But Hua wasn't his problem any longer.

Hua Minglan—and the Nagi controlling her—had a bigger purpose than simply masquerading as a man to join the army. Now, they would be the entire army. Only this time, Piao was the enemy.

With a shove, the Nagi threw Ru away from her and pulled herself onto Heima without a saddle. Heima bucked, trying to throw her off.

"It's okay, girl. It's Hua." The Nagi tried to soothe the beast.

But it seemed even the horse knew a lie when she heard it.

The Nagi kicked Heima, forcing her to take off down the road, dust kicking up into the night behind her.

She suspected Jian and Luca ran after her, hoping they could save Hua one final time. But she didn't look back to see how hard they tried.

CHAPTER 9

Jian

In a silent field, surrounded by dead men, Jian lost his faith.

"That wasn't her." Ru was the only person with the courage to speak what they all now knew. "Hua is gone."

Fa Minglan cried quietly into the dark while her husband stared down the road as if waiting for his daughter's return.

Luca kneeled beside one of his men, a young bearded fellow who could have been sleeping if not for the blood arching over the curve of his neck.

"My men are dead." It was the only sentence to pass Luca's lips.

Jian wasn't a stranger to losing his comrades. He put a hand on Luca's shoulder and squeezed. There were no words for any of them, nothing that could erase the sight of Hua holding a knife to her brother's throat.

Hua's grandmother looked to the bright stars above. "Protect her. Please." Jian didn't know who she spoke to. He closed his eyes for a brief moment.

Nainai pulled Ru into her arms. "No, dear. I don't believe that was your sister."

Those words made Gen pull away from his wife to approach his mother. "It is past the time for secrets, Mother. Where is my daughter? What does it mean that she's gone?"

Nianai rested her chin on Ru's head and settled her gaze on her son. "Our Hua has been chosen by a Nagi."

"That's impossible."

"No, it's not. The dragon that lives within her is strong. Ask Jian. He has seen it. If he believed he could catch her, he wouldn't be standing here talking to you or me."

She was right. The moment Hua mounted Heima, Jian wanted to give chase, to bring her back. Yet, he'd seen her in Kanyuan. If the dragon shifted—or even if she didn't—speed wouldn't save her. He had to come up with a different plan.

Jian rubbed his eyes. "The news hasn't reached Zhouchang yet." He'd never been more thankful for how remote the Minglans lived. "You know the city of Kanyuan was destroyed in a battle. It was the Nagi... It was Hua."

Gen stumbled back, his bad leg hindering his movements. "No."

Luca straightened, his face a mask of steel. "Hua… that was her? She killed without distinguishing between Kou warriors and Piao children. I can't… And now this…"

Flashes of the battle rolled through Jian's mind. He couldn't let that happen again.

"I thought dragons were supposed to protect us." Fa sniffled.

Luca's eyes flashed. "Generations of Piao emperors have hunted their descendants. Those of us with dragon blood have had to hide it our entire lives. Piao betrayed the dragons, and this is our retribution."

With each passing moment, the Minglans' grief choked the air. Fa dropped to her knees, collapsing in on herself while Gen stared into the night as if Hua would return. The family broke right in front of Jian's eyes. He'd only known them for a few weeks, but they didn't deserve this.

And Hua? What did she deserve?

He spent weeks sitting by her bedside, hoping and praying she'd open her eyes, that he'd get to see her strength, her courage even just one more time. Her presence kept him from folding under the weight of everything he'd seen, the people he'd let down.

Now, she was gone too.

"I have to save her," he whispered.

No one heard him as they continued to mourn the daughter they already considered lost. Jian wasn't ready to give up on her.

"She's still in there." He didn't know how he knew. Maybe it was a foolish hope, the last thread holding him together.

"Son." Gen hung his head. "If my daughter was in there, she'd never have let these atrocities happen."

He shook his head. "I..." His jaw clenched. "I'm going after her. Hua wouldn't give up on us." She was the most loyal person he knew, the soldier who'd have risked her life for the people she cared about. She already had. "She walked through fire to save me. Twice." When she arrived at his camp, a soldier with no idea of war, he'd been drowning in guilt, in pain. Hua Minglan was the only reason he was still standing.

"How will you find her?" Luca asked. He was the only one with a glimmer of hope in his eyes. He'd always believed in the good in life, despite hiding his heritage.

Jian knew where he had to start. There was one person who might be able to help him, but he didn't relish the idea of returning there. "I must travel to Prince Dequan's estate."

Gen opened his mouth to speak, but Luca cut him off. "She's not there."

"What?" Qara, Prince Dequan's healer, had to be there. She was the only person who could set him on the right path. "Did something happen to her?" Once, he'd loved Qara with everything he had, but she'd always known his future didn't lie with her.

"You must protect the dragon."

He was trying.

"Commander Yang drafted her to help the army find her brother."

General Altan. For weeks, Jian managed not to think of the enemy that still loomed over the empire. Qara's brother wasn't only a threat to Piao, he wanted Jian dead.

But thoughts of Batukhan Altan didn't bring forth the anger as they had only weeks ago. Not when the danger rested within Hua. "Where are they?"

"They set up camp among the ruins of Kanyuan to protect the mountain pass now that the village is destroyed."

He nodded. "Then that is where I must go."

Luca glanced at the dead men in the grass. "I want to bury my men, and then I'll join you."

"You can't."

"I care about her too, Jian."

Jian softened his tone. "I know you do." He glanced over his shoulder at the vulnerable Minglan family. "I need you to do something else for me. Protect them." He gestured to Ru. "Get them to your family like we talked about."

There was no argument left in Luca. He knew Jian was right. "I'll make sure they arrive at the farm near Dasha." He paused. "Jian…"

Jian waited for him to continue.

"Promise me you'll find her."

Their eyes locked. "I promise I won't stop trying while there is breath in my lungs."

Jian saw the truth in Hua's parents' eyes. They mourned their daughter as if they'd never see her again. When he pulled Ru into a hug, he whispered in his ear, "Protect Luca for me."

Ru nodded, his lip quivering as he sucked it into his mouth.

Nainai walked toward him, the night hiding the tears on her cheeks. "At night, she is the weakest," she whispered.

"What?"

"The Nagi does not have full control when she sleeps. Hua will fight her hardest then."

"How do you know that?"

She only tapped her nose in response.

Jian's eyes widened as understanding hit him. Nainai Minglan knew from experience. She'd once had a dragon inside her, yet here she stood.

He backed away, having no more time for questions.

As he mounted a horse and took off down the dark road, he realized what Nainai had given him with that knowledge.

Hua would never be gone. She just needed a reason to fight.

Chapter 10

Hua

Hua slipped further into her mind. Bit by bit, moment by moment, the small control she still had ebbed away, eroded by a river of fire within her.

Yet, there was one thing she could still do.

The Nagi howled, the sound echoing in every corner of their shared mind, as she tried to shift into the winged beast that had destroyed an entire village.

Hua wasn't quite sure how she did it, but she held on to the unravelling threads of control and prevented the Nagi from changing her form.

It was all Hua had left, that tiny satisfaction, a small victory.

Keeping the Nagi from shifting took every bit of strength Hua had left, leaving her with nothing to fight to regain her own mind.

"Where are we going?" she asked, the words not spoken aloud.

When the Nagi didn't respond, Hua focused on the leather reins in her hand, sliding them through her fingers to prove she could still feel something, anything.

She was past the point of fear, in part, because she was already lost. People feared the unknown when they didn't want to die, to disappear, but Hua no longer existed in this world.

She'd seen the look in her parents' eyes when they discovered the slain soldiers, the betrayal on Luca's face. When she'd held the cool metal to Ru's throat—little, trusting Ru—she realized it no longer mattered who controlled the actions of her body. In their minds, her parents would still see blood coating their daughter's hands.

Ru… Tears slipped down her face.

"Stop crying," the Nagi commanded, wiping her cheek. "Do not be a weak-hearted fool, Hua Minglan. I chose you for your strength."

"Loving my family is not a weakness." She tried to lift her eyes to the rising sun, but the Nagi didn't let her, instead focusing their gaze on Heima's matted mane.

The Nagi sighed, and it parted Hua's lips. "I let them live, did I not? I am not the monster you would like to think. The Minglans are of the dragon blood. They will not come to harm."

"And everyone else? The people of Kanyuan? Luca's soldiers?"

"They are my enemy."

"No," Hua shouted in her mind. *"Piao has long been an ally of the Nagi. Centuries ago, you protected us."*

"May I ask you a question?"

The Nagi's formality wasn't something Hua would ever get used to. *"Depends on what the question is."*

Neither of them spoke for a long moment, and the Nagi surveyed their surroundings. Wheat fields spanned the Piao countryside. Little changed in the three-day ride from Zhouchang to wherever they were now. Three days of sparse conversations where all Hua could do was picture her family the moment she became something cruel to them, something evil.

"We have two more days until we reach the mountains." The Nagi still hadn't asked her question.

"Are we going into Koulland?" Alarm jolted through Hua.

"We will cross the border, yes."

"Why?"

The Nagi didn't respond. She shifted in the saddle, her back straight. Hua didn't think the Nagi had slept the entire trip, and she hadn't let her defenses down enough for Hua to gain control.

"What was your question?" Hua asked.

"Your loyalty... I do not understand it."

"That wasn't a question."

The Nagi thought for a moment, guarding those thoughts in her mind from Hua. "It is true the Nagi's purpose was once to protect Piao. That was before the empire we died for began killing those we could return to. People like you. Why do you serve a master who does not serve you?"

Hua wished she could say something noble about putting the empire before herself, that she had a good reason for joining the fight. Instead, she only had one word. *"Revenge."* General Altan was responsible for her sister's death. Not directly, but he'd led the attack on Dasha.

Hua had wanted to protect her father when she stole his armor and joined Jian's camp, but it was the need for revenge that drove her, pushed her.

The Nagi nodded. "Revenge is a concept I can understand."

"That's why you're here, isn't it? You didn't come to save us from the Kou."

"I did not come to save Piao, but I am here to save you, Hua Minglan, and others of the ancient dragon lines. This empire will rue the day they cleansed our heritage from the earth."

All the vengeance, all the anger Hua felt in the days after Luna's death rang in the Nagi's thoughts, as if she pulled it from the depths of Hua's soul.

"What are you planning to do?" Hua had to find a way to fight, to prevent more destruction from coming to her home.

"I do not yet know." A village appeared over the crest of a hill in the distance. "But I will when we get there."

"Get where? Please, tell me something."

"I do not know."

Hua didn't know the name of the village they stayed the night in, only that it was larger than Zhouchang. Shops lined the road past the broken town gates, but most looked like they hadn't been open in a long time.

The afternoon sun hung above them by the time they rode through the narrow cobblestone streets. Arched roofs hung above ramshackle buildings.

Men and women rode rickety carts pulled by malnourished animals.

Hua wondered what she looked like to them as they cast curious glances her way. Days of sleeping on the hard ground without bathing or combing her hair. The Nagi had eaten nothing but a few raw fish she caught by hand in a stream two days ride from here, but Hua didn't feel the pangs of hunger or the aches from sitting in a saddle for days.

In the center of the village sat a monastery, its glazed tiled roof painted in an intricate flower design. Jade pillars not unlike those at the emperor's palace lined an overgrown walkway to a door that stood wide open.

Hua peered inside at the entrance that led into a courtyard with a pond in the center of it. A few shabbily-dressed monks tended dying flowers.

"What happened here?" Hua whispered, managing to force the words past the Nagi's guarded tongue.

The Nagi responded in her head. *"This is what occurs when an empire turns away from those that protect it."*

"You can't believe that."

The Nagi pulled on the reins, turning Heima away from the ruins.

Hua wasn't finished. "You were gone. The Nagi abandoned Piao centuries ago. You want to blame someone for our persecution? All fault lies with the ones who put this terrible duty on us."

"Hua—"

"No, I may not be able to control the words leaving my lips or the movements of my body, but at least for now, my thoughts are my own. I. Don't. Want. This. The dragon blood isn't some noble birthright. It's nothing more than a curse."

"You know not of what you speak."

"Sure. Okay. I'm just a simple farm girl. That's what people have seen my entire life. If you want to believe I don't matter, that my life is yours for the taking, fine. But I won't stop fighting you. I won't fade quietly into the abyss. Yes, Piao has betrayed people like me, but so have you."

She wished she could cross her arms and stomp away after her petulant outburst. That was the problem with sharing a mind. There was no escape.

The Nagi didn't respond to her words. There was no apology or explanation.

Instead, a deafening silence followed them all the way to an inn where, once again, the Nagi refused to sleep.

Hua tried to stay up into the night, but she no longer had the energy to remain alert in the Nagi's mind.

When she woke the next morning, she sat atop Heima outside the village they'd ridden through the day before. The Nagi allowed them hours in the night to rest—for Heima, not Hua.

The poverty she'd witnessed in the village stuck with her. The villages closer to the mountains had faced many hardships in recent years. Constant attacks by the Kou, and an empire that cared little for them. They did not represent the heartland of Piao as places like Zhouchang did, and therefore received little help

The farmlands around Zhouchang—including the Minglans' farm—fed a large part of Northern Piao. Their land was hearty, their harvests rich.

Hua never before considered how others in Piao lived.

"Ah," the Nagi said. "Right now, you're realizing there are more difficulties a person can have than the dragon blood."

"Get out of my thoughts." She wasn't wrong. The Minglans lived their lives hiding their true heritage, but they'd always had food on the table, new dresses and dolls for holidays.

Even Heima and Chichi were well fed as if they too were part of the family.

Until now, the dragon blood never stood in Hua's way, never prevented her from reaching her full potential.

The Nagi smiled. "And now you're contemplating how unfair it is that you and I met."

"We haven't just met. You took my life."

"I did no such thing."

"Then what would you call it?"

"You and I are now one. We must work together to achieve our goals."

Hua laughed, the sound not leaving her throat. *"Our goals? I just want to protect my family."* Jian. She'd tried not to think of him, of the brokenness in his eyes the moment she climbed onto Heima, and he realized she was gone.

In those eyes, she'd seen the Nagi for what she was. A usurper. An enemy.

"You must let me shift."

"No."

The Nagi sighed. "You are stubborn, girl, and it will be your end."

Hua gathered every bit of control she could, reaching her hand forward to run it down Heima's neck, needing to know at least one friend was with her before doing what she needed to do.

Guarding her thoughts, she closed her eyes for a long moment before ripping an arrow from the quiver hanging on the saddle and throwing herself sideways. Her shoulder slammed into the packed dirt road.

For her family, and other families in Piao, she could do this, she had to. Forcing her arm up, she aimed the steel arrowhead at her throat.

No one was coming to save her. It was up to Hua to save all of them.

Her hand froze as the tip of the arrow pierced her skin, drawing a bead of blood.

Hua tried to force it farther in, but she couldn't move. Breath rushed into her lungs with a relief that brought her shame. She should have been prepared to die if it meant taking the Nagi with her.

But in that moment, all she could think of was how glad she was to still be alive, to have a body that was not her own.

The Nagi exerted her will, pulling the arrow away from Hua's throat and wiping the blood clean from her skin.

"You would sacrifice yourself?" Confusion clouded her words as she cocked her head.

"Yes," Hua whispered in the back of her mind.

"Why?"

"Because I love them."

The Nagi's brow creased. "I won't kill the people you love, Hua. I proved that."

She thought of Bo, the emperor her sister loved. Of Jian, who loved his brother and his empire. What would happen if the Nagi succeeded in destroying the empire, in killing more people? Would any of them be able to live with themselves?

"Sometimes death isn't the worst thing."

CHAPTER 11

Jian

Kanyuan held the nightmares that plagued Jian every time he closed his eyes. The screams. The fire.

He'd never expected to return, especially not so soon after that destructive battle.

The front gates stood charred and broken, the rubble cleared away. Beyond them, a city of tents stretched through the cleared streets in the shadows of scorched buildings.

He rode into the city, not knowing the welcome he'd find. As far as anyone here knew, Jian Li died in the battle along with Huan Minglan.

It wouldn't be an easy explanation, but he didn't have time for long stories or jubilant reunions. It had been two weeks since Hua rode away from everything she'd known, since the Nagi took over her mind.

Two weeks with no news of dragons, despite the rumors circling Piao that the winged beasts had returned.

No one had seen the dragon since it destroyed an entire village.

The Nagi could be anywhere, doing anything, while Hua stayed trapped.

Jian reached the first row of tents and slid down from his horse to walk through the camp. A sentry stopped him.

"Who are you?"

Jian didn't answer the question. "I'm looking for Commander Yang. Where is he camped?"

The sentry put a hand on the hilt of the dao at his waist. "You expect to be given an audience with the commander?"

"Yes." Jian didn't have time for this. "He will see me. Send someone to tell him Jian Li has arrived."

The sentry gaped at him. "Commander Li? Forgive me for not recognizing you." He bowed, removing his hand from his dao.

Jian scratched at the beard forming on his cheeks and looked down at his travel stained robes. "I'm no longer a commander." He straightened and crossed his arms. "Why are you still standing here?"

The sentry bowed again before scurrying away.

A sigh deflated Jian's chest as he turned his eyes on the rest of camp. Soldiers eyed him with the distrust he'd expect after battle, none of them recognizing their disgraced, supposedly dead, former commander.

"Commander Li?"

Jian closed his eyes at the familiar voice. He'd hoped to get out of this camp without coming face to face with any of the men he'd failed. He pivoted on his heel to face Zhao Shi, the convict who'd been sent to Jian's camp to train and work off his prison sentence.

Upon seeing his face, Zhao bowed.

"Rise, soldier." Jian shifted. "I am your superior no longer."

"Sir, you will always be my commander." He lifted his eyes to Jian.

Jian appreciated the sentiment, but it was wrong. "You do not know what you say, soldier. Commander Yang deserves your loyalty more than me."

"He is a good leader, but you're the one who gave me a chance, who trained me and allowed me freedom after being in prison." Zhao never deserved prison. The man was as loyal as they come with a bravery and willingness to fight to match.

Jian stepped closer and put a hand on the man's arm. He couldn't look at him without thinking of the girl who'd trained alongside him, masquerading as a man. "I also failed you, Zhao. I could not protect you."

"This is war, sir. General Altan is an enemy unlike any other. It is up to us to protect ourselves. The only duty you had to us was to show us how. In that, you succeeded, or I wouldn't be standing here."

It was the most Jian had ever heard the silent man speak, and he tried to swallow the guilt building in him as he shifted his eyes away and hung his head. It was wrong, he knew that. He couldn't have predicted how the Kanyuan guard had switched sides, or that the Kou would attack their camp. That wasn't on him like the battle in the mountain pass was. And still, he felt like he should have done more.

"Commander!" Chen Yu sprinted between tents, knocking over a cooking pot full of rice porridge. He yelped as he stumbled forward before righting himself and barreling into Jian to wrap him in a burly hug.

Jian grunted in surprise as he tried to remain upright, his arms hanging limp at his sides.

"You're alive." Chen squeezed him so tightly Jian struggled for breath.

"Let the man breathe." Yan Sun, the remaining member of their group, approached. "Chen," he barked. "Let the commander go."

Chen didn't listen at first, but after a while, he let go and backed away.

Zhao jabbed a thumb in Jian's direction. "Says he's not our commander anymore."

Chen dropped into a deep bow. "You will always be my commander."

Yan swatted his head. "Stop being dramatic." The tall soldier met Jian's eyes. "Let him tell us how he survived being carried from the battle by a dragon."

That answered Jian's biggest question. They'd seen Hua save him.

"That wasn't any dragon." Zhao crossed his arms. "It was Hua."

"How—"

"I saw her change, so you can't deny it, Commander. I'm not the only one either. It killed her, didn't it?"

Jian rubbed a hand over his face. "No, she's alive." At least, he hoped she was.

Chen and Yan wore matching expressions of shock, their jaws hanging open.

Zhao grunted. "So, she has a Nagi inside her." He said it as a statement of fact instead of a question.

"How..." Jian shook his head, realizing Zhao's knowledge of the Nagi wasn't important as a cluster of soldiers marched toward them.

Chen eyed Jian. "Do not leave this camp without telling us the entire story."

The soldiers stopped in front of them, no expressions on their faces. "Commander Yang will see you now."

Jian nodded to the men who'd been under his command before following the soldiers on a winding path through the camp to a home that stood intact while the buildings around it lay in ruins. Jian recognized the wooden structure as the house once belonging to the captain of the Kanyuan guard, the man who'd been killed when those under his command chose to aid the Kou.

"You may enter." One of the soldiers pushed open the painted door while two others took up stances on either side of it. Jian stepped into the front room, noting a broken table next to the door. Was this where General Hanan struggled for his life?

Beyond the front room, an archway led into an open-air courtyard. A fountain sat lifeless above a coy pond with green water covered in a film of scum.

The stone walkway circled the courtyard leading to an outdoor kitchen at the back. A soldier led Jian to an open door near the kitchen, and he walked into what must have been Hanan's living room. A black mark stretched up one wall behind the small sitting area.

Commander Yang looked up from his spot in a high-backed wooden chair, a pair of spectacles perched on his long nose. His eyes widened before a smile graced his lips. "Jian Li." He stood and crossed the room.

Jian bowed. "Commander."

"You are supposed to be dead."

Jian rose and met his superior's scrutinizing gaze. "Well, I'm sorry I'm not."

Commander Yang's laugh boomed through the room as he waved away the loitering soldier. "You may go. This man is who he says he is." He gestured for Jian to take a seat on the bench near the window. "When my man told me someone claiming to be Jian Li wanted to speak with me, I was angry someone would impersonate a dead man—and a great one at that."

"I am no great man, sir." Jian folded his long frame onto the small seat.

"On that, we must disagree. If it weren't for you, we would have been overrun at Kanyuan. I don't know what you did, but it lured the dragon away."

Jian couldn't reveal Hua's identity to the commander, even if he did trust him. It wasn't his secret to tell. "To be honest, sir, I don't remember anything that happened once the dragon took me from the battle."

"Well, that is a shame. I have new orders from the emperor. We are to continue to defend against a Kou invasion while also seeking out this predator." He leaned back in his chair and removed his glasses to rub his eyes. "A dragon. I never thought I'd see one in my time. What I don't understand is why a creature that history calls a protector of Piao destroyed one of our largest villages? Surely it could have defeated the Kou without forcing us into the position of protecting the mountain pass without our high walls."

"Sir, may I speak freely?"

"Please do."

"History is also full of emperors seeking out those with dragon blood and murdering them. My brother's own father, Emperor Anxu Xu Wei, lured them to the dragon festival for their own executions. If you were the Nagi and you came back into a world like that, would your loyalty be to the people who had shown no loyalty to you?"

He put his spectacles back on and nodded as if he were deep in thought. "Nagi… that's what she calls them as well."

"Who?"

A proud grin spread across his face. "Jian, if we are to have dragons of old back in our midst, don't you think it's time we make use of our seers once again?"

"Commander," a soft voice called through the house. "You sent for me?" Qara froze in the doorway, her wide eyes gleaming. "Jian," she whispered before rushing forward, stopping only feet from him.

"You two know each other?" Commander Yang asked.

Jian couldn't take his eyes from the tear tracking down her face. "We did."

"I can't believe this." She wiped away the tear. "I heard stories of the dragon carrying you away, yet here you sit, alive."

She was the reason he'd come to Kanyuan, but he couldn't find the words he needed to say to her, the questions he needed to ask. Not when she looked at him with a broken heart in her eyes. They were no longer in love, but he realized right then, they'd always love each other. If anyone could help him, it was Qara.

He cleared his throat, a signal to her that they'd speak in private. She nodded. "Would you like some tea? I was just about to bring some to the commander."

Commander Yang shook his head. "She's determined to make sure I eat, drink, and sleep, despite my constant reminders that she is not a servant."

She smiled. "But I am a healer, and your health is of the utmost importance." She left them staring after her.

"What has been happening here?" Jian had been desperate for news of Altan and the Kou army, but Luca only had bits of information for him.

"We have had no sightings of the Kou since the battle." He sighed, rubbing a hand over his face. "Like us, it destroyed a large part of their force. I don't believe they are gone, but I am using this time to allow my men to rest, heal, and build up our defenses. We've started on a new wall to the north, but it will be a futile pursuit if the Kou attack before it is complete."

"It seems you also have a problem with deserters, sir." Jian relayed the story of General Yu and his men setting fire to the Minglan home.

Commander Yang bent forward, his elbows resting on his knees as he ran a hand through his short-cropped, dark hair. "We have too many fronts on which to fight, Jian. Our beleaguered forces cannot win this war if we are forced to fight the Kou, search for a dragon, and chase our own men."

"General Yu is still roaming the countryside, but his men

are no longer a danger to Piao. Gen Minglan and I took care of them."

"That poor family. They lost their first daughter to the attack on Dasha and their second to the Kou. Then their home..."

"They're being taken care of. I hope you can spare Luca for the time being."

"Of course." He rubbed his face. "I'm pleased he found you. What of his men?"

Jian's heart jumped into his throat as he thought of Hua killing Piao soldiers in their sleep, of the vacant look in her eyes when she faced him. But he couldn't tell the commander what she'd done. "Dead, sir. I'm sorry."

"Was it Yu?"

Jian nodded. When he lifted his head, he found Qara watching him from the doorway, a tarnished silver tray balancing on her hands. Did she know the truth? Had she seen it?

She approached them and set the tray on the small wooden table in front of the chairs. With slow, delicate movements, she poured tea into three painted porcelain cups.

Jian lifted a cup, examining the chips along the rim that told a story of struggle and strife. Staying with the Minglans had been different, almost idyllic. Their farm prospered, and the family lived far from war and poverty.

Ru and Chichi spent their days running across rolling green hills, their laughter ringing out behind them.

And all of that was gone, just another casualty in this war.

His appetite for tea disappearing, Jian set the cup down.

Commander Yang sipped his before lowering it. "So, Jian

Li, you have not returned only to bring me news of deserters. Are you here to lend your considerable knowledge to the cause?"

Jian wished it was as simple as that. That he wanted to become a soldier again and throw himself back into a life he knew well. Instead, he had to find a girl he couldn't stop fearing for, one with a beast controlling her every action.

And he had to do it before she did something she couldn't take back. "I'm afraid not, sir. Luca told me of Qara's presence in your camp, and I must speak with her."

The hope in the commander's eyes faded. "We are fighting for the very existence of our empire, Jian."

"I promise you, Commander, I am fighting too."

Commander Yang shared a look with Qara Jian couldn't decipher. The older man steepled his fingers, tapping them against his chin. "I will soon be sending a unit of men into the mountains."

"Across the border?" Jian sat up straighter. "Into Koulland?"

Commander Yang nodded. "We know where Batukhan Altan is."

That single phrase flipped Jian's entire world upside down. He'd spent so much of the past few years wanting nothing more than to get his revenge on the man he thought killed Qara, her own brother. Every action he'd made as the commander was to that end.

Yes, he wanted to defeat the Kou and prevent them from taking his brother's empire, but it was more than that to him. It was personal.

"Where?" The single word came out hoarse.

"There is a Kou village." The commander nodded to Qara.

Qara sat beside Jian and folded his hand in both of hers. "I saw it. A village we call Xiǎo Miányáng."

"Little sheep," he whispered.

She nodded. "Don't let the name deceive you. This village is the most heavily fortified in all of Koulland, but one wouldn't know that at first glance. It looks like a sleeping village, a little sheep, when in fact, it is quite deadly. The greatest Kou warriors have been trained in the yards of Xiǎo Miányáng."

"How do you expect to get to him?" He shifted his gaze from Qara to the commander.

"Qara has great knowledge of the defenses. She has seen her brother there and the new measures they've put into place. There is a way in. We're going to get him, Jian. If we capture Batukhan Altan, this war will be over." He stood, towering over Jian, and put a hand on his shoulder. "I would like you to lead this mission."

It was the kind of mission he'd dreamed about, one that would bring him everything he'd ever thought he wanted. Glory. Revenge. Redemption.

But as he pictured Altan's smirking face, the desire to chase him, to fill the chasm inside Jian's chest with a thirst for a single man's blood, no longer controlled him.

"Sir..." He pushed out a breath. He had a mission, one that meant a lot more to him than Batukhan Altan ever had. Protect the girl who'd taken him into a world where lore was more than a story, and the people on his side were more important than the ones standing across the battlefield.

Qara smiled with understanding in her eyes. Had she seen this decision coming? A choice between what he'd always wanted and what he needed? Who he needed.

"I am grateful for the opportunity you've laid before me, Commander." Jian met the commander's gaze. "But my battle no longer lies with General Altan."

"All of our battles are with that man."

Jian stood, bowing his head in deference to the great man before him. "My presence on the mission will not decide its success or failure."

Commander Yang sighed. "Well, I can't say I expected you to accept the offer. I merely hoped. How long do you plan to stay in camp?"

"Only the night. I must leave at first light."

"I see. If you have need of anything, you only have to ask."

Realizing he was being dismissed, Jian looked to Qara, trying to communicate his need to speak with her.

Bowing once more to the commander, Jian turned toward the door.

Qara led him out. "Come with me."

They barely spoke as they walked side by side back into the city of tents, winding around groups of soldiers rolling dice and drinking wine.

Qara stopped outside a tent that looked no different from any other and pushed him in.

Jian stumbled through the opening and found Chen and Yan sitting on piles of furs that served as beds.

They both jumped to their feet as he entered.

"It's the seer," Chen whispered, garnering an elbow from Yan.

"Don't be a fool, Chen." Zhao entered the tent behind them, his large frame making the already small space more crowded.

Chen smoothed out his blanket and patted his bed. "You can have a seat, Commander."

Jian grunted as he sat. "I told you not to call me that."

"Then what are we to call you."

"Jian."

Chen's eyes widened as they met Yan's. "J-jian? We couldn't possibly—"

"You're being a fool." Zhao gestured for Qara to sit and remained standing. Chen and Yan both returned to their furs, their eyes darting from Jian to Qara.

Qara nodded at each of the men. "Jian, Zhao Shi has been chosen for the mission into Koulland." Something about those words comforted Jian. After training the man for months, he trusted Zhao.

"Congratulations."

Zhao only grunted.

Chen leaned forward. "Enough with the news of this war. Tell us about Hua. Where is she? Is she really the dragon?"

Jian sighed as he surveyed the surrounding men. "It is true that she lives."

Qara put a hand on his arm. "You can trust them, Jian. You need to."

He'd never get used to the eerie way in which Qara spoke now, like she just knew things. He supposed she did. That was what it meant to be a seer.

And he trusted her with his life, but did he trust her with Hua's?

He lowered his voice so those outside the tent couldn't overhear. "During the battle of Kanyuan, Hua shifted into a dragon to save us." They already knew that part.

"And then burned the entire city." Yan shivered. "I don't

think I'll ever get over the horrors we witnessed. She burned children, Jian. Children!"

Jian closed his eyes for a brief moment as the smell of charred flesh wafted up his nose, like the memory latched onto every one of his senses. "That wasn't Hua."

"But you just said—"

"The Nagi... the dragon has gained control of her."

No one spoke for a long moment until Zhao's voice filled the tent. "What can we do?"

"Keep fighting the Kou. I cannot search for Hua with a contingent of men at my back. It has to be me and me alone." He didn't know how he was so certain what she needed, but he knew it in his bones. "She has fled from me, from her family. But I refuse to believe she is gone. Hua is still in there somewhere, and I'm going to bring her back."

"For Piao," Chen whispered.

Zhao shook his head. "For all of us. Hua Minglan is the best of us. She always has been."

Jian couldn't refute the words. Even when Hua portrayed herself as a man named Huan, he'd seen something in the soldier, a warrior's spirit, an irreplaceable strength. She refused to be broken. They'd bonded over their shared need for revenge, but it became so much more than that.

He respected her.

Qara took his hand in hers. "I must speak with Jian alone."

The other men didn't protest her obvious dismissal from their own tent. Instead, they filed out with nods of acknowledgement.

Jian focused on the feel of Qara's hand in his, the warmth where their skin touched. There'd been a time he'd have given anything to feel that again. Now, all he wanted was to see Hua's eyes blaze in defiance as she refused to back down from his harsh words.

He wanted to feel impact reverberating up his arm as their daos clashed together in the sparring ring.

He pulled his hand free of Qara's. He didn't deserve her comfort when Hua was trapped in her own mind.

"You care about her a great deal." Qara's voice was sad.

"I…" What could he say to that? "I'm sorry."

She smiled sadly. "Don't be, Jian. You were one of the great loves of my life, but I have always known I was not your future. When I told you the dragon needed you, I did not yet know what it meant. Do you love her?"

How could he? For most of their time together, he thought Hua was nothing more than a pain-in-the-butt soldier. They barely knew each other, yet he was drawn to her in a way he couldn't explain. He'd spent weeks sitting beside her bed in the Minglan home watching her face for any kind of sign she'd come back to him. "I don't know." It was the only thing in any of this that made sense to him.

A tear tracked down Qara's cheek. "She needs someone to care enough to bring her back."

"You believe she's still in there?"

Qara's watery gaze met his. "I don't think she is, I know it. Hua is a fighter, Jian. She holds a strength few possess. And you were right to find me. I know where she has gone."

"Tell me, please."

She wiped a thumb under her eye. "There is much we don't know about the Nagi. They've always been a mystery. But there is a place high up in the mountains in Koulland, a monastery. Legend says the monks have kept histories of the Nagi that have never been seen in Piao."

"So, this thing that has stolen Hua's body wants a history lesson?"

She shook her head. "I do not know why she has gone there. My visions don't contain an explanation. But you must leave immediately. The longer Hua is trapped in her own mind, the harder it will be for her to come back."

Jian shot to his feet. "Now. I'll leave now." As tired as he was, he couldn't afford to wait until morning.

She stood to face him. "Ask Chen to gather some supplies for the journey. It is a three-week ride across dangerous mountain passes. I will find some ink and a quill to draw you a map." She moved to the door, but Jian put a hand on her arm to stop her.

"Qara?"

She turned to face him, and he crushed her to his chest like he'd done so many times before. "Thank you."

"I hope you save her, Jian."

CHAPTER 12

Hua

Lóng Băolěi. The dragon fortress sat nestled in the Shan Mountains beyond the border separating Piao from Koulland. Its domed roofs rose up seemingly from the rock itself, glittering gold beacons in the morning sun.

Hua couldn't take her eyes from the sight of the monastery before her. A chill had lived in her bones since reaching Koulland. She'd spent so long wanting to fight the Kou and never imagined doing so would bring her such a distance.

Her breath curled in front of her face as she took in the

high stone walls. Two red double doors stood closed against intruders.

"How do you know this is where we need to be?" she asked the Nagi in her mind.

The Nagi spoke her answers aloud. If anyone watched the lone Piaoan girl from the tiny circular windows, they'd think she talked to herself. "Do you ever tire of that question?"

"No." Hua wished she could hug her arms across her body to protect herself from the cold. She wanted to pull the furs tighter around herself. But her arms didn't move. They were no longer hers and words were all she had. *"We traveled weeks and crossed onto enemy lands to reach this place no one has heard of. I deserve an explanation."*

The Nagi clicked her tongue as she gripped Heima's mane to keep her at her side. "You humans have odd thoughts about what you deserve." She brushed hair behind one red-tipped frozen ear. Snow crunched underneath her boots as they made their way to a stone path that didn't look like it had been walked on since the last snow fell.

"Please."

The Nagi sighed. "There is someone here we must see."

"I gathered that, but how do you know? I didn't even know there was a monastery hidden in the mountains."

"I sensed him."

"Sensed?" A fear Hua couldn't explain stole the next words from her lips. *"How did we not know of this place?"*

"I do not pretend to know how your limited mind works, Hua. Now, be quiet. I need my mind clear of your insipid thoughts." A wall slammed up in her head, and Hua jerked backward, hammering against it to no avail.

She froze when a groan shook the ground and the giant

red doors opened, revealing a dark hallway, untouched by the morning light.

Hua watched a small boy run toward them, his robes billowing around his legs. Long auburn hair was tied back in a top-knot, revealing soft features.

He couldn't have been much older than Ru. He stopped in front of her, his forest green eyes scanning her from head to toe. "I have been sent to find out what you want." His high voice reminded Hua so much of her younger brother.

The Nagi's brow creased. "And they send a child?" She shook her head. "No matter. Take me to your master."

"I have no master." His eyes narrowed with a stubborn pride that would have made Hua laugh under different circumstances.

A deeper voice interrupted their conversation. "I wondered when you would come to me." An ancient man walked through the snow with no shoes on his feet. His eyes blazed red when they landed on the Nagi, and Hua shrank back into her cage.

Because she now knew why they'd come.

This man also had a Nagi inside him.

The man did not speak again as he led Hua into the monastery. Flames flickered to life from the torches that hung along the walls of the long, dark hall.

Cold seeped through the stone walls, and Hua wanted more than anything to turn around and escape from this place.

The child ran behind them, his little footsteps breaking through the eerie silence.

The old man turned into an open doorway, and Hua's heart stuttered. A sea of red-patterned carpeting stretched across the room where large bamboo chuang benches sat in front of a roaring fire. Decorative stone provided the railings to the furniture where four red-robed monks sat soaking in the warmth.

The old man gestured Hua forward, and the Nagi propelled her body past high cherry wood shelves filled with leather-bound tomes and papyrus scrolls.

The monks at the fire finally took notice of the stranger in their presence and scrambled to their feet. They bowed, none of them uttering a single word.

"They are under a vow of silence," the old man said. "None of them will speak to you." He turned to the bowing men. "You may go back to your studies, brothers." The monks dispersed to where books sat on the floor near the fire.

"What is this place?" The question wasn't the Nagi's, and Hua shocked even herself by managing to push it past her lips.

The old man cocked his head, his intense gaze latching onto her as if he saw all her secrets. "Lóng Bǎolěi."

She already knew the name of the monastery but couldn't get another question out. As if sensing her frustration, the old man smiled. "I am Master Delun. Welcome to our home." He put a hand on the small boy's head. "This is Boqin. I expect you are staying?"

The Nagi nodded, but Hua wanted to scream, to tell this strange man and his friends they couldn't keep her here.

"We are pleased to host both of you." Hua's eyes widened, or at least she thought they did. He knew. "We have much to discuss, but first, warm yourself. Boqin and I will get you something to eat from the kitchens. It will not be much, I'm afraid."

The Nagi bowed her head. "We have been on the road for weeks. Your hospitality is appreciated."

The man smiled again before ushering the boy away, giving Hua the chance to hammer against the Nagi's wall once more.

The Nagi rubbed her temples. "That causes me pain, Hua Minglan. Stop."

"Oh, I'm sorry. Have I hurt you? At least I didn't take over your life and force you into Koulland to some strange mountain fortress no one knows about."

"Do not be a child. Soon, you will not have to worry about me at all."

"What does that mean?" Hua practically growled the words. *"What are you going to do?"*

The Nagi ignored her as she moved toward the fire, holding her frozen fingers out in front of it. The monks didn't pay the Nagi any mind as she joined them, sitting on the soft carpet and shrugged the furs off her shoulders.

Warmth from the fire thawed her icy limbs, but Hua's mind was elsewhere.

"Heima?" she asked, realizing the Nagi left the horse out in the cold.

Master Delun returned. "Is that the name of the haggard horse you rode in on?" Had Hua said her name aloud?

The Nagi nodded. "The human in my mind is worried about her beast."

"It's not your mind," Hua screamed despite no sound leaving her mouth.

Master Delun watched on in sympathy. "Don't worry, dear. Your friend has already been taken to our stables where she will be given fresh hay and water. We heat the stables with coal in order to keep our mules from succumbing to the cold, so don't worry about her."

The Nagi took an offered porcelain cup from Boqin and sipped the steaming tea. Hua felt the heat slither through her and sighed in relief. "This human worries about many things. I have a lot I must accomplish and cannot do it with her moral questions constantly holding me back." She set her tea on the tray next to a plate of dried meat. "I wish to rid myself of her."

"Ah." Master Delun lowered himself to the floor beside her and held a cup of tea against his lips. "A Nagi's pursuits are noble pursuits and must be held to greater import than those of the humans."

Hua cried out for escape, but it was like a hand clamped around her throat, choking the sound at its source. Tears built in her eyes, but the Nagi wiped them away before they could fall.

"So." Master Delun wrapped an arm around Boqin. "You have sought out the only Nagi you felt in this world in hopes I can train you to wipe the human from your mind?"

"Only then will I be able to fulfill my purpose."

"And what purpose is that?"

The Nagi leaned forward, her voice deepening. "Our people have been hunted and destroyed. Anyone with a connection to us has been slaughtered time and again. I could not protect them before coming to this earth, but the time has come for a reckoning."

Master Delun continued to sip his tea. "Hmm. Interesting. And what will this reckoning consist of?"

"Revenge. I will bring Piao to its knees."

Hua shrank away from the words, unable to pull them back, to make them not true.

The Nagi was going to destroy her home. The only question was how.

And if she succeeded in her mission, Hua wouldn't be around to stop her.

CHAPTER 13

Hua

Hua needed to see Heima, to make sure she was okay, but they'd been here for days, and no one seemed concerned about what she wanted.

The monks continued in their silent study, walking through the cold stone halls with measured steps, almost like a dance.

Boqin, Hua had come to learn, was a child orphaned when his village in Piao turned on his parents upon learning of their dragon blood. Master Delun, traveling the region at the time, saved him.

That could have been her if things went differently. What if the village of Zhouchang had learned of her family's heritage? Would the shopkeepers her father frequented betray him? Turn him in to the emperor?

When her family first received a summons to Dasha for the dragon festival, they'd worried they'd been found out, that their secret belonged to them no longer. And still they went. For Luna. If the emperor knew the Minglans had dragon blood, what would he have done to her?

Luna should have been standing here right now, not Hua. She'd have known what to do. Hua shivered as an icy blast lifted the hair from her neck. Standing on a balcony overlooking the vast valley between two of the Shan Mountains, she longed to run away. To force the Nagi out of her body so she could cross that valley and disappear, forgetting the things she'd felt her hands do.

Blood was sticky and warm. It carried life with it as it poured from small slits in the skin. She tried to close her eyes but couldn't as she pictured Luca's men lying dead in the grass beyond her family's charred home.

How much responsibility did she bear for their deaths? How much guilt did she owe the world?

Jian and Luca... her family... none of them would ever see her the same way.

Good, she thought. If they remembered her as a monster maybe it would hurt them less when she didn't return.

Master Delun stepped up beside her, but when he spoke, she had no illusions that the words were for her. They were from one Nagi to another, one body-usurper to another.

"Clear your mind," he whispered. "Focus only on the human inside."

Hua strengthened her thoughts, sending them bouncing in every direction inside her own head. *Murderer. Traitor. Beast.*

The Nagi rubbed her forehead. "She is strong."

"But you are stronger."

Not a chance. Hua refused to fade away like she was never there at all.

"It's not working." The Nagi groaned. "Pain… that's what I feel when I think of her. She's flashing through memories of every time she's been hurt in life. The fear… is this really how humans live?"

"Their existence is full of turmoil."

A snowflake landed on her cheek, melting instantly, but it wasn't alone. Hua tried to urge the Nagi to ask to go inside where the fire never seemed to go out in the library, but it was no use. She couldn't make herself move.

The Nagi turned to Master Delun. "Why have you stayed?"

He pulled his fur wrap up to cover the bottom half of his face. "I do not understand the question?"

"We Nagi have missions. Once we complete them, we can choose to leave this plain of existence and all its… turmoil behind."

He was quiet for a long moment, and Hua strained to hear him, needing to know about this whole Nagi can leave thing. "My human and I… we have an understanding that works quite well for us. And we do not yet know if we have completed our mission."

"That's impossible," the Nagi scoffed. "Humans do not make accords with Nagi. I have to constantly fight to remain in control of this mind." She tapped her head.

He sighed. "It is possible, young one. You come to Lóng Bǎolěi seeking a way to rid yourself of the human this body belongs to, yet you do not plan to stay once your mission is complete. Explain why I should help you."

"I was sent here to avenge our descendants, the hunted and the slaughtered. I cannot do that with a human and her odd sense of morality holding me back. They seem to think it's okay to wage war against other empires, killing warriors and innocent civilians alike, but then question themselves when faced with doing what is necessary to their fellow Piaoans."

The Nagi stepped forward and leaned against the stone wall surrounding the balcony. Snow and ice covered the surface where she rested her arms, caring little for the cold. "They think their greatest enemy is the Kou, but what separates Koulland and Piao but an invisible line in the mountains? No, their greatest enemy is the empire they pledge loyalty to. If our duty is to protect Piao, do we not need to protect them from themselves?"

Master Delun didn't get a chance to respond as the heavy oak door flung open and Boqin stood on the threshold breathing heavily.

"Boqin, what is it?" Master Delun turned to face him.

"There's a sickness in the barns. Two mules, five sheep, and a horse were found dead in their stalls."

Heima. Fear coursed through Hua. She couldn't lose the last connection she had to her old life.

Master Delun put a hand on the boy's shoulder. "Follow our guest to their room and make sure she has dinner." He sent the Nagi an apologetic smile. "Our animals are the greatest source of food for us. I must see to this."

"Of course." The Nagi bowed.

Hua screamed at the Nagi to go after him, to follow him to the barn and make sure Heima was okay. She hammered against the walls in her mind until all strength left her and she shrank into a dark corner where she could hope all of this would end soon.

Hua groaned as she rolled over on the hard bed and froze. She groaned. *She* groaned.

Lifting her head off the scratchy pillow covering, she surveyed the dark room with its sparse furnishings consisting of a single cot and a small desk. The stone walls closed in around her.

A smile spread across her face. She'd never been happier to feel a rough woolen blanket scraping against her skin. Because it was hers. Not the Nagi's. This body belonged to Hua Minglan. Lifting her hand, she flexed her fingers, cracking her knuckles one at a time.

She couldn't remember the last time she'd been able to do that.

Not even the chill of the room could dampen her spirits. Sliding out from under the blanket, she set her bare feet against the cold stone floor and stood.

The wool robe Master Delun provided for her to sleep in settled around her legs. Tentatively, she stepped forward, enjoying the flexing of her calves and even the shivering of her body.

Because for so long, she'd felt almost nothing.

Immediately, she thought of how she could get out of the

creepy silent monastery. Inching toward the door, she pushed it open, revealing a long, narrow hallway devoid of any light.

Slipping into her boots by the door, she stepped into the hall. There was no one to stop her or make her turn back, and only one thought kept her moving. *Heima.* She had to get to her horse. No one had come to tell her if the sickness in the barn had reached Heima, and she'd spent most of the night worrying over her friend.

She pushed her way into the inner sanctum of the monastery, a courtyard open to the sky. Black roses that seemed to have no problem blooming in the harsh weather sat covered in a fresh dusting of snow.

Hua hurried through the deep snow in the odd garden to part of the monastery she hadn't yet seen. When she stepped inside again, melting snow coated her hair. But she didn't care. Not when she could feel it for the first time.

Forcing her stiff legs into a run, she sprinted down the back hall where the monks' dormitories branched off. At the end of the hall was a door that led to the outside and, she hoped, the stables.

When she forced the heavy door open, freezing air rushed in, sending a flurry of snow across the hall. She didn't hesitate before stepping out and yanking the door shut.

Her eyes found the barn, its white paint standing out against the darkness of the night. A cracked sliding wooden door separated her from the animals inside. She used every bit of strength she possessed to pull it open, letting a waft of animal smells escape.

Choking at the scent, she pulled her robe up to cover her mouth and nose before entering the barn. Hay littered the ground, escaping from the bales stacked against the far wall. How did they get supplies this far up in the mountains?

Sheep bleated as she walked past their pen. Rows of mules stood in warm stalls. She didn't know how they kept the barn from freezing. Maybe hot coals like they'd mentioned, or some kind of dragon magic. She almost laughed at the ridiculousness of the thought.

Dragons might exist, but there was no such thing as magic.

When her gaze connected to familiar brown eyes, her entire body sagged with relief. "Heima." She ran toward the stall and fumbled with the lock before pulling it open.

The horse backed away from her.

"It's okay, girl." A tear slipped down her cheek. "It's me. I promise."

Heima took a step toward her, her movements cautious.

"I don't know how long I have, girl."

The horse lowered her head, rubbing it against Hua's shoulder. Hua threw her arms around her friend's neck. "I missed you," she whispered.

Heima's warm breath melted the remaining snow in Hua's hair.

"I won't let the Nagi erase me." She pulled back to meet the understanding brown eyes. "I'm not so easy to get rid of." Running a hand down Heima's nose, she didn't hear the footsteps coming her way.

A throat cleared, and Hua turned to find Master Delun watching her. She shrank back against the horse, but as she looked at the old man, something was different.

And she knew what it was.

"Your Nagi," she breathed.

He nodded. "Tonight, I am truly Master Delun, not the dragon sharing this body. Come, Hua Minglan. We have much to discuss."

Hua hesitated, not wanting to leave Heima.

"Your friend is well cared for. The sick animals have been removed and we turned over all the hay. She'll be okay." He gestured to the door. "Please, come."

Hua kissed the side of Heima's nose. "Love you, girl." She followed Master Delun from the barn and across the snowy landscape. He led her through the maze that was the monastery and into the library where a fire blazed in the hearth, emitting an orange glow.

She rushed toward the warmth, holding her hands out to rid herself of the ice rushing through her veins. At least with the Nagi controlling her, she'd been spared most of the discomfort on the journey here. Now, every blast of cold, every ache and pain was magnified as if hitting her all at once.

Master Delun slid the door shut and waited with a finger pressed to his lips. After a moment, he nodded. "We are alone."

Hua wondered if she was ever truly alone. She searched the recesses of her mind for the Nagi, finding only silence. A breath rushed out of her.

"Have a seat, child." Master Delun gestured to one of the long benches. The seat was as deep as a bed but much harder. The mute monks seemed against any sort of comfort.

Hiking the ends of her robe up, Minglan climbed onto the bench and scooted in until her back hit the carved rail. Many questions ran through her mind as she watched the old man stoke the fire. "How am I here? How are you here? What is this place?"

Master Delun leaned the fire iron against the wall beside the hearth and turned to her. The square sleeves of his robe covered his hands save for the tips of his fingers. He pulled them up as he sat on the bench facing her. "What has your Nagi told you?"

"Nothing useful. She came here to rid herself of me so she can destroy my kingdom."

He pursed his lips. "Ah, a young Nagi. They are rather passionate."

"Passionate? She destroyed an entire village, killing all those within."

Sadness curved his lips down. "Piao has not been kind to those like us, Hua." She started to protest, but he held up a hand to stop her. "That is not to say revenge is needed. But your Nagi's desire for it is understandable. Mine, on the other hand, is an old Nagi who has been with me for many years. He desires nothing but solitude and silence as he waits to complete his mission. We are one."

"I don't want this thing. I want my family." *Jian.* She'd tried not to think of him, but it was hard when she had little to do but think and remember.

"You asked me how you are here." He paused. "A Nagi must sleep—though less than us—and that is when they are at their most vulnerable, their minds having less control. The day is theirs, but the night is very much ours."

That was why the Nagi refused to sleep on their journey. She had known. Now that they were here, she must have been too exhausted to fight.

"I don't want to die." Hua said the words so quietly she

wasn't sure he heard them at first. Focusing on her hands, she refused to look him in the eye.

"We all die in the end."

She lifted her eyes, a burst of anger coursing through her. "But this is not my end. She's going to erase me." Hua pounded on her chest. "This body is mine. I refuse to let her steal it."

"The Nagi does not want your body, dear child. She wants her own."

"Her own..." Hua shrank away from him as understanding struck her.

"Tell me." He cocked his head. "How do you keep her from resuming her form?"

The truth was she didn't know. She'd felt the Nagi trying to transform into a dragon on their journey—probably to speed it up—and each time, Hua gathered every bit of strength she could and expanded her thoughts to fill the Nagi's entire mind, flooding her with images of the battle for Kanyuan. "I don't," she lied.

He tapped his chin. "I very much doubt that. You are strong, Hua Minglan. It will be no easy task for the Nagi to push you from her mind."

"And if she does? What happens to me then? Do I go into my next life, or..." She couldn't speak the words she'd feared since learning the Nagi wanted to erase her. If Hua's body didn't die, would she be allowed into the next life? Or would she wink out of existence, never to reach Nirvana after many lives of struggles?

"I do not know. I am sorry. I wish I had the answers you seek."

Hua's shoulders slumped. Maybe this was her final night

on this earth, the last time she'd ever feel breath entering her lungs or the pulse pounding in her head.

She lifted a hand, flexing her fingers and wondering how she'd never considered the wonder of it all, the magic of being able to move one's legs in coordination with the direction of her mind.

Tears built in her eyes, and she let them fall, imagining what it would be like to never again feel the wetness on her cheeks.

"Hua." Master Delun's bald head shone in the firelight as she met his gaze. "You cannot force the Nagi to obey you, to let you remain, but you can make her believe she has succeeded in her mission."

"What do you mean?"

"The Nagi wishes you gone, so you must cease to exist in her mind."

"But—"

He cut her off with a wave of his hand and stood. "Come, sit in front of the fire."

To her surprise, he lowered himself to the floor and folded his legs in, resting his elbows on his knees. He was much more flexible than a man his age should be.

Hua took a seat across from him and tried to match his pose, but her legs wouldn't bend that way. She tried to lift one foot over her knee, and the movement threw her off balance. She let out a groan as her side slammed into the cold stone floor.

Luna would have laughed at her before striking the pose with ease.

With the sudden fierceness of a battering ram, she missed her sister. Luna was always smarter than her. She'd have known what to do. Hua could hear her melodic voice in her mind. *"It's going to be okay, miemie."* Hua would give anything in that moment to hear Luna call her little sister again.

But Luna wasn't there, and Hua had to do this on her own. She straightened and folded her legs in a more comfortable way before lifting defiant eyes to Master Delun.

If anything was going to save her, it was the fact that she'd never done what anyone told her to. Defiance was her weapon, anger her tool.

The Nagi didn't control her destiny.

"Teach me," she demanded.

Master Delun nodded, and she'd have sworn she saw a smile forming. "You must let the Nagi become the dragon, let her control your heart as well as your mind."

Hua's eyes widened. No. That was one thing she couldn't do, not after the horrors she'd witnessed. "I can't."

"You must. There is a darkness in a Nagi's mind when they are in control."

Hua nodded. She knew it well. When she wanted to wallow, she shrank away from the Nagi and hid.

"You have to let yourself fall into the darkness completely. No thoughts. No actions. You must disappear."

Hua looked away to hide the fear in her eyes. Each time she inched toward the darkness, it took all of her strength to come back. If it covered her completely… she didn't know if she'd ever return. "What if I can't come back?"

"Then the Nagi will win."

Fear raced through her hard as she shook her head, tears clouding her vision. "No."

He squared his shoulders, lengthening his spine as he put his palms on his thighs. "Close your eyes."

Releasing a long breath, she let her eyelids flutter closed.

"Breathe," he whispered. "In. Out. Let all the tension in your mind escape into the world."

Hua's shoulders relaxed as she focused on her breathing.

"Now, think of the Nagi."

Hua flinched as images of the battle flashed across her mind before settling on her home outside Zhouchang. The rolling hills held a peace to them she'd never see again. Their quiet lives were destroyed the day they lost Luna; they just hadn't known it yet. She saw her parents, Nainai, Ru—

"I see a man." Master Delun's voice held a hypnotic tone.

"Jian," she breathed.

"This man… he is meant to aid the dragon."

"What?" It couldn't be true.

"The seer has foreseen it."

"Qara?" Her eyes popped open, but Master Delun continued to squeeze his shut.

"He is coming here."

"No." She scrambled to her feet. "How do you know all this?"

He jerked back, his eyes popping open as if he'd just remembered she was there. "We are connected, Hua. Every Nagi that walks the earth can look into another's mind."

"Are there many?"

He shook his head, sadness entering his gaze. "You are the only other I've felt in many years. That is how you found us. I led your Nagi here."

"You…" She stepped back, noticing the darkness now swirling in Master Delun's eyes. "Your Nagi…" He took back control while they sat in front of those flames.

"Master Delun sends his regrets." He rose to his feet.

Hua's gaze darted to the door, but she'd never be able to outrun a Nagi even if he appeared to be an old man.

"Hua Minglan, I do not wish you harm."

She whirled on him. "Harm? Harm! You wish to force me into the dark, never to return. But you listen to me, I am not as weak as you think. I won't be erased without a fight. Nagis have no place in this world. You aren't human!"

He turned his back on her to stare into the flames. "You are right. The Nagi are no longer of this world. We existed on this plane of existence to protect Piao. It's ingrained in our very structure, but how do you protect an empire that has betrayed you?"

That was why Master Delun and his Nagi lived in a silent monastery in the mountains of Koulland. They no longer believed in Piao.

"Piao is no longer controlled by blood-thirsty emperors who hold onto their power by eliminating the dragon lines. But we are at war. You might live up here doing no damage to my empire, but this Nagi inside me… she has a plan that I can't figure out, something to make Piao pay for the pain. If you help her erase me…" She sat down on one of the benches, exhaustion weighing her down.

It was too much. The fate of the empire sat on her shoulders, and she didn't know what she could do. Unchained from human emotion, the Nagi could wreak havoc throughout Piao, the likes of which had never been seen before.

If Master Delun's Nagi was anything like the old man, he'd understand without needing her to spell it out.

The door opened and two red-robed monks appeared.

Master Delun—or rather, his Nagi—sighed. "Hua

Minglan, it is time you return to your rooms. My master was wrong to let you in here." He bowed. "Sleep. All will be right when the Nagi once again takes hold of your mind."

She tried to protest, but a hand clamped down on each of her arms and pulled her away. She bucked, trying to free herself. Still, Master Delun did not turn away from the fire.

"I won't go," she yelled. "You can't erase me."

The monks dragged her down the long, dark hall and shoved her into her room before slamming the door shut, cutting her off from any light.

As Master Delun told her before his Nagi returned, the darkness would be her friend. She'd let herself sink into the inky black void of the Nagi's mind, but she'd return.

For her family. For Piao.

For Jian.

She'd fight.

CHAPTER 14

The Nagi

"Try again." Master Delun stood on the windy balcony facing the Nagi. "Do you feel her?"

The Nagi searched the recesses of her mind for the girl who'd been a constant companion for what felt like her entire life, finding only emptiness.

Thoughts rattled around her head, finding no one else to latch on to. For the first time since inhabiting this body, the Nagi was truly and utterly alone.

What should have been a satisfactory moment only left

her feeling odd, like this body didn't belong to her. Of course, it didn't, not truly. But now the disassociation was more pronounced.

"Nothing," she said.

Master Delun didn't smile, he didn't congratulate her. They were both Nagi but had very different goals. The old man still felt Piao needed to be protected as their mandate bid them.

The Nagi inhabiting Hua wanted the empire stripped down to its core. And there was one way to begin.

But not if she couldn't transform into a dragon. Without Hua in her mind keeping her from her true form, the shift should have been easy.

Master Delun pulled himself up onto the stone wall encircling the balcony. He threw his arms out to keep his balance on the slick surface before reaching a hand down to the Nagi.

If this worked, she would be one step closer to her goal. If it didn't, this body would break. How did humans survive in such weak forms?

Taking Master Delun's hand, the Nagi pulled herself up, almost falling as her foot hit the snow-covered ice. Frigid air blew in their faces, and the Nagi closed her eyes, savoring the feel against her burning skin.

"Ready?" Master Delun asked.

The Nagi only nodded as she looked out into the valley below the balcony. Peaks rose in the distance, separated by dips in the land and snow-covered hills.

Lifting her face to the snow falling from the heavens, the Nagi stepped forward, letting her entire body drop off the balcony. Her stomach flipped as she tried to force the dragon form to come, sending surges of power straight through Hua's heart.

A scream left her lips as the ground rushed closer. She braced for impact, but at the last moment, scales burst free, overlapping Hua's skin. Giant scaled wings with ragged edges emerged and issued one powerful flap, their tips brushing the ground she came so close to meeting.

The Nagi rose as the wind caught underneath the wings. A bubble of glee rose in her before she released a stream of fire, carving a wide lane through the snow.

She swooped lower, brushing clawed feet through the fresh powder. Above, Master Delun soared through the sky, spinning and twisting with joy.

This was how a Nagi was supposed to live, free from human bonds and high above their meaningless woes.

If Hua could experience a feeling like this, she wouldn't waste another thought on a man who'd led her into war or a sister who no longer walked this earth.

Dark emotions had no place high above the earth.

The humans believed in Samsura, the cycle of suffering one endured before reaching Nirvana.

But this flight… this freedom… if they let the Nagi return and show them what it meant to fly, they'd never have to suffer again.

As the Nagi circled the bleak monastery, she spared a single thought for the girl she'd banished from her mind, wishing Hua too could see this.

But Hua put chains on her, preventing the Nagi from transforming.

The Nagi had no choice but to rid herself of the human burden.

It was the only way to continue on a path for justice.

CHAPTER 15

Jian

"She needs someone to care enough to bring her back."

Qara's words were the only thing keeping Jian moving through the snow-deep mountain passes. He'd crossed into Koulland days before, but he didn't know how much longer he had to travel to reach the monastery.

Ice crusted his gloves as he wrapped chilled fingers around his horse's reins and focused all his strength on just staying in the saddle. He'd fallen off periodically throughout the day, but always managed to get back up.

When was the last time he'd slept? Each night, he set up a

tent to keep the wind at bay, but the cold never went away, leaving him shivering as he lay awake.

He'd switched horses at each village he found, but there hadn't been another village in days.

Weakness enveloped his very bones, and he pitched forward, clinging to the saddle, trying to keep the darkness encroaching on his vision from overtaking him.

Hua. He had to get to Hua. Qara was right. She needed someone to care enough to bring her back. He wanted to believe she could do it on her own, but if Hua was in control of her actions, she'd never have killed Luca's men.

He'd have given anything to have Luca at his side, but his best friend's mission was just as important. If Jian managed to help Hua defeat the Nagi, he refused to have to tell her anything happened to her family.

Jian's job was to bring her back. Luca's was to make sure she had something to come back to.

Jian's vision went blurry as he tilted to the side, unable to keep himself upright.

His body went limp as he slid from the horse, but Jian didn't feel himself hit the ground. He didn't sense the snow closing over him.

Because he was already gone.

Warmth seeped into Jian where he lay on a small cot.

Wait, a cot? He hadn't brought any such thing with him. In fact, he'd been sleeping on the cold ground inside his tent.

His eyes slammed open, and he instantly regretted it as pain pierced his skull.

Where was he?

A domed tent surrounded him, held up by a ring of wooden poles. Vibrant reds and yellows decorated the cloth from floor to vaulted ceiling, making the space seem bigger than it was.

The bed he was in served as one of the few pieces of furniture other than a small stove across the space.

In the center of the tent was a hand-woven blue carpet and low table.

A wooden door kept the weather from entering.

As he sat up and peered closer around the tent, his eyes widened. This was no Piao military tent.

"A yurt," he whispered. The favored homes of the Kou, easily movable, sturdy and able to withstand harsh weather. Jian remembered the structures well from his time in Koulland.

Was he a prisoner?

He pushed off the furs someone had piled on him, finding a woolen robe and pants adorning his frame rather than the clothes he'd had on last.

Someone knocked on the door and pushed it open. The older woman hesitated only for a moment. "You're awake. That's good." She crossed the room and held out a chipped black ceramic cup. "Milk tea. You drink."

He didn't reach for it. "Where am I?"

"Take tea." She thrust it toward him again.

With a sigh, he did as she asked.

"Drink," she ordered.

He lifted the cup to his lips and savored the steam rising from the top, letting it warm his face before he took a sip.

How long had it been since he'd had a simple cup of tea?

He'd traveled for weeks now but couldn't manage to keep a fire lit long enough to heat a kettle when the winds and snow blew it out constantly.

The woman nodded in satisfaction and pointed to herself. "Sarnai." She pointed to him. "Soldier."

"No." He sat up straighter. "Not soldier." Not anymore, at least. "My name is Jian. I am searching for someone."

She pursed her lips like she didn't believe him.

"Mama," a voice cut off her next words.

The older woman turned and rushed from the yurt as a younger man entered, ducking his head at the door. He couldn't have been much older than Jian, but he looked every bit the Kou warrior. Swirling black tattoos stretched up his thick neck. His red robe hung off his massive frame with gold threading depicting the image of a dragon.

An image forbidden across the border in Piao.

"Forgive us." His voice held little of the Kou accent his mother's had. "My mama speaks very little Piaoan. She has not been trained as a warrior."

"And you have?" Jian would never trust anyone loyal to Koulland.

The big man sighed. "Something like that. My name is Khenbish. Most people call me Khen. You and I have a lot to discuss, Jian Li."

"How do you know who I am?" Jian freed his legs, his eyes searching the room for the sword he'd had with him. "Are you Altan's man?"

Khen rubbed the back of his neck. "We only belong to one master."

"Who?"

"His name is Delun, and he has been awaiting your arrival."

"He knew I was coming?" That didn't make any sense. Unless…

"Yes." The man turned to the door. "His Nagi is very eager to meet you."

A young girl with wide eyes rushed in with a wooden bowl in her small hands. She had to be around Ru's age. Jian stared at her, wishing he could see the young boy he'd come to love instead.

But Ru wasn't his brother, and he needed to make sure the kid saw his sister again.

"Thank you, Baya." Khen took the bowl from her and dipped his head with a smile.

The girl scurried back out into the cold.

"Eat." He shoved the bowl at Jian.

Jian lifted the wooden spoon and eyed it. Rice porridge? It was standard army food in Piao, and the familiarity brought a strange sort of comfort. He set the bowl in his lap and shoveled food into his mouth as if he hadn't eaten in days.

He barely had.

By the time the spoon scraped the bottom of the empty bowl, Jian found some of his strength returning.

Khen sat on the rug in the middle of the room, his legs crossed.

Jian put the bowl on the bed beside him and leaned forward, his eyes never leaving the Kou man who held him prisoner. "My horse?"

Khen's expression didn't change. "The animal did not survive the cold, I'm afraid."

A pang hit Jian. "Am I your prisoner?"

Khen lifted one shoulder in a shrug. "You may leave, but you will never make it off this mountain alive, and the truths you seek will not be known."

"This man, your… master, he is a Nagi?"

"No, he has a Nagi living inside him. Lóng Bǎolěi is the home of the dragon."

"And you serve it?"

Khen's dark brows drew together. "We do not serve the creature, only the man it possesses."

Something in his tone sounded off. "Are there those who serve the Nagi?" He still couldn't wrap his head around the fact Hua wasn't the only human with a dragon living inside her, but there was much left to learn.

Khen nodded. "The twelve dragon disciples as they are known. The monks of Lóng Bǎolěi."

"Why were you searching for me?" Jian rested his elbows on his knees and peered down at the man. "Why did this Master Delun want me to live?"

"Ah, but that is not for me to know, Jian Li, Commander of the Piaoan armies and brother to Emperor Bo Xu Wei."

Jian's eyes widened. How did they know so much about him?

Khen wasn't finished. "You led men into the mountains only to face slaughter at the hands of General Altan. And in the great battle of Kanyuan, a dragon flew you to safety."

Jian opened his mouth to speak, but Khen cut him off. "Master Delun knows everything Hua Minglan knows. Their Nagi are connected."

"Hua?" Jian jumped to his feet. "Has she been here? Is she

okay?" His pulse hammered in his throat. He was wasting valuable time sitting here.

Khen ignored the question. "My family has served Master Delun for a long time, and it is rare travelers come through here."

"Because the mountain passes are dangerous?" He knew that well enough.

But the Kou man shook his head. "Because this is not the direct path to the monastery."

"I don't understand." Jian had a map, one drawn by Qara herself. He never imagined she'd lead him astray, let alone send him on a more perilous journey than it needed to be.

Khen stood and walked to a chest hidden at the end of the bed. Pulling open the heavy lid, he retrieved thick furs and tossed them to Jian. "Come with me."

Jian clad himself in the warm furs and followed Khen through the wooden door into a clearing surrounded by a circle of yurts. It looked so similar to the village he'd first met Qara in that he stopped breathing for a moment, waiting for Altan to appear at any moment.

The Kou were enemies of Piao, no matter if they served the man harboring a Nagi or not. But then, the Nagi were no longer protectors of Piao, at least, not the one residing in Hua.

Yet, as he watched children dart from one yurt to the next followed by women carrying kettles and baskets, he couldn't help but think of the normalcy of it all. If these people lived in Piao, no one would know the difference. Yet, here they were on the far edges of society, going on with life and just surviving.

A few men lingered about, daos hanging at their waists. Guards?

What was this place?

"This is my family's camp," Khen explained as they walked between two domed yurts to the ice fields beyond. "We are messengers of Master Delun and his Nagi."

"And what does the Nagi say?" The viciousness of Hua's Nagi would never leave his mind. It was a dragon seeking revenge and nothing more. Khen spoke as if Master Delun and his beast were aged, and they lived high in the mountains, away from the empire that slaughtered those with dragon blood.

What did it want? There was always something.

Ice broke underneath Jian's boots as he trudged across sheets of it that covered the vast plains of the valley stretching to the next rise of the mountain. A frigid wind blew snow across his cheeks, and he pulled up the fur cloak to cover the lower half of his face.

Khenbish kept going as if the cold didn't bother him. He left his face exposed to the wind, and snow dusted his dark hair.

Jian didn't know where they were going or how much farther he could travel. "Are we going to the monastery?"

Khenbish glanced sideways at him. "We do not enter the sacred place. No, Master Delun will come to us when he's ready. He knows you are here."

They stopped at the base of a hill, and Jian looked up at the bleak gray trees cresting the top of it. He never imagined he'd long for a yurt.

He'd give anything to be back at the Minglans' house,

huddled in front of the fire with the family who'd accepted him before Hua even woke.

To hear Nainai's stories and dig his frozen fingers into Chichi's brindled hair.

With a sigh, he followed Khenbish up the hill, his legs threatening to give out with each step.

By the time they reached the trees, Jian was ready to collapse.

"Not much farther now." Khenbish pulled aside a branch and ushered Jian through.

Frozen sticks and pine needles stuck up through the snow—which had thinned once they reached the tree cover.

At the edge of the trees, Jian froze.

It wasn't possible.

The hill dipped down into another valley, but this one wasn't as empty as the land behind them.

Fires dotted the land, kept going by ramshackle shelters built over them to keep the winds and snow at bay.

Yurts—hundreds or maybe thousands of them—stood in rows, their tan pelts covered in white powder. Between them, men walked in full armor, but not Piao armor like Jian was used to seeing.

They wore the leathers and furs typical to the Kou, the most dangerous fighting force in the land.

"Who are they?" General Altan didn't have his men stationed this far into the mountains. They'd once discussed how the snows made it an impossible feat.

"General Altan has controlled the Kou army for two decades. He forces young boys from their homes and pushes them into intensive training until the only thing they know is loyalty to him. The Kou warriors are brutal and skilled because all they've known is battle."

"That didn't answer my question."

"Piao isn't the only empire that needed the dragons to protect them. The Nagi were supposed to keep our world from being destroyed by human idiocies. Their very presence prevented wars. The men and women in this camp have left everything behind in pursuit of something other than the life of strife they inherited."

"You're saying these are Kou refuges?"

"Many of them are warriors and many are not. But, Jian, you'll find their greatest desire aligns with that of Piao—to free Koulland from the yoke Batukhan Altan has placed around its neck."

The problem with General Altan was that there'd never been anyone to rein him in. Koulland had no central ruler, only elders who controlled each village. Altan and his fighting force were never challenged.

It made sense now. Jian stepped back. Qara knew. She'd given him a map that would take him through these valleys instead of a more direct path to the monastery because she wanted him to see this.

But what did it mean?

They were high in the mountains. Even if they'd agree to come to Piao's aid, there would be no time to get a message to them.

It was just as useless as any of Jian's other plans to find Altan. He turned away. No, the way to save Piao led through Hua, not these unknown and untrustworthy Kou.

Hua was more dangerous than any number of enemy warriors.

CHAPTER 16

Hua

Darkness was no friend, only a foe.

Hua held on to the tiny thread of her old mind, not allowing herself to look out through eyes that were once her own. If she rose to the surface, the Nagi would know she failed, that the girl she'd tried so hard to erase was too stubborn to let herself fade away.

It wasn't strength that allowed Hua to carry on, not even fearlessness. No, she refused to let the Nagi win. It was the same stubbornness that led her to disguise herself as a man and go to war, the very same that had once wanted to find the man responsible for her sister's death no matter the cost.

But some costs were too high.

The irony was this beast inside her body was probably the only thing that could help her get the revenge she'd so desperately sought. If she allied herself with the Nagi, they could force General Altan to his knees.

But what then? The Nagi destroyed both the Kou warriors and the Piao army inside Kanyuan. It hadn't differentiated between soldiers.

Just like Hua once called revenge her mission, so did the Nagi.

What would Nainai say? She'd probably spout some ancient wisdom about revenge turning the soul bleak.

Her father would bow his head in acceptance of the emotions raging through her. He grieved Luna, but his life hadn't been ripped in two by her absence. Luna was half of the whole that created the Minglan sisters.

And Jian? The man who'd made it his mission to get his own revenge on Altan, what would he say?

We do what we must, Minglan.

She let the warmth of his imagined voice cocoon her in comfort. When she'd been part of his unit, she'd felt safe, secure.

We do what we must, Minglan.

He'd forgive her for everything she'd done, everything she had yet to do. He'd understand why she surrendered her remaining power without knowing if she could come back.

She'd let the Nagi take flight once again from the monastery, believing she had gained her freedom. It took everything in her to remain silent when the Nagi left Heima behind.

I'm sorry, girl.

And now, all Hua could do was wait to see where the next battle would begin.

CHAPTER 17

Jian

Jian had been in Khenbish's camp for two days when the riding party came. The sound of horses thundering through the mountain pass drifted into the yurt. Khenbish got to his feet and set aside the dao he'd been sharpening. "They are here."

"They? How do you know who it is?" Jian got to his feet.

"No one approaches this camp except for our master."

Their master. Jian rubbed the back of his neck before rearranging the knot on top of his head. Master Delun, the man who might know where Hua was, the only other living person known to have a Nagi inside him.

Shrugging on a fur cloak, Jian wiped his palms on his wool robe and followed Khenbish from the yurt.

In the clearing, an elderly man dismounted from a familiar horse. Jian couldn't breathe. This was it. He'd found her against all the odds. Heima lifted her head and snorted. Jian ignored the men surrounding the old man as he rushed for the horse, needing to thread his fingers through her tangled mane. He reached for her, and Heima stepped forward as if drawn to him just as much as he was to her.

His breath returned as he rubbed her nose and stared into her wide brown eyes. It was like getting part of Hua back.

The old man cleared his throat, and Khenbish ran forward, dropping into an elaborate bow. "Master Delun, we are honored by your presence here."

For the first time, Jian studied the man, taking note of the haze of his eyes. The true Master Delun wasn't in control.

"Nagi," Jian growled, inching toward him. "Where is she?"

Khenbish stepped between them, bowing again. "I am sorry, sir. He is not versed in our ways."

Master Delun eyed Jian, his gaze as cold as the snow beneath his feet. "This is the man I sent you to find? The one I saw coming?"

"Yes. He was close to death just as you knew he would be."

Master Delun's keen eyes scanned Jian from head to toe. "General, I do not have time for your hatred of my kind. The girl you seek is not here."

Everything in Jian deflated at those words. He took a step back, pressing himself against Heima. "But she was." She had to be. There was no other explanation for the horse's presence.

"The Nagi left hours ago."

Hours. He'd missed her by mere hours.

But wait. "She has a name, one belonging to a woman whose life has been stolen. Hua Minglan. I want you to say it."

"The Nagi has taken full control of Hua in a way I would never imagine doing with my own human. He and I are a team. The young Nagi…" He sighed and there was something sad about the man. "She has tried to erase her human."

Jian's eyes narrowed. "Tried?"

"Your human girl may still be in there or she may not. I do not know, but the Nagi has been released from her cage."

"And you just let her leave? I thought you Nagi were supposed to protect Piao." His shouting drew others from their yurts, and the crowd formed around them.

"Jian Li, some Nagi have left those vows behind. Our young Nagi is preparing to betray the empire we were meant to protect."

"How?"

"That is not something I have foreseen."

Jian paced in front of the crowd, growing more agitated with each moment. He was so close and failed. "You should have stopped her if you knew I was coming."

"I do not interfere in the affairs of another Nagi, Jian. What will happen will happen. I'm sorry, I cannot tell you more than she has gone to Dasha."

"Dasha?" He froze, turning on his heel to face Master Delun. What could the Nagi possibly want in—Jian flushed with anger. The Nagi wanted revenge on Piao. If she desired destruction, there were more populated areas than the capitol.

The true enemies of the Nagi weren't the people in villages scattered across farmlands and hills or the ones in the coastal cities dealing with traders from far kingdoms.

No, who held the dragon festivals where the blooded were slaughtered?

Who lured descendants of the last dragons to Dasha for their own deaths over the years?

The emperors.

Hua was on her way to the capital to kill Bo—Jian's brother.

"Come, Jian Li." Master Delun held out a hand. "I could not stop the girl, but you can. We must help you reach her." He dropped his hand and stepped back from the others, putting distance between him and the horses as black scales slinked down his arms and up his neck.

Jian kept the old man's gaze as his eyes yellowed and widened. The horses whinnied and stomped their feet in agitation, but the men who'd accompanied Master Delun held their leads, not letting them run away.

The only horse that didn't try to get away was Heima. Instead, her eyes latched onto the beast's.

Because she too had seen this before.

The Nagi shed his human form, his body expanding and bones twisting until he lifted his long, jagged neck and peered down at Jian. The mountains stood at his back, the white snow unmarred by this dragon's darkness. He opened his mouth and fire built in the back of his throat, an orange glow ready to explode.

But the flames didn't come. Instead, the dragon sat back, its tail carving a path in the snow.

Khenbish's voice beside Jian made him jump. "He is ready."

"Ready?" Jian looked from Khenbish to the giant beast that should strike terror through his heart. But Jian had known fear, real, deep fear. It didn't come from the creatures of this world or the battles they fought. He wasn't scared of his own demise.

The thing that scared him most? Watching someone else live Hua's life, inhabit her body.

Losing Bo.

He wouldn't let either of those futures come to pass.

So, instead of fearing the dragon before him, he stepped forward. The dragon's heat thawed the ice in Jian's veins. A nose nudged the side of his head as Heima stepped up beside him. He bowed to the dragon offering to help him.

The dragon dipped its head in response.

"Take us to Dasha."

CHAPTER 18

Hua

Luck. Power. Truth.

The lore of dragons in Piao held many contradictions. Contradictions Hua had plenty of time to consider as she lived in the darkness of her own mind.

Little by little, she clawed herself back to the surface, enough to know her feet now stood in Dasha Square. No, she couldn't see her surroundings, but she'd never forget the sounds of the place that took her sister's life, the shouts of shopkeepers crowded together, the way carts sounded as they rumbled from stone to marble.

Maybe it was fitting this was where she too would meet her end and join Luna in the next life—maybe. Then the fear came again. Not of death, but of her mind dying while her body remained whole. What would that mean for her spirit's journey?

Footsteps echoed off the cobblestone square. She could almost picture it, the marble steps leading up to the emperor's palace were a beautiful testament to the city and a horrible reminder of what took place there.

She flinched as she saw Luna's body hit the step and imagined the girl Hua used to be, hovering over her in the middle of the attack with arrows bouncing off her skin as they failed to pierce flesh strengthened by a Nagi.

And still, Jian had risked his life for her that day, a total stranger. She only wished she was strong enough to do one last thing for him.

Because the Nagi had a plan.

Bo Xu Wei stood no chance against the wronged dragon.

It was time. As soon as she pulled herself into the light, the Nagi would know she had failed in erasing Hua, but Hua had no choice now, not as the Nagi picked up her pace.

Hua cried out, the sound echoing in the recesses of her mind, and the Nagi froze.

Another scream, and the Nagi searched inward, letting her thoughts and attention shift to her mind rather than the world around it.

Which was just what Hua needed.

Gathering all her will, she leaped forward in her mind, grasping onto the Nagi's waves of thoughts and using them to scratch her way to the front of her mind.

The Nagi convulsed, a greasy haze flittering across her

brain before she collapsed, slamming Hua's head into the ground and jolting her into control.

Hua lay still for a long moment, pain rocketing through her limbs. Warm blood trickled from the back of her head, soaking into her hair. Slowly, her eyes opened to find a crowd hovering over her.

Their quiet questions and concerns hit her louder than they could possibly voice, and she covered her ears with her hands, needing to block out the sounds as they closed in on her.

Only one thought filtered through her mind. She'd done it. She was back.

Reaching out, she felt the bottom of the imperial palace step and used it to push herself up as anxiety buzzed along her skin. A full moon hung overhead, casting an eerie glow across the square.

Two guards sprinted down the palace steps, their chain-mail clinking together. They parted the crowd of onlookers and stared down at her.

"Miss," one of them started. Hua waited for him to ask if she needed help, but instead, he frowned. "You cannot ascend the palace steps."

The second guard scowled. "Do you belong here?" He meant at the palace, but as Hua's eyes flitted past the crowd, taking in the same paper lanterns that had hung during the dragon festival where her life changed, she shook her head. Hua Minglan didn't belong in Dasha.

She'd come to kill the emperor, after all.

A young man ran down the steps, his feet light. "Is she okay?" He tried to get past the guards, but they blocked his way.

"Prince Duyi," one of the guards growled. "You are not to be out of the palace."

The prince stopped pushing them. "My brother was just taking me out to walk the square."

Guard number two crossed his arms. "The emperor should know better than to venture out at night without guards."

"I'm sure he was going to ask you to come." Hua could tell by his tone he was lying. Duyi and Bo had meant to sneak down the steps into the square.

One of the guards grabbed the prince by the arm and forced him back up the steps.

Hua lifted her gaze to the palace, peering past the columned splendor to find a young man she'd only met once before standing in the doorway, his eyes meeting hers.

She couldn't let the Nagi harm him.

"You can't stop me," the Nagi said in her mind.

"Watch me."

A middle-aged man wearing a short cloak over his pale green silk robe crouched down in front of her. "Are you okay, dear?" He looked up at the others. "Go. Leave us."

As if this man had some authority, they scattered with only a few murmured protests. He gripped her elbow and helped her to her feet.

Hua clutched the man's arm as the world spun around her, and she almost lost her footing. "I… can't…" Her head throbbed as the Nagi clawed and thrashed in her mind. It wouldn't be long before she lost control again, and she needed to be far away from here when that happened. But at the moment, she couldn't make her feet obey her command to walk forward.

"Come." The man slid her arm over his shoulders, his strength keeping her upright as they stumbled across the square together past blackened buildings, burned during the attack at the dragon festival. Some lay in ruins while others were in various stages of being rebuilt.

Hua spared few thoughts for Dasha after the Kou destroyed the city. She'd thought of the attack many times, but not the city left behind in the rubble. Many of the people living in the capitol and running businesses had lost everything.

Some even gave their lives. Like Luna.

And she'd come to cause them more pain.

"Like the pain they caused us," the Nagi whispered inside her mind. *"Isn't vengeance the reason you joined the army?"*

No, not vengeance. She'd done it to save her father. At least, that was what she'd told herself. The truth lay somewhere in between. Was the Nagi's desire for revenge any less noble just because she sought Piao's destruction instead of Koulland's? Hua wanted to avenge her sister's death. The Nagi sought to make up for generations of slaughtered descendants.

"Ah, we're beginning to understand each other."

The man helping Hua led her into a storefront that still had a black burn stretching across the stones over the newly crafted wooden door. A sign hung in the large-paned glass window. A healer.

That was why the crowd gave deference to him. Healers were important, revered. "Why did you help me?"

He grunted under her weight as he led her to a cot near the back of the threadbare room. "You were injured."

He didn't know what he'd just brought into his home, the danger he embroiled himself in. "What is your name?"

"Liqin." He helped her onto the cot. "Stay."

She didn't argue as he entered another room at the back.

"Liqin," the Nagi said. *"He is not dragon blooded."*

"He's helping us, me. You will not harm him."

"We will see."

A growl reverberated in Hua's throat. "What is wrong with you?" She spoke the words out loud without realizing it.

The Nagi didn't respond.

Liqin returned a moment later with a tarnished silver tray. "Did you say something?"

She shook her head, wincing at the pain the movement caused.

Setting the tray on the cot beside her, he passed her a white ceramic cup. "Drink this. It will help."

He removed a wet cloth from the bowl on the tray and dabbed her head. "You will be fine. Just a minor cut that I do not need to sew. What you need now is rest."

"Rest?" Her head jerked up. "No. I can't rest." She got to her feet, her legs wobbling beneath her.

"You have suffered a fall. The pain will ebb away while you relax and then you can be on your way."

"I'll go now." He obviously didn't want her here, a near stranger. He'd never even asked her name. She stumbled toward the door. The teacup tumbled from her fingers, crashing into the ground and shattering, sending a spray of glass near her feet.

"Don't move."

Hua couldn't have moved if she tried. Her limbs stood

frozen in place as Liqin retrieved a broom and swept away her mess.

"I-I'm sorry."

He cleaned up the remaining glass before reaching a hand toward her. "You look like her."

Hua had no more energy to fight. She set her hand in his and let him help her back to the cot. "Like who?"

"Consort Minglan."

Tears sprang to Hua's eyes unbidden. She neither wiped them away or let them fall. "You knew my sister?"

Liqin nodded. "My daughter was so proud the day she was chosen to be a servant to a consort. She loved your sister with her whole heart and said she'd never met a kinder woman of her station."

"Luna was just a farmer," Hua whispered. "A village girl." That was how she remembered her—in woolen robes with dirt under her fingernails from helping their mother in the gardens. But the people in this city knew her as something else, a woman of stature in silk clothing with jewels adorning her hair.

"I saw you at the festival with her," Liqin continued. "I was walking with my daughter as she attended to Consort Minglan."

"You daughter…" Hua could hardly get the words out as her eyes scanned the surrounding room that so lacked a woman's presence.

Liqin met her gaze in some kind of shared pain. "She died in the attack along with my wife and young son."

"I am sorry."

He bowed his head in acceptance. "As am I. This city loved Consort Minglan. She was the only member of the palace household who frequented our shops rather than sending servants to make her purchases. We have mourned her loss along with the loss of so many others."

Maybe it was because she'd finally met someone who could understand her pain, or maybe because he was a stranger with a trustworthy aura, but Hua needed to tell him she'd tried to avenge the deaths of all those they loved. "I tried to fight the Kou." Her story of joining the army disguised as a man poured out of her. She'd done it for Luna and everyone else who'd died because of the Kou. Once she'd finished, she lowered her voice. "And I failed."

"Dear girl, this is not over yet." He put a finger under her chin and tilted her face up so she met his gaze. "Do not claim a failure that is not yours."

Hua's entire body relaxed at his words, and she scooted farther back onto the cot. The edges of her vision grew fuzzy, but she held on to consciousness as much as she could. "I can't..."

"Sleep, child."

She shook her head, her oily hair sticking to her cheeks. "No. You don't understand." Her tenuous grip on the moment slipped, and her eyes fixated on where the cup had broken on the floor. "What did you—"

"Just a bit of silk bark tea." He smiled as if he'd done her a favor. "It will help you sleep. Just for a while. You need to regain your strength."

Hua slumped back against the bed. She tried to sit up again, but it was no use. Her entire body relaxed into sleep, letting her mind go blank as she lost control once again.

CHAPTER 19

Jian

Jian never imagined his search for Hua would take him back to a farm he knew so well. It was difficult to wrap his mind around how he'd gotten there, taking only a single day for the massive black dragon to fly him and Heima to the fields surrounding Dasha.

It wasn't something he'd ever forget. It gave him hope.

If Master Delun and his Nagi could live in peace together, causing no harm, then maybe he could see the light in Hua's defiant eyes again and know it was her and not the beast inside.

Master Delun carried Jian and Heima in his claws and set them down in the middle of a golden winter wheat field stretching as far as the eye could see. The high grasses bent to make way for the winged beast, giving deference to him.

Heima launched herself away from the dragon as soon as her hooves touched down, and Jian couldn't blame her. He too wanted to run. Instead, he turned to Master Delun and bowed in thanks.

The dragon's yellow eyes bore into him as his head dipped once before he jumped into the air with an earth-shaking flap of his wings.

Jian shielded his eyes against the sun as he watched it disappear on the horizon. "Heima, I don't think that happens every day."

Heima ran circles around him, stomping the wheat in her path.

Jian lowered his hand and surveyed his surroundings. The ring of fields circling Dasha like a crown were legendary. All travelers used the roads between the fields to come and go from the capitol, but there was only one field that surrounded an ancient gingko tree. Its twisted branches stood bare this time of year, but still, it dragged memories from the depths of Jian's mind.

How did Master Delun know to bring him here?

To the farm he'd spent so much time on as a boy? The empress had liked finding ways to torture the young bastard child of the emperor's consort, but she didn't realize his time working alongside Luca on his family's farm was no torture at all.

Luca's father was a great general in the civil wars, but he'd always preferred his simple family life to any other.

Luca was of the same mind. He'd follow Jian wherever he led, but what he truly wanted was a home to call his own.

"Heima," Jian called with a cluck of his tongue. "If the Minglans made it here, we must tell them she is still lost to us."

He wasn't sure how long it had been since he left them with their hopes scattered on the wind. Weeks? But how many? Six?

And still, he had no good news to tell them other than that she was in Dasha. But was it good news when he knew her reason for being there?

He looked over his shoulder to the roads leading into the city, winding past the far edge of the fields, but he wouldn't reach it by nightfall, and the weariness started catching up with him. Heaving a sigh, he closed his eyes for a brief moment.

He was home.

Well, the only home he'd ever known.

The palace had never been a welcoming place to him, but each time he set foot on this farm, he belonged. It was the power of the Kais. The Minglans had it too. An ability to take people in and make them family.

Heima walked up behind him and nudged his shoulder. He reached up to rub her nose. "I know, girl. This is going to hurt them." He gripped the saddle and pulled himself up.

Strands of wheat brushed his calves as he urged Heima into a trot, doing all he could just to remain in the saddle.

In the last few days, he'd almost died in the snow drifts, been rescued by a strange group of people in Koulland, found an entire Kou army who was not under the control of

General Altan, and was carried through the skies by a dragon.

Now, he rode toward the people he wasn't yet ready to see. If Luca did as he asked, the Minglans would be in the manor house he saw as he crested a small hill past the tree he'd climbed so many times.

Heima emerged from the wheat stalks as the ground beneath her hooves hardened into a dirt path meandering toward the large white house. An arching black roof pointed toward the sky. Jian couldn't focus on the familiar barn across from the house or the straw littering the ground outside the front door.

He slid from Heima, keeping one hand on the horse to steady himself.

The front door opened, and a girl he'd know anywhere stood frozen in the entryway. "Jian?"

"Song." His shoulders sagged in relief at the familiar face. Her hair, normally hanging to her shoulders as befit an unmarried girl, was pulled back in a simple knot. But her eyes, those hadn't changed. She still looked at Jian as if he hung the moon.

"It is you." She rushed forward. There was a time when Luca's sister wanted to marry Jian. She hadn't cared about his lack of position as a common soldier. It wasn't until Bo came to power he had any prospects in life.

But she'd never evoked the kind of fear he had for Hua. Fear of losing her. Fear of failing her.

Song wrapped Jian in a hug more befitting siblings than old friends. He let himself soak in the comfort for a long moment before pulling back.

"We've been so worried." A smile graced her red-painted

lips. "But you're okay. You're here. I must tell Luca and Baba. Their hearts will sing with joy."

Jian shook his head. "No singing with joy yet please. Just Luca. I need Luca. Have him meet me in the barn. Please speak of this to no one."

She nodded. "Yes. Of course. You know I'll do this for you, Jian."

He did know, but he didn't get a chance to thank her as she rushed back into the house. Jian crossed the small field to the barn and pulled Heima through a side door. It took all his strength to remove her tack and saddle before leaving her in a stall. Luca could feed her.

Dropping down onto a hay bale along the wall, he folded in on himself, dropping his head into his hands. How was he supposed to save Hua and Bo when he could barely lift his head?

A thought came to him. Maybe he didn't have to tell Gen and Fa Minglan at all. At least, not yet. He could let them hold on to their last shreds of hope a while longer. It probably made him a coward, but he couldn't face them until he knew for sure if Hua was coming back to them.

The barn door opened, and he turned his head, expecting to see Luca. Instead, Ru ran toward him with Chichi dogging his heels. The dog jumped at Jian, swiping his tongue across Jian's cheek.

"Chichi," Ru's high pitch voice squealed. "Bad dog. Jian is not a honeycomb. You can't just lick anyone you please." Ru crossed his arms and stared at the dog with stern eyes before settling that hard gaze on Jian. "And you… where is my sister?"

If Jian wasn't so far down the road to hopelessness, he'd

have laughed at the indignant kid. "Your mama and baba can't know I'm here, Ru."

He stuck out his lip in a pout. "I thought we were friends."

Jian sighed. "We are." He cared about Ru like he cared for his own brother.

Tears gathered in Ru's eyes. "Then why weren't you going to come see me?"

Jian opened his mouth to protest but closed it when he decided he wouldn't lie to the kid. Ru had been through too much trauma in his life. "You see too much, you know that." He patted the hay bale beside him. "Sit, and I'll tell you of the dragon that brought me here."

Ru's eyes widened, and he did as Jian asked, hanging on his every word as Jian recounted the flight. It was the only way he knew to avoid the subject of Hua.

Chichi paced the length of the barn and stopped outside Heima's stall, letting out a shrill bark.

"What's wrong, Chichi?" Ru jumped up and ran toward him, his feet skidding to a halt. "Heima? But…" He turned accusatory eyes on Jian. "Hua took her. I saw it. Where is she?"

"A question I'm sure we'd all like to know." Luca's voice came from the doorway where he stood with one foot propped on the frame. "Ru, you will speak of this to no one. Go back to the house. You have not finished your chores for the day."

"Luca—"

"I said go." Luca did not raise his voice, but the command was the same, leaving no further room for argument.

Ru's sad eyes locked on each of them once more before he

kicked open the barn door and slammed it shut once Chichi scurried through.

Luca scrubbed a hand over his face. "He will not say a word. The kid is scared of me."

"Of you?" Jian had never met anyone scared of Luca Kai unless meeting him on the battlefield. The man had a personality opposite of Jian's gruffness. But now, his eyes did not sparkle with mirth.

This was hard Luca, General Luca, the man marching into battle. He stared at Jian for a moment longer before rushing forward and pulling him up into a hug. "When we didn't hear word of you, we thought you'd died. Again." Luca pulled back. "You were supposed to go to Kanyuan to seek Qara and then meet us here."

Jian lowered himself back onto his seat. "I went into Koulland."

Luca's jaw fell open. "Well, I wasn't expecting that."

"Neither was I. There's a place far in the mountains called Lóng Bǎolěi. I did not set foot inside, but my search brought me many answers. I know what the Nagi wants, where she has taken Hua."

Luca held his gaze. "I'm not going to like this, am I?"

Jian closed his eyes and hung his head, swinging it back and forth. "None of us will."

Jian didn't know how long he slept. After telling Luca everything he'd seen, everything he'd learned in their time apart, he'd nestled into the pallet bed Luca prepared for him in the room attached to the barn. He'd laid there for the longest time listening to farmhands rub down horses and oxen at the end of the day before he'd let himself rest.

Luca promised they'd find Hua, that nothing would happen to Bo, but Jian heard the uncertainty in his voice.

And still, he'd forced Jian to sleep, to gather the threads of his strength, a strength he'd need in the coming days.

While Jian slept the next morning, Luca sent Song and a retinue of servants to Dasha under the guise of buying wares for the house. But Song sought information instead, knowledge of dragon sightings or strange events.

Light spilled into the barn as a door opened, and Ru appeared with a bowl cradled in his hands.

"Has Song returned?" Jian sat up, his mind clear for the first time in weeks. He'd barely slept on the road through the mountains.

Ru extended the bowl toward Jian. "No. Luca says it takes over an hour to ride into the city from here. She left at first light."

Jian gripped the bowl, finding fluffed millet with a whipped egg overtop. "Thank you, Ru."

"Chichi tried to eat it, but I scolded him."

"I'm glad I have you watching over me." He offered him a tiny smile.

Ru's cheeks reddened in pleasure, but his eyes dipped to the ground. "You're going to find her, aren't you, Jian? You're going to bring her back?"

Jian dropped the wooden spoon into the still-full bowl and set it aside before standing. He put a hand on each of Ru's shoulders and bent so they were eye to eye. But what could he say? A promise was meaningless when Jian didn't know how possible his mission was. He didn't want to give

Ru empty words. He couldn't make him wish for something Jian might not be able to deliver.

Wasn't that what Jian had been doing himself? Seeking hope, searching for the girl who could give it to him?

"Ru, I will do everything in my power to save Hua." That was all he could give.

"Don't die, Jian." Ru's eyes glassed over. "Everyone dies." He sniffled. "Luna… Hua—"

"Hua isn't dead." He pulled the boy against his chest, letting the boy's tears soak his robe.

"She might be," Ru whispered.

Jian couldn't let himself think that. He couldn't fathom a world in which Hua Minglan's angry eyes never settled on him again. None of them knew if Hua lived inside her own body still.

Horse hooves pounded into the road outside the barn. Jian released Ru and went to the door to peer out into the cloud of dust kicked up by Song and her companions. He couldn't leave the barn in case the rest of the household were to see him, so he waited like the useless soldier he'd started to feel like.

Ru ran past him to greet Song with a hug, and Luca appeared from the house. When his father and Gen Minglan walked out behind him, Jian retreated into the barn. Picking up the discarded bowl, he ate absently, barely tasting the food. For the first time since he'd left Kanyuan, he was rested and well fed. It was time to set out again. He wasn't made to sit around in hiding.

"Leave your horses," Song's voice called to her servants. "You've all been very gracious traveling to Dasha so early for the opening of the shops. My brother will care for your beasts while you go get cleaned up."

There was a smattering of praise for the kind lady.

"You could help me, you know," Luca grumbled as he led two horses into the barn.

Song skipped ahead. "Quiet, brother. I am a married lady now. I answer to my husband, not my brother."

"Married?" Jian leaned against a stall door as Song walked past him.

Luca spared a glance for Song, but she seemed distracted by Heima. "To a soldier."

Jian's heart sank. That was why she lived with her father still. If her new husband was a soldier, he was away with the Piao army, keeping the Kou at bay. He stepped up beside her and rubbed Heima's nose as Luca busied himself removing tack and saddles from each of the horses before retrieving the others from the courtyard. "Did you learn anything in Dasha?"

She pulled her hand away from Heima. "This horse is special, isn't she?"

Jian shrugged. "I don't know." Although, he did. Heima was more than an animal, she was a part of Hua, and they loved each other.

"I think she is. I can sense it." A sad smile curved her lips. "I always wished you'd love me one day, Jian."

"Song—"

"Let me finish. I know about the Kou woman. Luca told me of her long ago to dispel me of any notion that we might marry. In truth, I'd already given up. I didn't believe the great Jian Li would ever love anyone more than his empire."

"I am not a great man."

She touched his arm. "I know you will always see yourself as the unwanted son of a consort, a ward of the emperor who was not welcome, but try to look through my eyes, through Luca's or Bo's. We see a noble warrior who will protect us and never fail us. A true commander."

Jian's stony expression didn't change. She said the same words Bo had been spewing for many years, but they were lies crafted by their love for him. It was impossible to see every fault when love was involved.

Song wasn't finished. "What does Hua see?"

He stepped back away from her. "The same man as everyone else."

"I do not believe that. Does she see your love for her?" Song's tone held a sad note, but she covered it with a smile.

Jian continued to stare.

"She does." Song nodded in confirmation. "Love is hard to hide, Jian. You have the same problem with words you have always had, but your actions do the speaking for you. She no doubt fell in love with you the moment she showed up to train at your camp." The Kai's must have heard the stories of soldier Huan Minglan from Luca. "But not you. Men are always a little slow."

"I didn't know she was a woman. For months, she deceived me."

Song covered her mouth as a laugh escaped. "You must have been confused by your feelings. Answer me this, Jian. Does she challenge you? Because the Jian Li I knew was always a little too demeaning. He needed someone who'd turn his world upside down."

He pictured Hua standing among the men with her chin lifted in defiance, how she'd fought with him and spent all night training on the course in the dark. "She challenges everyone."

Luca finished unsaddling the final horse and wiped sweat from his brow. "I don't know why father doesn't hire stable hands."

Song lifted a brow. "Because it is almost time to harvest the winter wheat. All the men are busy in the fields. Something you'd know if you spent as much time here as you did with the army."

He ignored her barb and dropped onto a hay bale. "Tell us what you learned in the city, sister."

Song sighed. "There have been no sightings of a dragon, but you should have seen the looks shopkeepers gave me when I asked. It was as if their greatest fear had been realized—that Dasha will suffer the same fate as Kanyuan."

Jian wouldn't voice the possibility aloud, but if Hua was in the city as Master Delun claimed, that very thing could happen.

Leaning his head against the wall, Jian groaned. "So, we're back at the beginning with no news of Hua?"

Luca, looking just as forlorn as Jian felt, shook his head. "The Nagi is not just an animal waiting for the will of a human to be made clear. She thinks for herself. If she is here to cut out the heart of Piao, she wouldn't have landed within eyesight of the city. That would have only incited terror in the streets." He scratched his cheek. "Tell me this, though. Why wouldn't she want that? We both saw the Nagi lay waste to Kanyuan. Why not do the same to Dasha?"

Jian pushed away from the wall, hope filling him for the first time in weeks. "Because Hua is still in there. She wouldn't let that happen twice."

Song pursed her lips. "That's a far conclusion to reach."

"Can you tell us anything else?" Jian pleaded. "Any news from the city."

Song started to shrug, but her shoulders stopped midway. "Well, I tried to go see the city healer this morning. A man named Liqin. But his shop was closed up, strange for mid-week. So, I asked about him at the baker's and then the smithy. Both recounted the same story. Yesterday, there was a commotion near the bottom of the palace steps. A young girl collapsed and Healer Liqin forced a crowd to disperse so he could help a woman back to his shop. They say even the young prince was involved."

"Duyi?" Jian shared a look with Luca. Duyi was the only one of Empress Yanyu's children who didn't despise Jian. "What does Duyi have to do with anything?"

Song finished her shrug. "Nothing, I think. He was just there. But here's the thing, no one has seen Healer Liqin since he left the square with the girl."

CHAPTER 20

The Nagi

He came for her.

The Nagi perched atop the flat roof of the healer's shop in human form, letting the darkness hide her as she watched over the square throughout the night.

Few people walked the cobblestone paths and fewer still came anywhere near the healer's shop.

Except for him. Or rather, them. Two men peered into the darkened window, searching for something they wouldn't find. Hua. She wasn't here right now.

One of the men was Jian Li, the soldier Hua forced the

Nagi to carry from the battlefield after the destruction of Kanyuan. And the other? Luca Kai, Hua's betrothed and another dragon blooded.

A smile curved the Nagi's lips.

"Dearest Hua, did you know two men love you?"

Hua didn't respond. She'd been silent since that useful healer gave her the sleeping tea. What other reason would Jian and Luca have for seeking out a Nagi than love? Their mission would only end in their deaths, and they had to know that.

The Nagi didn't consider herself cruel or unkind. Only determined, focused. She was no different from all the people down below in their homes who wanted the Kou dead for what they'd done to their people. The dragon blooded hadn't had anyone protecting them. They hadn't had armies going to war to defeat their enemies because their enemies were the army, the emperor, everyone meant to keep them safe.

The Nagi breathed in deeply as she focused on the fear, the pain those people must have felt. Their screams echoed in her mind, stealing away her peace. There would be no peace until Piao paid for what they'd done. The empire tried to take away any chance of the Nagi returning. By killing the blooded, they erased the vessels in hopes they'd never witness the work of a dragon again. The Nagi didn't want to feel for the people, but their fear was intertwined with her species' plight.

"You can't do this." Hua finally woke, but her thoughts were weak.

The Nagi sighed. She didn't want to hold one of the dragon blooded hostage. She didn't want to erase Hua

Minglan from this world and the next. But what choice did she have? *"Why do you protect them?"* It was the question plaguing the Nagi since she first awoke within Hua. Why did she serve her enemy? Why did she protect those who would not protect her?

Hua didn't respond for a long moment, and the Nagi assumed she'd fallen asleep once more. She shook her head and straightened out of her crouch to get a better look down below.

"Because I am better than them." Hua's voice was little more than a whisper in the Nagi's mind. *"For centuries, they have hunted my ancestors and all those like me, but I believe in change. I believe what has happened does not have to happen again."*

"Those in power always repeat the mistakes of the ones who came before them."

Hua sighed. *"Sometimes, we have to have enough faith to know the stars can change. The sky does not remain dark unless you close your eyes."*

The Nagi didn't believe in change. Each time they came into this world, they found people very much the same as they'd left them. Selfish. Cruel. Illogical.

They warred with each other, killed each other, and for what? A kind of power humans could never hope to possess? To rule over all humans?

The Nagi lifted her face to the sky, letting the starlight wash over her skin. Above, guiding stars created the points of a dragon, only visible to those who were willing to see it, those open to the possibilities of the Nagi.

"Do you see the stars, Hua?"

"Yes." Hua went quiet for a long moment. *"I see them."*

Movement down below had the Nagi jerking her head

toward the square. Jian and Luca were halfway across now, heading toward an inn.

"Don't go after them," Hua begged. *"Please."*

A pang of sympathy struck the Nagi, a new sensation, but she shook it off. There was a mission to complete, and Jian Li and Luca Kai were standing in her way. They had to be dealt with before the Nagi could move on to the Imperial Palace.

This would have been easier if she could shift, but just like before, Hua had found a way to prevent that.

The Nagi leaped off the roof, sailing through the air until her boots slammed into the stones. Vibrations rocketed up her legs, but she felt no pain as she took one last look back at the healer's shop. As a reward for unknowingly helping the Nagi regain control, she'd left healer Liqin alive. He laid on one of the cots at the back of his shop, unconscious. Tomorrow, he'd wake with no knowledge of where his patient had gone.

Jian and Luca reached the inn across the square, so the Nagi picked up speed, keeping to the shadows of the buildings as she sprinted through the inky blackness.

As she ran, she pulled a knife free of the belt on her waist. One of the men had already entered the building by the time the Nagi slammed into the other, knocking him to the ground.

A curse flew from the man's mouth as the Nagi pinned him to the stones and looked down into the wide eyes of Luca Kai, a man she didn't want to kill.

"Hua," he wheezed.

The Nagi bent, holding the knife inches from Luca's throat. "Wrong."

"Let him go." The tip of a dao flashed in front of the

Nagi's face, and she lifted her eyes to the broken expression twisting Jian Li's features.

"Jian." Hua's whisper sent a tremor through the Nagi, but she gripped the knife tighter, turning it so the silver light of the moon reflected off the flat blade.

This body no longer belonged to Hua, but in that moment, the Nagi realized there was one person in this world who could aid Hua. It wasn't another Nagi. Not the Kou general or the emperor who had armies at his disposal.

Jian Li was more dangerous than any of them, because he gave Hua strength.

CHAPTER 21

Hua

He was here.

The man Hua hadn't known if she'd ever see again.

And her body prepared to fight him against her will.

The Nagi pinned Luca to the earth and lifted a fist. Hua tried to scream as she brought it down, and Luca's body went limp.

The Nagi climbed off him and turned to face Jian. He'd changed in the months since she'd seen him last. His eyes, once stern, now held a wary sadness. Stubble coated his normally clean-shaven cheeks. He looked like he'd seen too much, worried too much.

She wanted to reach out to him, to smooth the crease between his brows.

Instead, her stance widened, and she drew her dao, brandishing it in one hand with her knife in the other. Her actions were not her own, but she still felt the betrayal enter her heart at what her body was about to do.

In a fight, Jian Li would have beaten Hua Minglan almost every time.

But the Nagi?

"Please don't." She had to make the Nagi see reason, make her understand vengeance against Jian wouldn't bring her peace.

Hua knew that better than anyone. Fighting the Kou didn't take away her grief over losing Luna.

"This must happen, Hua. If we are to fulfill our true purpose."

Hua's sobs echoed in her own mind, not pushing past the lips she couldn't control. Weakness thrummed through her, aftereffects of the sleeping tea.

Jian held his dao aloft, reluctance in his gaze. "I do not want to hurt you."

"Then you will lose." The Nagi's voice held no emotion, only logic.

"If that is what must happen." Jian flicked his eyes to Luca once before lowering his dao, letting it clatter to the ground. "I won't hurt Hua."

"No!" Hua battered against the walls in her mind. *"Fight, Jian. Don't let her win!"*

The Nagi cocked her head. "Hua wishes you to fight."

His jaw tightened, his eyes going wide. "She's there?"

"Fight!" the Nagi roared, heat searing through her throat. She advanced, forcing Jian against the side of the building and slamming the dull side of the dao into him.

Jian released a grunt, but still, he didn't move to lift his dao.

The Nagi flipped her knife and jabbed the hilt into Jian's shoulder with jarring force.

Jian cried out in pain, but he didn't waver. His eyes remained on the Nagi's as if searching for something in them. "I won't hurt you, Hua."

Anger burned through Hua, the Nagi's anger, as she sliced her knife across Jian's side, cutting through his robe. Blood left a trail of red.

Hua hammered harder against the walls of her mind, but she couldn't break through.

Jian touched his side, pulling his blood-coated fingers away to stare at them. "Hua is still in there." He lifted his gaze. "I won't give up on her."

The Nagi sneered. "She is gone. There is no hope for you. Soon, you will join her in death. I will not let anything stop me in my mission."

Indecision warred in his eyes, and Hua wanted to cry out, to tell him it was okay to choose his brother over her. If he didn't stop the Nagi, the emperor would pay.

And still, he remained in place, weaponless.

The Nagi lifted her dao. "I have had enough of this game. Kneel."

"They will stop you." Jian dropped to his knees.

"Who? There is no one left."

"There is everyone. Piao will protect its emperor."

The Nagi rested the blade against Jian's neck. "Like they

protected Piao's citizens? Those with dragon blood? Enough words. They are meaningless in the end." She drew the blade away, swinging it back in a methodical arc.

Pain ripped through Hua as she screamed, her voice reaching every space of her mind, pushing past barriers as she watched the path of the dao while the Nagi prepared to take Jian's life.

It started with one finger, the sensation. It twitched against the hilt of the knife at her side. Little by little, her body came to life as she pushed further to the forefront of her mind.

The dao knocked Jian's knife away before she forced her arm to freeze. Blood dotted the blade as she pulled it back and released her grip, letting it fall at Jian's side.

His dark eyes were glassy moments before his end, but now they studied her.

Hua's knees shook beneath her before collapsing. She fell against Jian, a sob escaping her lips.

"Hua?" he whispered, his tone disbelieving.

"Jian," she cried.

Jian pulled her into his arms, holding her against his chest as she trembled.

"I almost killed you." Even if she wasn't responsible for her actions, her hands would have still been coated in his blood.

"Shhh." He brushed her hair back and rested his chin on her head. "I thought I failed you."

She pulled back to meet his gaze, hearing Healer Liqin's voice in her mind. "Do not claim a failure that is not yours."

His eyes settled on something over her shoulder, and she

scrambled away from him as she remembered everything the Nagi had done.

"Luca." She crawled to his side as his eyes slowly opened.

"Hua?"

Tears coursed down her cheeks as she nodded. "It's me."

He blinked away tears of his own as he tried to sit up.

"We need to get off the street." Jian searched the square for anyone who might have seen them, but they were alone in the dark with only empty storefronts facing them. He helped Luca to his feet and slid one arm over his shoulder. "Are you okay to walk, Hua?"

She nodded, standing on shaky legs and following them through the door into the jiuguan. A woman came rushing toward them. "Sirs, are you okay?"

"Bandits." Jian half carried Luca to the stairs despite his own injury. He didn't pause for further explanation. "We will require fresh water and something to eat."

The woman nodded and scurried away.

Hua peered through the inn to the courtyard garden it centered around before following Jian up the narrow wooden staircase. Peeling paint told stories in intricate designs, but she was too tired to examine any of it.

"We have two rooms." Jian stopped outside one of them and shouldered the door open to reveal sparse furnishings. He deposited Luca on the small bed. "Are you going to be okay?"

Luca nodded. "You need rest, Jian. Go take care of your injuries, I'll be fine."

Jian ran a hand over the top of his head and heaved a sigh. "Hua, you'll stay with me. I'm not taking my eyes off you." With a grunt, he walked back into the hall.

Hua stared at the door for a moment before turning back to Luca. "Are you really okay?"

He nodded. "Your Nagi friend didn't do too much damage." His eyes ticked toward the door. "He has been scared, Hua, and the Jian I know does not scare easily."

She wrung her hands. Jian had gone from relieved she was with them to the commanding general quickly. "I know. He is worried what happened to Kanyuan will happen to Dasha with me here."

Luca shook his head and then groaned as if regretting the gesture. "He does not fear losing Dasha, Hua. He fears losing you."

A knock sounded on the door, and Hua answered it, letting an older woman come in with a tray of cheeses and breads. Hua slipped out to find Jian waiting for her in the corridor. He didn't speak as he led her into a room down the hall from Luca's.

Hua's gaze swept the same sparse furnishings. A bed sat along the far wall opposite a cold hearth. Two chairs and a table took up the center of the room.

Jian closed the door and untied his sword belt. He hadn't thought to retrieve his dao, so the belt hit the floor with barely a sound.

Untying his cloak at the throat, Jian folded it over one of the chairs before dropping into it. "Are you cold?" He didn't look at her.

Hua rubbed her hands up her arms but not from the chill. The Nagi's heat coursed through her, warming her from the inside out. "I'm okay." Was she? The words felt strange as they left her lips. She'd spent the last two months wrestling for control over her own body, her own mind. She'd killed people and almost been erased entirely. The people she loved felt as far away as ever, and there was a voice in her mind telling her she had to kill the emperor her sister had loved.

No, she was most definitely not okay.

Someone knocked, and she opened the door, moving aside for two servants to enter. One carried a tray of food like they'd brought to Luca. The other set down a bucket of water with a cloth hanging over the side. "I'm sorry, Taitai." The servant bowed as she issued the term of respect. "We do not have wash tubs here."

"This will do." Hua's voice was small, quiet from disuse.

The servants started a fire in the hearth before leaving Hua and Jian alone once more. Hua wasn't sure what to do or how to act.

She hadn't been alone with Jian—while she was in control —since that night at Prince Dequan's estate where they looked to the stars for answers, for hope.

A part of her still felt like the incompetent soldier who'd shown up at his camp, hiding her identity. And he was her intimidating commander.

A hiss passed Jian's lips as he shifted, and their past fell away. They were no longer those people. Hua rushed toward him, taking in the injuries she'd almost forgotten about. "The Nagi hurt you."

"I'm okay," he wheezed. That word was just as wrong as when she'd said it only moments ago.

"Sir, we can't know that until we look at the wounds."

"Sir." He grunted. "I know you too well for you to call me sir, Hua. I sat by your bed for weeks on end after the battle of Kanyuan. Your family became mine. I watched you and tracked you for months. But you don't remember any of that, do you?" He sighed. "You don't know me at all."

She wished she could tell him he was wrong, but she only knew him as her commander, the man riding at her side into battle. There was something bonding in that, but it was nothing to the look in his gaze. "I'm sorry."

He shifted his eyes away. "It is no fault of yours."

It didn't mean she didn't care for him. She hadn't stopped thinking of him since the first time he challenged her during training, the first time he treated her like she was capable. He'd believed in her, trusted her.

Reaching out slowly, she felt the cut in his robe. Blood soaked the fabric. "You need to take this off."

His eyes locked on hers, and she couldn't move. In the recesses of her mind, she felt the Nagi squirm, trying to break free, but she held it back, not wanting to leave Jian again, not wanting to let him down. It took every ounce of strength to stay here with Jian, but she'd give everything she had to fight the Nagi.

With a simple nod, he reached for the bottom of his robe and slid it up. Hua moved closer to help him as his face twisted in pain. Each movement revealed more smooth skin until she yanked it over his head, leaving him in only his silk pants.

Muscles rippled in his chest, creating dips and valleys she wanted to run a hand over, to feel the strength underneath his skin.

Kneeling beside his chair, she dragged over the bucket and dipped the cloth in it. "I'm sorry I did this to you." She dabbed the cloth against the wound in his side.

"It wasn't you." He clenched his teeth. "You might not

know me like I know you, but I don't believe you'd ever do this to me."

The cloth froze against his skin as she lifted her eyes. "Jian, I do not remember your time at my home, but everything else is still fresh in my mind." She returned her attention to cleaning the wound. "Only you could have helped me regain control."

His hand reached down and grabbed her wrist. "Why me?"

She didn't answer him. Instead, she finished cleaning the wound before methodically cutting a bandage from the bottom of his robe. Getting to her feet, she gestured for him to do the same. She wrapped the silk bandage around his torso a few times and tied it as tightly as she could. "It's only temporary. You should go see the healer in the morning."

He put a finger under her chin and tilted her head back so she looked at him. "Hua?"

She swallowed. "Do not ask questions that will do us no good to answer."

"Why me?"

She held back the Nagi's incessant drumming in her mind. It was a constant reminder that whatever time Hua had was temporary. Soon, she'd lose control once again, and the ones closest to her would pay. The Nagi had already nearly killed both Jian and Luca.

"It's not important." Her breathing slowed.

Jian's gaze hardened, and he stepped back. "Thank you for cleaning my wound."

Hua nodded. "You're welcome, sir."

"You should rest. Tomorrow, I will bring you to your family."

Fear snapped through her, and she stumbled back, shaking her head. She couldn't go anywhere near her family, not with the Nagi living inside her. They'd never be safe from her.

"I would never hurt the blooded, Hua." The Nagi whispered in her mind.

"I don't trust you."

"They are my family too."

Those words filtered through Hua, bringing her anger simmering to the surface. "No," she shouted. "They're not." She scrambled away from Jian and his sympathetic eyes.

"What's not?" Concern entered his gaze.

"They don't belong to it." Her family descended from the last dragons as were all dragon-blooded in Piao and Koulland, but that is where their affiliation ceased. Hua would not let her family have any connection to the enemy inside her.

"I am not the enemy, Hua."

Hua gripped the sides of her head as tears sprang to her eyes. "Get out of my head."

"I can't. I am you. You are me. We are together in this."

"No!" Hua lunged for the knife that had been discarded on the table. Her fingers fumbled for the hilt, and she lifted it to her neck. "I don't belong to you. I could slice through my neck right now, and you'd die. You. Can't. Stop. Me."

"Hua." Jian tried to reach for her, but she sidestepped him. "Think of what you do."

"I know exactly what I do." Her eyes begged him to stay back, to let her choose her own fate.

"Hua Minglan." The Nagi's screams echoed in her mind. *"Lower that knife."*

Her eyes met Jian's. "It's scared. I can feel the fear coursing through my veins. The Nagi let's arrows bounce off her. She walks through fire. But nothing is invulnerable." She pressed the blade hard enough against her skin to draw blood and satisfaction rolled through her. "You see that? Blood. The neck is the most vulnerable part of any creature." She lowered the knife to her arm, drawing it across her skin, a line of red following in its wake. Yet, she felt no pain.

"Hua!" The Nagi demanded she listen, that she obey.

But Hua Minglan was done listening.

Now, she was in control.

Jian held up a hand, begging her to stop.

She shook her head, letting her tears fall free. "If I die, this will be over. Your brother will be safe. *Piao* will be safe."

"This isn't you, Hua." Jian's eyes glassed over. "Please."

"You don't know me."

His gaze softened. "The day Huan Minglan appeared at my camp, my life changed. I didn't realize it then." He stepped forward. "He was strong and determined, the best warrior I had."

"No, he wasn't." She sniffed, not lowering the knife.

He took another step. "He was. Not the most skilled, but he had the kind of bravery I can't teach. And now I know why. Huan Minglan was a woman, and not just any woman, one fighting battles in her own heart."

"I can't stop her." Hua blinked away more tears. "The Nagi is going to destroy everything."

Another step. "I have spent months searching for the woman who saved me from a battlefield in Kanyuan." He stopped in front of her but didn't take the knife. "You've saved me time and again. This time I wanted to save you."

"You can't."

"I know." His gaze latched onto hers. "You have to save yourself."

"This is how I do that. I won't ever be free, Jian. Not until the next life. At least let me protect everyone I love."

"I didn't travel all the way into Koulland searching for you only to lose you again."

Her mind barely registered his words. He'd gone into Koulland for her? Her grip on the knife weakened.

"Listen to him, Hua," the Nagi crooned.

Hua's fingers flexed around the hilt. This was what the Nagi wanted, for her to lose sight of the real issue. She'd come to Dasha to kill the emperor.

The man Luna had sworn her life to, her heart.

The man Jian loved with his whole being.

"I have to stop it," she whispered.

Jian's hand closed over hers, forcing the knife down. "And we will. We'll find a way, Hua. Together."

She stared into his dark eyes, losing herself in their fathomless depths. Their breathing struck a rhythm as they remained locked in a trance, as they held the knife in both their hands.

Jian was wrong. They wouldn't find a way. But she could. A plan formed in her mind, one that would take her from the man she couldn't imagine leaving behind. If this was her last night in this life, she needed to make it count.

Reaching up on her toes, she crashed her lips to his for what could be both her first and last kiss. The knife slid from their grasp, clattering to the floor as his hands wound through her hair.

Hua slid her palms up the ridges of his chest, feeling the

muscles flex beneath her fingers. He walked them backward toward the bed, not taking his lips from hers. He consumed her, everything she was, everything she could have been.

At least she would live on in this memory forever.

She pushed him back onto the bed, and he sank down, wincing as his side stretched. Careful to avoid his wound, Hua hovered over him, her hair hanging down around them.

He kissed her like they'd do this for the rest of their lives.

She kissed him like it was the end.

Hua pulled her robe over her head and tossed it aside. The moment her skin touched his, warmth spread through her.

"Hua," Jian whispered. "Why do I feel like you're telling me goodbye?"

She answered him with a kiss, letting him interpret that as he would. It was a moment she'd yearned for since first meeting the stern commander, one she'd never dreamed would become her life.

But this wasn't her life. It now belonged to the beast inside her.

All Hua had were moments like this, fragments of a life she could have lived.

Tears dampened their kiss, and she rolled onto her side, pressing herself to him as tightly as she could. His arm wound around her waist, refusing to let go.

"Is this okay?" Jian asked, dragging his lips down over her collarbone.

More than okay. If she was going to die tomorrow, she'd still feel the touch of his lips as she left this life.

"If I have to suffer in life before reaching Nirvana." She

lifted his chin so their gazes connected. "I want one night of joy."

Samsura wouldn't defeat her. This life, the Nagi, was only one more cycle of the suffering she had to endure before reaching final peace.

"Hua." He pulled her lips back to his because there was nothing else he could say. "I love you." Except that.

She averted her eyes, blinking away tears. "Don't say that."

"Why not?"

Because it made it that much harder to do what she needed to. "You can't love me."

"There was a moment when we were looking at the stars on that rooftop. You looked at me and I could see a future I'd never envisioned before, one beyond wars."

She closed her eyes. "That's the problem, Jian. I am war. I am blood and death. I am fire. You cannot love me because that love will be the end of you." She rolled away from him and reached for her robe, shrugging it over her head.

Jian looked at her with such pain in his eyes, like she'd taken the sun from his world. "You can't make me stop loving you."

She nodded, a tear dripping from her nose. "I know. But I can keep myself from loving you back." Even as she said the words, pain shattered through her heart. Loving Jian had never been a choice, and neither was walking away from him.

She couldn't meet his tortured gaze as she slipped from the bed. "You need rest. I'm going to check on Luca."

The fire popped, breaking the silence as she hurried toward the door and yanked it open. Letting it shut behind her, she slipped down the hall and into Luca's room. She slid down the door to her butt and pulled her knees to her chest as sobs wracked her body.

"I'm sorry, Hua." The Nagi's voice filled her mind. *"Truly."*

Hua didn't let herself think of what the next day held for her lest the Nagi try to stop her. She ignored the beast in her mind as the Nagi continued to talk like they were friends, or worse, family.

"I'm not going to sleep."

"Eventually, you will."

Hua leaned her head back against the door, letting herself listen to Luca's soft snores.

The next time she slept, she would never wake again.

Chapter 22

Hua

It was still dark when Hua picked herself up off the floor of Luca's room. Jian had knocked on the door a few times in the night, but she told him to go away. If she saw his face, looked into the eyes that saw every part of her, the resolve she'd crafted would waver.

She'd put all of Piao at risk.

Inching toward Luca's bed, she looked into his serene face, wondering what life would have been like without the Nagi, without the war. Would she have married Luca like her family wanted? They'd have been happy together, even if they wouldn't have fallen in love. Life would have been a lot simpler.

She glanced over her shoulder to the door she expected Jian to barge through at any moment. He wouldn't give up, but then, neither would she.

Luca Kai was a good man, a kind man, but they'd never been meant for each other. He didn't light a fire inside her with a single look. Only one man had ever done that, and she'd repaid his offer of love with a lie.

I can keep myself from loving you back. Was the lie meant for Jian or for herself? She lifted a finger to her lips, hating how his touch already faded from her mind.

"Is there a reason you're hovering over me before the sun has even risen?" Luca's eyes opened.

She sucked in a breath and expelled it with a rush of words. "I need you to take me to the palace."

Luca sat up with a groan. "Well, that was effective in getting me up. What do you really need?" His eyes searched hers. "It is you, Hua, right?"

She nodded. "I'm not kidding. I need to go to the palace, but I can't just walk up the steps. I need to be sure to see the emperor."

"Bo?" He gripped his head as his face twisted in pain. "I'm not taking you anywhere near Bo."

His distrust stung, but she understood it. As long as the Nagi lived inside her, none of them could trust her. "Please."

"Hua." He slid his legs over the edge of the bed, planting his feet on the wooden floorboards. "You almost killed me last night. Why would I help you get close to the emperor?"

She wrung her hands together. "The Nagi wouldn't have killed you."

"Oh really? I have a splitting headache that tells me otherwise."

Hua turned and paced the length of the room as she searched her mind for the Nagi who'd gone quiet. She couldn't stop moving. If she did, her mind would settle, her determination would waver, and she would lose the battle warring within her.

"Hua." Luca sighed.

She kept pacing.

"Hua!"

At the sound of his stern voice, she stopped and pivoted on one heel. The Nagi's presence flooded her mind, filling every empty space with her words until they tumbled past Hua's lips. "I would never have killed you." She bowed her head through no will of her own. "You are blooded."

Luca stood and crossed the room, approaching her with caution. He dipped his head to meet her gaze. "Are you Hua or the Nagi?"

Hua struggled to the surface of her mind. "Please, Luca. I need your help. I need to try to save him from this thing inside me."

Indecision warred in his eyes before he stepped back. "I want you to know, I will protect Bo before I protect anyone else. Even you."

Relief flooded her. "Thank you, Luca."

He grunted. "Jian is going to kill me for this."

She tried to avoid thoughts of Jian by picking up Luca's cloak and tossing it his way. He stepped into his boots and laced them up. Neither of them said a word as they walked into the dark hall and passed the door behind which Jian slept, thinking he'd see them when he woke.

"I'm sorry," she whispered.

The Nagi growled in her mind, but she suppressed the sound. When they reached the inn's courtyard, Luca held a hand out to stop her. "Promise me this is the right thing."

She pushed past him. "What is right, Luca? Maybe there is no such thing." Sparing one glance for the stars she knew so well, she said a silent prayer to the skies. Would Nainai be proud of her? Would she understand Hua's decisions? Her sacrifice?

Luca stopped at the three-stall barn, and Hua peered in, her chest tightening when she met Heima's eyes. She had so much to say to her friend, but no time to voice the words. Instead, she rubbed Heima's nose and moved on to Luca's stallion. "We only need one horse."

"Hua." Luca's brow creased. "I thought we were going to the palace together."

She nodded. "We will. As soldier and prisoner."

"Prisoner?"

"It's the only way."

His eyes widened as he stared at her with a new understanding in his eyes, a new respect. "I could stop this, stop you."

"But you won't because you can see this is the only way."

He didn't move for a long moment before he reached for her and pulled her into a tight hug, his arms keeping her pressed against his chest.

"Hua Minglan," he whispered into her hair. "You are under arrest for harboring a dangerous beast, a Nagi. For hiding your dragon blood from the empire and the murder of innocents in the Kanyuan province."

The words sent a chill down her spine as she pulled back to meet the gaze of the first friend she'd made in the army, the man who'd protected her secrets, and now the one making her pay for them. "Thank you." The words were barely audible over the hammering of her heart.

"I have no choice but to take you to his Imperial Majesty." His voice thickened with emotion. "No choice."

She shook her head, a tear breaking through. "None."

His breath released in a long hiss as he turned away from her to saddle his horse.

"Hua," the Nagi pushed to the front of her mind. *"This will not end like you hope it will."*

"I am in control now." Control of her actions, her words. Control of her destiny. All she had to do was remain awake until the emperor delivered her fate.

Luca lifted her into the saddle before leading the horse from the barn. He looked up at the inn one last time before climbing up behind her and snapping the reins.

The first light of dawn rose on the horizon as they continued through the cobblestone streets of the main square in Dasha. The Imperial Palace stood like a beacon raised above the city, representing everything Hua wanted to protect. Black marble pillars lined a walkway at the bottom of the steps, and Hua couldn't tear her eyes away as memories flashed through her mind.

Sitting with Luna and laughing during the festival.

Hiding from the attack.

Meeting the emperor.

Jian.

That night changed her life forever, setting her on a path to vengeance and destruction, bringing her back to where it all started.

Searching inwardly, she spoke to the Nagi. *"Why did you choose me?"* It wasn't a question she'd ever thought to ask before. All dragon blooded had minds that could open to the Nagi, but this one hadn't chosen anyone else. If Hua was going to destroy the Nagi—and herself in the process—she had to know why.

The Nagi didn't respond at first, and Hua let her mind drift to the feel of the horse beneath her, her friend at her back. As soon as her eyes closed for the final time, she'd forget these moments.

But the moments would never forget her.

"You and I are the same." The Nagi's voice was quiet. *"Your desire for vengeance called to me, and I realized we belonged together."*

"I will never belong with you."

"You yearn for blood."

Hua closed her eyes. She had yearned for blood, for revenge. Those early days of her war were tainted with anger and hatred. A piece of her died when Luna did. Luna was the sun, the brightness in a dark existence.

"Are you having second thoughts?" Luca's voice rumbled against her back.

"No." Hua's jaw clenched. If Hua backed down now, if she gave in to the beast, that was when they really would be the same. She lifted her hands, turning them over to stare at her palms. The Nagi had done terrible things using these hands. They were forever stained with blood.

After today, Piao would remember Hua forever. She'd become part of their lore, but not as the hero.

Hua Minglan was the villain of many of their stories.

Two guards rushed down the steps as they approached, but the rest stayed near the ornate golden doors at the top.

"Ting," one of the guards called, ordering Luca to halt the horse.

Luca pulled back on the reins.

"Who goes there?"

Lifting his chin, Luca stared at the two guards. "I am General Luca Kai." He swung his leg over the horse and slid down, pulling Hua with him. He shoved her forward, keeping a tight grip on her arm. His lips formed a snarl. "I bring a prisoner for the emperor."

One of the guards removed his helmet to examine her more closely, his brown eyes scanning her from disheveled hair to wrinkled robe. "What has she done?"

Luca pushed her down to her knees, keeping a hand on her at all times. Hua bit back a cry as her knees slammed into the stone.

"He won't do it," the Nagi said. *"He loves you, and that is the ultimate weakness."*

Hua lifted her eyes to Luca, imploring him to finish what they'd come here to do. He only had to utter a single line to bring the might of the emperor down on her. She swallowed roughly as time ticked by, and she began to wonder if the Nagi was right. Luca cared too much for her to put her at the emperor's mercy.

His tongue darted out to lick his lips, and he cleared his throat. "Hua Minglan has come to kill the emperor."

The words struck Hua with a force she hadn't seen

coming, and her shoulders slumped under the truth of them. Because that was why she'd come to Dasha, and she hated that it wasn't a lie.

Luca met her gaze once more, an apology in his eyes.

The Nagi sighed. *"I see now."*

"What?"

"He loves you, but there is someone he loves more."

CHAPTER 23

Jian

The moment Jian woke, he knew something was wrong. He could feel it, a pain in his chest. He jolted up in bed, cursing himself for falling asleep at all.

Hua never returned, but he'd tried to reach her throughout the night, tried to tell her everything was going to be okay, that he wouldn't let anything happen to her. At least, that was what he'd planned to say each time he pounded on Luca's door.

She'd refused to open it, refused to see him.

He rubbed his eyes, trying to ignore the sharp stab of pain

radiating out from the wound in his side. Glancing down, he stared at the blood-stained bandage.

Blood had seeped onto the bed, too much blood.

The smart thing to do would have been to search for the healer, to take care of the wound.

But Jian didn't want to be smart. He only wanted Hua, to look in her eyes and know it was still her, not the beast bent on killing his brother.

He couldn't shake the feeling of wrongness as he stood and reached for his clothing, the skin pulling against his wound. Unable to lift one arm, he managed to pull the robe over his head with the other and squeeze his weak arm through the square sleeve.

A wave of dizziness washed over him, and he gripped the back of the chair until it passed. There was no time for injuries or weakness, not when Hua and Bo's lives were at stake.

A curse flew from his lips as he stumbled to where he'd left his boots by the door and bent to pull them on, tying them with one hand. It took all his remaining strength to straighten once more and pull the door open. He stumbled into the hall, stopping when he saw the door to Luca's room open.

Using the wall for support, he inched forward to peer in, finding it empty save for a single maid bent over cleaning the hearth.

"They have to be downstairs," he whispered to himself. Would Luca and Hua have left him sleeping to seek their breakfast? His heart wanted to believe he'd find them as soon as he descended the stairs, but his head knew better.

Gripping the rail, he took the narrow steps one at a time,

trying not to fall as his unsteady legs shook. He reached the bottom and pressed a hand to his side. Blood seeped through the silk.

Only hours ago, Hua carefully tended to his wound, her strong fingers flitting over his skin, making him forget about the pain or the fact the only bandage they had was a strip of cloth cut from his clothing.

He crossed the small courtyard to the front room where two women bustled around crowded tables, plates of food balancing on their hands. One of them looked up, catching sight of him leaning against the doorframe. It was the only thing holding him up.

A smile curved her lips. "Sir." She approached him and bowed. "May we serve you?"

He shook his head and tried to push away from the frame before falling back against it. "I was staying here with another man and a young woman."

She nodded. "Yes. General Luca, I remember him."

"His room is empty."

He didn't ask a specific question but understanding lit in her eyes. "One of the stable lads was waking for the early morning work when he saw the general and his lady riding across the square."

His lady. Jian's jaw clenched. Hua was Luca's intended, but she wasn't his, not really. "Do you know where they went?"

She smiled in apology and shook her head. "But I can't imagine what would have been so pressing at such an hour. They rode toward the palace, and the shops near the steps will only just now be opening their doors." Her eyes lit up. "Maybe they went to fetch healer Liqin to help you."

Jian wanted nothing more than to believe that, but the moment she mentioned the palace, his blood ran cold.

There were only two reasons Hua would go there, and it depended who was in control for each.

If the Nagi controlled her movements, she was on her way to kill Bo with Luca as her prisoner. But then why would she have left him unharmed?

And if Hua chose that road... Jian twisted away from the serving girl without another word and half-walked half-ran out the front of the inn. He swallowed down a bout of nausea and kept his hand pressed to the wound. It didn't matter what happened to him, only that he made it to the palace before Hua or Bo did something they couldn't take back.

He managed to reach the barn without collapsing. Heima picked up her head when she saw him, releasing a braying sound.

"Heima." He reached up with his strong arm to touch her between the eyes. "Master Delun brought us here for a reason. It's time we do something useful." His eyes searched the stall, landing on the saddle hanging on the wall. He wasn't strong enough in that moment to saddle a horse, much less with one hand.

"Do you trust me, girl?" He'd been through a lot with Hua's horse, and it seemed their adventures were never ending.

Heima snorted.

"Well, I trust you." He clicked his tongue, leading her from the stall to a row of hay bales sitting at the far end of the barn. Gathering his remaining strength, he stepped up on the hay and gripped a fistful of Heima's mane. She shifted as he pulled himself on, situating himself along the curve of her back.

It seemed as if with every move she made they were more connected. Heima was the strength Jian no longer had.

"Come on, Heima." He nudged her forward out the barn door.

A few people lingered nearby, sparing him passing glances.

But Jian only had eyes for one thing, a shining palace in the distance. In his mind, he was the hero racing to save the woman he loved, galloping across a battlefield for her.

In reality, he inched across the square on Heima, unable to prod her into a trot without losing his seat. It was all he could do to keep his seat on the horse. A few shopkeepers called to him as they opened their shops. It wasn't every day they saw an injured man riding bareback in their city.

His breath curled in front of his face with each puff of air. Every inhale was harder than the one before it.

Jian's vision went dark for a moment before he blinked the blackness away and sat up straighter. His robe stuck to the wound, a sticky reminder of his weakness.

His heart, pounding in his ears moments before, slowed to a low rhythmic beat. He focused on his breath. In. Out. In. Out.

As if sensing Hua, Heima walked toward the palace with little direction from him.

He didn't know how long it took to cross the square, or how he made it without succumbing to the darkness, but the clanging of armor made him jerk upright as Heima stopped.

Guards ran down the steps, their footsteps like a thundering herd.

"It's the commander!" one of them yelled.

No, not the commander. Not anymore. Now, he was just a man who'd failed in his vow to protect Hua Minglan.

Guards called to him, but he didn't hear them as his legs loosened their hold on Heima and he pitched to the side, only vaguely aware of the ground rushing up to meet him before his head hit the bottom step and everything faded away as he whispered one final word.

"Hua."

CHAPTER 24

Hua

Exhaustion warred with determination in Hua's mind. She wouldn't let herself fall into slumber, not while inside the palace.

She'd expected to be taken to a prison cell, but instead, the guards stuck her in this ornate room, unfit for someone with plans to kill the emperor. Gold coated every surface from the trim of the wood-paneled walls that had been painted with intricate designs of roses, to the table and chairs centering the room.

It was some kind of sitting room with a wide, blue-velvet

settee in front of a gold-rimmed hearth. No fire warmed the chilly room, and at least that discomfort made sense. Prisoners didn't get to be warm and comfortable; they didn't get to experience luxuries at the Imperial Palace.

In Piao, those not of the emperor's council or household weren't supposed to enter the palace at all. Yet, here she stood. She crossed the dark marble floor before pacing back. Where were the guards? They should be preparing her for a quick execution. This was supposed to end.

She'd stopped fearing death because the alternatives were much worse. If the Nagi managed to erase her before her body died, she wasn't sure she'd move on to the next life. And then what? The Nagi would terrorize Piao, and no one she loved would be safe. That was what scared her. It was why she'd first donned her father's armor and joined the army in his stead.

It had never mattered what happened to her.

Noise sounded outside the door and voices filtered through. "If my life is in danger, I will face my enemy."

The emperor.

She closed her eyes, willing him to walk away.

The door opened, and he froze on the threshold, his eyes finding hers.

The emperor looked no different from when she'd first met him at Luna's side. A top knot sat on his head, pulling his hair away from his face. But that was where the severity ended. His face held a softness that made him instantly likable, trustworthy. And even now, upon looking at his would-be killer, his eyes held kindness.

She didn't know how long she stared, not bowing or addressing him, before he spoke. "I know you."

Swallowing back her memories of Luna, she shook her head. "No, your Imperial Majesty."

He looked behind him to the lingering guards. "You removed all weapons from her?"

Murmured responses came from the guards.

"Good." The emperor stepped into the room and shut the door despite the protests from his guards. He pulled out a key and stuck it in the door, turning it until it clicked. Squaring his shoulders, he faced her once more. "I will hear about this from my advisors, no doubt."

Snapping out of her stupor, Hua bowed.

"Stop that," the emperor snapped. "You have come to kill me. Don't play at respect." He pointed to the settee. "Sit. Now."

Bo Xu Wei was not an intimidating man, not in the way his father was before him. There was nothing stern about him, nothing hard. Hua had seen it in the way Luna spoke of him, and the way he'd looked at her. They'd admired each other. Hua looked away, unable to meet the eyes of the man her sister loved.

Hua lowered herself onto the settee, waiting for the emperor to tell her he'd set her execution. That was the punishment for treason, and she needed him to follow through with it.

The emperor paced in front of her, his arms clasped behind his back. The purple robe swished around his ankles. "General Kai has told me how he uncovered your assassination plot."

She cleared her throat. "He speaks true."

He didn't stop moving. "My advisors wish me to throw you into the darkest cell until we can throw an execution like no one has ever seen—as if it's some kind of party." His lip curled in distaste. "But something here doesn't make sense to me. I have known Luca Kai my entire life. I cannot read anyone as well as I read him. And that is how I know he does not speak the whole truth."

Hua kept her eyes trained on the cold hearth. "I came to Dasha to kill you." The words were true. The Nagi was here to kill the emperor, it didn't matter if Hua wished him dead as well. She squeezed her eyes shut to prevent tears from falling. She waited for the words of hatred, for the condemnation and reminder Piao would forever remember her as a traitor.

Instead, the emperor put a hand under her chin to tilt her face up. "Why?"

Hua swallowed. "The emperors of Piao have forced my kind into hiding. The dragon blooded have suffered too much." She held her breath, waiting for his reaction. It was the first time she willingly revealed the blood inside her that was once a mark of death in Piao.

The emperor's hand dropped, and he stepped back, his gaze going to the door where his guards pounded against the wood, their fear for him evident in their yells. His brow creased and she couldn't tell if he wanted to retrieve his worried guards or hear more of what she had to say.

When he met her eyes again, recognition sparked in the depths of his irises. "Hua Minglan."

Fear coursed through her. If he recognized her, he'd know her entire family was blooded. "No."

He covered his mouth with his hand. "You look so like her."

Hua jumped to her feet and backed away from him. "I don't know of whom you speak."

His eyes glassed over. "I have mourned Luna since the day she died."

Hua couldn't hold back the tears any longer as everything she'd felt about Luna's death poured out of her.

"Is that why you have come to kill me? Because Luna died in my service?"

"Haven't you heard anything I've said?" The words burst out of her. "I am dragon blooded. That's enough reason. Take me to a cell, kill me like your father killed so many of my kind."

He wiped his eyes. "I am not my father. I knew of Luna's blood, but I made a promise to her that I would do better than my predecessors. She was my best friend. The day she died, I felt like I had too."

"She was your consort. Not your friend."

The emperor sighed and sat on the settee. "What would she think of you coming to Dasha for this purpose?"

Hua turned away from him. He was supposed to hate her, to spew vitriol that would have made everything easier. "I don't know. She's dead." If she was at the palace for any other reason, she'd laugh at the thought of Hua Minglan having a private conversation with the emperor. The day Luna was chosen as consort, the sisters had been terrified, but also excited. It meant Luna moved into another world Hua could never have dreamed of.

Yet, here she was.

Rage filled her, but it didn't feel like her own. She drew her fingers into fists, clenching them at her sides as she turned back to the emperor.

"He killed our kind, Hua." The Nagi's voice echoed through every part of her until it was all she heard.

Hua hadn't slept since her time at the healer's, and with each passing moment, her weariness grew and her control slipped.

"He is the enemy."

"This is what we came for, our purpose."

"You can fix all of Piao's problems right now."

Each time the Nagi filled her head with her words, Hua inched closer to the emperor, her lips forming a snarl.

She tried to make herself stop moving, but it was no use. Her strength slipped away as the Nagi whispered a few final words.

"Luna is dead because of him."

She lunged, knocking the emperor from the settee as her hands closed around his neck.

"Hua," he wheezed. "Stop."

A tear fell from her lashes. "I can't." Her grip on him tightened as something boomed against the door.

"It will all be over soon," the Nagi whispered.

She stared into the eyes of the man her sister had loved, the one Luca was loyal to. Jian's brother.

There was no coming back from this, but then, she'd never wanted to come back.

Heat seared down her arms as the emperor bucked and thrashed beneath her. He was no match for the Nagi's strength. It wasn't like before. This time, the Nagi didn't take complete control of her mind. Instead, she weaved their consciousnesses together.

Hua knew exactly what it was she did. She could feel every bit of it. The tears were her own.

But the Nagi controlled the actions of her body.

Another boom rent the air as the light faded from the emperor's eyes. Sobs wracked her body, but she couldn't stop.

Wood splintered inward, spraying across the room before a man dove toward her, tackling her to the ground.

"Bo." Luca's cry cut through her heart as she saw her friend drop to his knees and pull the emperor into his lap. "Wake up, Bo. You have to be okay."

It wasn't until that moment Hua understood everything the Nagi had said before. Luca loved Hua, but there was one person whose life he wouldn't risk to save her. He'd brought her to the palace for an execution to save the emperor.

The Nagi continued to fight, but three guards held Hua down, pinning her to the wood-strewn marble. She couldn't take her eyes from Luca as he pressed his forehead to the emperor's. A crack widened in her heart. How many more people was she going to hurt?

She released a breath when the emperor's eyes opened slowly, and a sob shook Luca's back.

"You're okay," Luca whispered.

The emperor searched his surroundings until his eyes found her. "She almost…" Fear entered his gaze, a fear Hua put there.

Luca helped the emperor to his feet and addressed the guards. "She is not to be left unattended. Four guards must watch her at all times. Do not be fooled by her small appearance. Hua Minglan is the most dangerous enemy Piao has ever faced."

"Luca," Hua whispered.

But he didn't look at her. His jaw clenched as if he'd heard his name. He paused for only a moment before helping the emperor from the room.

Hua looked to her hands as two guards hauled her up. What had she done?

"What we had to."

CHAPTER 25

Jian

A groan rattled through Jian's throat as he shifted and froze, feeling the soft bed underneath him—softer than the bed at the inn. His eyes slammed open, and his breath caught in his throat as his gaze connected to the man hovering over him, one of the few people who knew every part of him.

"You're awake." Bo pushed out a breath and ran a hand over his face, pushing back the dark hair that had fallen free of the knot on his head.

"Am I…" Jian tried to sit up but fell back on the bed.

"At the palace?" Bo grimaced. "Yes. My guards found you

collapsed at the bottom of the steps with a wound in your side." He sat on the edge of the bed. "You could have died, Jian."

Died. He jolted up, a spear of pain ripping through his side. "Hua, she's here. Did Luca bring her? Have you… is she okay?"

Bo's jaw tightened, and he put a hand on Jian's shoulder, forcing him down. "You'll tear the wound open again. Don't be an idiot."

Bo was the only person other than Luca who spoke to him in such a way, the only one who cared enough to drop formalities or disdain. Jian let himself relax for just a moment as he took in the sight of his brother. Everything he ever did was for him. The battles he'd fought, the missions he'd undertaken.

Bo's lips drew down, and it was only then Jian noticed the marks on his neck.

"Lean down." Fear spiked through Jian as he issued the order.

In that moment, the emperor was not the leader of Piao. For that beat in time, he was only Jian's brother.

Bo leaned forward, a sigh escaping his lips. "It happened yesterday."

Red fingerprints burned across the skin of his neck like someone wrapped scorching hands around his throat. Jian closed his eyes as his worst fears rose to the surface. The Nagi was in the palace. Not only Hua, the girl he didn't know how to save.

"Where is she?" Jian waited for Bo to tell him they'd executed the girl who tried to kill him. He waited for the heart to stop beating inside his chest.

"Luca had me put her in our strongest cell beneath the palace. He tells me she has a Nagi inside her." He stood and paced the length of the room.

"Bo."

He didn't stop moving. "She came here to kill me, Jian. And she nearly succeeded. Luca says Hua wanted me to execute her before this Nagi got the chance to succeed in her mission."

"Bo."

He whirled on his heel to face Jian. "But she's... she's..."

Jian slid his legs over the side of the bed and forced his body up, using the post to remain steady on his feet. His bare toes curled in the plush velvet carpet, and he skimmed a hand along the wall for support as he lumbered toward his brother.

Bo's shoulders shook as Jian reached him and pulled him into a hug, ignoring the pain spreading over his skin underneath the thin robe. Bo didn't hesitate to shrink against Jian as if his entire body collapsed in on itself.

They borrowed each other's strength to remain upright, and Jian closed his eyes, reminding himself he wasn't alone in this. For months, he'd traveled on his own in search of Hua, but now he'd found her, and he didn't need to be a single man fighting a dragon anymore.

"Brother," Bo whispered. "I almost died." He pulled back. "You almost died." His face glistened with tears he'd never let the rest of Piao see.

The emperor's mask was a facade. To the rest of the empire, he was a kind and benevolent ruler, but also strong, unwavering.

To Jian, he'd always be the emotional older brother, the

one Jian protected from his other siblings when they bullied him.

"We're both still here." Jian stumbled back, his legs unsteady. He walked back and grappled for the edge of the bed before lowering himself. "A lot has happened, Bo."

Bo nodded. "I have been kept apprised of the news. I need to ask you a question you won't want to answer, one that could decide the fate of the girl sitting in my cells."

Jian swallowed. "Go on."

"Was Hua… this Nagi of hers… is it the dragon who destroyed Kanyuan? The beast who killed an entire village of innocents?"

Jian sucked in a breath and pressed a hand to the wound at his side. He knew what his answer would mean for Hua. It was the reason she'd come to the palace. She wanted to face her own execution, to end the Nagi's hold on her. "Yes."

Bo's expression fell like he'd been hoping for a different answer, a simpler answer. "What am I supposed to do with this information?"

"Have you spoken to your advisors?" Jian needed to know who else knew of Hua's situation.

"I don't trust a single one of them." Bo pulled himself onto the end of the bed and crossed his legs. "You and Luca are the only people in this world I trust. We can't tell them until we've decided what to do."

"What to do? Bo, she came here to kill you and nearly did. She destroyed an entire village—one we need to protect our borders from the Kou." Jian would have done anything to protect Hua, even after everything, but Bo barely knew her.

"No, the animal inside her did those things." Bo leaned

forward. "Hua Minglan is Luna's sister. I won't let Luna down or you."

"Me?"

"You arrived here hours after Hua and Luca, despite your injuries. Luca hasn't told me how Hua is connected to either of you, but I know you better than anyone. You care for her and that means I do too."

The knot squeezing around Jian's heart loosened just the slightest as he relaxed back onto the bed.

A knock sounded on the door moments before Luca entered without either of them answering. He brushed hair out of his eyes as he flicked them from Bo to Jian.

"You're awake." He grimaced. "Look, I was only trying to protect Bo. Coming here where she expected an execution was Hua's wish. She only ever wanted to do what was right for Piao. You can hate me for helping her, but don't hate her for trying to do the right thing." His chest heaved as his words trailed off.

Jian sighed. "And yet, having her here almost got Bo killed, anyway. Sit down, Luca." He pointed to a wooden chair next to the bed.

Bo cast a nervous glance at Luca, and their eyes locked.

"Tell him, Luca." Jian was tired of secrets and lies. It was time they all had every piece of information available to them.

Luca, seeming to guess what Jian meant, hunched forward, resting his elbows on his knees. "Bo… Hua is my… betrothed."

All sound in the room ceased as Bo went still save for the expanding and contracting of his chest. Jian had spent most of his life observing Bo and Luca as they avoided the connection between them, knowing it wasn't possible to be anything other than friends. Bo had his consorts—as every emperor before him—and the duty to produce heirs. Luca had his intended, though Jian wouldn't let that wedding happen.

None of them spoke for a long moment before a maniacal laugh burst free of Bo. "Wait, so, Jian fell in love with your intended?"

Jian bristled at that. "She never wanted to get married, only to fight in the war."

Bo's eyes widened. "A woman fought with you? Not just in her dragon form?"

Jian met Luca's eyes. It was time Bo knew everything. "It started the day she showed up for training." He told his brother the story of Hua Minglan from training her to watching her walk through fire.

He spoke of battles and dragons and moments staring at the stars.

Through it all, he saw himself fall in love with her again little by little, moment by moment. There wasn't a singular moment when he realized what she meant to him. Instead, she'd crept up on him with her stubborn stares and determined training, her profound words and incredible bravery.

"She isn't the Nagi inside her." His voice rose. "I don't care if she thinks death is the only way to end this. We can't let the beast win." His eyes locked on Bo's. "Please."

Bo rubbed the mark on his neck and shifted where he sat. "Hua Minglan is a warrior of Piao, and we don't let our warriors down."

CHAPTER 26

Hua

Stay awake.

Don't let the pull of sleep overwhelm you.

Hua repeated those words in her mind over and over. She'd managed to keep her eyes open for two days now, but it wouldn't be long before she couldn't handle it anymore.

"Just give in." The Nagi had been her constant companion in the prison cell.

Hua sat on the small bed inside the dark cell and pulled her knees in to her chest. The iron bars taunted her, and she wondered if the Nagi would be able to rip through them.

She'd managed to keep the Nagi from shifting since they arrived in Dasha, but it was only a matter of time.

And then nothing could hold her back.

Hua unfolded herself and stood, crossing to the bars. She wrapped her fingers around the cool metal and called out to the guards. Luca made sure there were four of them watching her at all times. "Has the emperor determined my fate?" She lifted her voice. "Please. Just tell me what's happening." Her knees shook beneath her, and when she received no response, she stumbled back to the bed.

How long did it take to set up an execution? Surely by now Luca had told the emperor how quickly it needed to happen. Tears built in Hua's eyes at the thought, and flashes of her family ran through her mind. She'd never again sit under the stars with Nainai or spar with Baba. Mama wouldn't ever chastise her for the dirt underneath her nails, and Ru... A sob shook her.

At least she might see Luna in the next life. She sucked in a breath, willing her tears to stop. Death was not the end. She must face it bravely and with honor. It was the only way to rid this world of the terror she'd become.

She searched inward, speaking only for the Nagi. "You've taken everything from me."

"I am sorry for that, Hua."

Sadness wound through her, intertwining with her own. The Nagi's sadness. Piao killed the descendants of her kind. She couldn't imagine the pain. For most of Hua's life, being dragon blooded didn't define her. Sure, she'd had to hide it, but her grandfather was killed for his heritage long before she was even born. The dragons and their blood had only been stories to Hua and Luna, a strange obsession they saw in Nainai.

But for the Nagi, there was no escaping what had been done to their people. On some level, Hua understood her actions.

"He's different, you know." Hua rubbed her eyes. "Piao is different than it used to be. Bo Xu Wei does not hunt us. He has brought a new understanding to the empire."

The Nagi was quiet for a long moment. *"And yet, here you sit in the emperor's prison."*

"Maybe that's because you tried to kill him." She didn't believe the emperor would have imprisoned her for any other reason. He'd looked at her like she was the reincarnation of Luna, his consort brought back to life. There was love in his gaze, sadness as well.

"Do not fool yourself into thinking we mean anything to them. They will end us."

"I hope so." Hua leaned her head back against the wall as she yawned. Her eyelids drooped, but she jerked up when footsteps echoed off the stone. Was this it? Had they come for her?

Jian stepped into the dim light outside her cell, and the breath clogged in her throat. She had known he'd come, but part of her hoped it would have been too late when he did.

"Hua." He gripped the bars of her cell and leaned against them.

She scrambled from the bed. "Jian, you are injured. You shouldn't be down here." How long ago had she left him? Three days? Four?

His eyes didn't leave her face. "What did you do, Hua?" His voice cracked on her name.

Tears clogged in her throat as she met his broken look. "This has to end."

"Not like this."

She approached the bars. "I almost killed the emperor, Jian. What if I succeed next time? You know as well as I this cell can't hold the Nagi forever."

He rested his forehead against the bars. "There has to be a way."

Reaching through the bars, she let her fingertips skim over his hand, wanting, needing more. She pulled back. More wasn't possible for her. This wasn't an epic adventure with a happy ending. "How is your injury?"

He grunted. "A healer sewed it. I'll live. Don't change the subject."

"What subject? Seems to me you only wish to speak of things that have already been decided."

He closed his eyes for a brief moment. "Hua. Please."

At the brokenness in his voice, her defiance faded away, leaving only weariness behind. "I'm so tired, Jian, and not because I haven't slept in days. For months, I have been a prisoner in my own mind. I have done things I can never take back. An untold number of people are dead because of me."

"It's not you."

"Isn't it? No matter who controls them, these hands are still mine." She lifted her palms. "The blood will never wash away. I can't keep causing so much pain."

He shook his head. "There has to be another way."

"It's okay." She reached for him again, this time taking his hand in hers. She'd told him she could keep herself from loving him, but that had been a lie. Hua fell in love with her commander before he even knew her true name. "Look at me, Jian." Her smile concealed the sadness behind it. "Please."

He met her eyes, denial flashing in the depths of his dark gaze. "I can't—"

"I was wrong before."

He swallowed. "When?"

"I thought I could control my feelings, that this would be easier if you never knew how I felt." She squeezed his hand. "I love you, Jian Li. And I get to love you until my last day." She reached up to touch his cheek. "And that is a gift, the kind I never saw written in the stars."

He held her hand against his cheek. "I'm not going to let this happen."

Her hand drifted down to his waist. "I know." She yanked his dagger out of his scabbard, and as a cry left his lips, she plunged it into her stomach.

Pain sliced through her until all she felt was numb as she pulled the dagger free and let it drop to the ground.

"Guards," Jian screamed. "Open this cell."

Hua's knees hit the stone, and she pressed a hand to the wound, feeling the blood seep out through her fingers.

The door to the cell rattled as two guards yanked it open. Their hands clamped down around her arms, but she barely noticed them as her mind folded in on itself, focusing on the Nagi inside.

"I've won." A smile curved her lips as blood trickled from her mouth.

The Nagi sighed. *"That was a stupid thing to do."*

Heat seared through Hua, burning up her arms and down into her torso, an inferno pulling her into the flames.

A scream echoed in her mind. Maybe Hua's. Maybe the

Nagi's. The sound ripped through the cell, bouncing off the walls as the fire within Hua blazed hotter, radiating out from the stab wound.

Jian pulled her onto his lap, but his words were nothing but white noise in her ears.

As Hua sank into the depths of her mind, she gave up the remaining pieces of herself.

It seemed not even death could defeat the Nagi.

CHAPTER 27

The Nagi

Humans thought they were intelligent, that they could trick a Nagi into death.

Their bodies were fragile, yes, but the Nagi gathered her strength, spreading it through the girl's limbs like wildfire, burning away the weakness.

The Nagi focused her energy on the life seeping from the hole in Hua's stomach. The girl's consciousness wavered before she sank back into her mind, letting the Nagi take control. The heat seared along her skin, burning flesh together to stop the damage.

Strength radiated out from the Nagi as she enveloped Hua and forced her eyes open. Jian clutched her body as his desperate pleas grew quieter and quieter. The guards watched in panic, uncertain of what to do.

The Nagi groaned. "Release me."

Jian's head jerked up, and his eyes locked on Hua's. "You're…"

"The girl is alive." The Nagi shoved away from Jian and rolled to her feet. Hua's consciousness pulsed in the back of her mind, weak but present.

"You healed her?" Jian wiped his eyes and sent a panicked look to the guards.

"I healed myself." She stepped back, shaking her head to bring forth clear thoughts. Hua had come to the palace hoping for her own execution, and it wasn't the first time she'd threatened to kill herself. But… the Nagi sank down onto the bed, her hands shaking. She never expected Hua to actually cause harm. And for what? To protect an emperor who hailed from a long line of those who persecuted the blooded?

Jian looked to the guards. "Retrieve supplies to clean this cell and then return to your posts. Lock this door behind you."

The Nagi lifted her head. "You're… staying?" She could hurt him, of that there was no doubt. Yet, as the lock turned, Jian remained.

His expression tightened. "I'm not leaving her."

The Nagi didn't move to hurt Jian. Despite the battle a few days before, the Nagi realized Jian was not her true enemy. He didn't have dragon blood, but he loved Hua, a girl who did. If there was any doubt of that before, seeing the commander staring in hatred rather than fear was proof enough.

They sat in silence until a guard opened the door again, passing a wooden bucket of water and rags to Jian. Jian dropped to his knees and held one of the rags in the water before pulling it free, letting it drop over the blood-stained stone. Without a word, he bent forward, scrubbing vigorously.

The Nagi waited for him to stop, to tire. A man such as him would not be used to cleaning and shouldn't have the patience for it.

But he kept going, never slowing, never looking up.

The water tinted red with Hua's blood, and still Jian scrubbed.

The Nagi sat on the tiny bed watching the great commander she had trained under as Hua. The man she pulled from the battlefield because she couldn't separate Hua's feelings from her own. He should have died that day. If he had, would Hua still be holding on so tightly? Would it have broken her?

"I shouldn't have saved you."

Jian stilled. His eyes stared down at the stone that had been covered in Hua's blood but now showed no proof of what happened there. "Why did you?" He sat back on his heels and threw the rag in the bucket. Red water splashed over the sides, dampening Jian's robe. He didn't seem to notice.

The Nagi released a sigh. His question was one she'd asked herself before. What did Hua's feelings matter to her?

For the first time since the Nagi wrested back control, a spark of life came from Hua.

"Because you care for me."

The Nagi released a breath. Hua was still there. Only days ago, the Nagi tried to erase her, and now the thought of losing the girl in her mind struck an unfamiliar fear through her heart.

Jian's brow creased as if something in the Nagi's face confused him.

So, the Nagi spoke the most honest words she knew. "Because Hua asked me to."

Jian shifted onto his butt and leaned back against the bars of the cell, his gaze on the scrubbed stone. "She tried to leave me." He closed his eyes and breathed deeply.

The Nagi pulled her legs up under herself. "She tried to leave us both."

Jian's eyes snapped open at the admission. "She's still in there. Please, tell me she's still in there."

"I'm here, Jian." Hua's voice was no more than a weak crooning in the recesses of the Nagi's mind.

The Nagi nodded. "She hasn't left us yet."

"You saved her."

"I saved myself." She'd said it before, but it was only partially true.

Jian met her gaze. "You have come to Dasha to kill my brother. You'd like to bring about the destruction of my empire. Many are dead because of you. And now, you will take the woman I love. Bo will have no choice but to execute you. For the safety of his people." His voice hitched. "And I will have to let him. It's what Hua wanted, why she came here. For her own death." He sucked in a breath and held a hand to his side as his face twisted in agony.

The Nagi's lip curled. "I do not have to answer to you, Commander. You say I have done evil, but your people hunted mine. I hold the memories of the blooded, of all the Nagi. Your stories say we have disappeared, but we have been here as the emperors of Piao slaughtered our descendants at their dragon festivals. Men. Women. Children. They all died for their heritage, a heritage that was once considered regal, royal, until human men decided their blood was a threat to the destiny of the empire." She crossed her arms. "You will get your revenge on me. I cannot escape this place. I know this. But what about my vengeance? Who will avenge the lost dragon blooded? Who will protect the ones still living?"

"The danger is gone." Jian's voice sounded tired. "Bo Xu Wei is not his predecessors. He will protect all those of his empire."

A harsh laugh broke free of the Nagi. "We believed we were protected many centuries ago. We will not be so naïve again."

"Sir." A guard stopped outside the cell, ignoring the Nagi and focusing on Jian.

Jian rose to his feet. "Yes, soldier?"

"You have guests come to see you."

Jian flicked his eyes toward the Nagi. "I cannot see anyone just now."

"Sir, one of them said to tell you Nainai Minglan is here and will not leave until she sees her granddaughter."

Warmth spread through the Nagi at the thought of

Nainai. No, the family belonged to Hua. Yet, she couldn't stop the smile from spreading slowly across her face.

"You should go to them." The Nagi nodded toward Jian. "Hua is in no danger now. I am with her."

Jian's eyes darkened. "That has always been our greatest fear."

Chapter 28

Jian

Leaving Hua felt wrong, like he was letting her down.

But he wasn't the only person scared for her. His footsteps echoed off the low stone ceiling as he thundered up the stairs.

The guard led him to the palace grand entry where a number of people hovered near the ornate gold-framed doors. Empress Yanyu was the first to see him. Just what Jian needed. He'd avoided being in her scathing presence since coming to the palace in search of Hua, but she had to know he was there.

A flash of distaste crossed the old empress' face as she rushed toward him. "Jian Li," she barked. "This palace is sacred ground in Piao. We cannot allow just any farmer to walk through the doors searching for a consort's bastard."

Ah, yes. Their time apart hadn't improved their relationship. But Jian had no time or energy for her vitriol.

"This palace belongs to the people." He walked past her without a glance. "It's time we acted like it."

She tried to follow him, but Prince Duyi ran toward them and stepped into his mother's path, blocking her next attack. "Mama, stop."

One corner of Jian's mouth curved up, but he didn't hear the rest of what was said between them. The prince had grown up since Jian saw him last.

A dog's bark snapped his attention to the Minglans as Chichi barreled toward him at full speed, launching himself through the air to slam into Jian. Jian stumbled back, a surprised laugh escaping him. Guilt came next. There should be no laughter at a time like this.

Ru followed in Chichi's wake, wrapping thin arms around Jian's legs. "Jian. I missed you." Jian bent to look in the kid's eyes. It couldn't have been more than a week since he saw him last in the Kai's barn, but it felt like a lifetime. He lifted Ru into his arms as he approached Nainai Minglan. The old woman looked out of place among the marble and gold of the palace, but she held her chin high like she belonged.

"Jian." Her weathered face held immense sadness. "Where is my granddaughter?"

Ru clung to him tighter. "Hua. Where is Hua?"

Jian searched behind them, expecting Fa and Gen to appear.

"They decided not to come, not to face their daughter in this state." She spoke as if reading his mind and clutched her hands together. "Ru told me Hua was in Dasha, that you and Luca left to search for her. There was news in the city of Luca bringing a prisoner to the palace."

Jian's shoulders dropped as two worlds crashed together. In one, he was the bastard son of a long-ago consort, the brother to the emperor. And in the other, he was just Jian, the man who'd joined the Minglan family and promised to bring Hua back to them.

In both worlds, he'd failed.

Duyi appeared at his side, his eyes widening when he saw the dog. "No wonder Mama is angry." He bent down, calling Chichi to him and scratched his nose.

"Duyi, I must speak with this woman." Jian looked to Ru. "Do you think you can watch the boy and his dog? Make sure they don't cross the empress or any of the consorts."

Duyi nodded. "We'll go find Bo. He'll love seeing a dog messing up the too-clean palace." An impish smirk appeared on his face as he took Ru's hand and pulled him away. Chichi barked as he followed them.

Jian and Nainai stared at each other for a long moment before she stepped forward and enveloped him in a hug. "You found her, Jian. Now, take me to my granddaughter."

He couldn't let her see Hua like that, not with the Nagi controlling her. It wasn't something anyone could forget. "We need to talk." He turned and led her through the grand entrance hall to a room at the back that overlooked the courtyard and entrance to the temple. Once he closed the heavy wooden door behind him, he released a breath and lifted his eyes to the sitting room. Bookshelves lined the back wall, their expensive leather-bound tomes for appearance and not practicality. That was what Bo's father taught them when they were boys playing in this room. It had been their sanctuary away from the empress and her children.

Two settees faced each other over a handwoven rug with an intricate design made to look like stained glass. A large window spanned the back wall, where they could view the dormant fountain in the center of the courtyard. In the summer months, water poured from the center statue of a young boy.

Now, like everything else in Piao, it seemed bleak and without magic.

Jian gestured to one of the settees, and Nainai sat with a weary sigh.

"Tell me what has happened to Hua." She folded her hands on her lap as if to appear calm, but the tremor in her voice gave away her fear.

Jian sat across from her, his heart hammering against his ribs. He'd seen the Nagi with his own eyes. Even if Hua kept her from shifting, the Nagi controlled her. Yet, voicing those words out loud seemed an insurmountable task.

"She is here." He scrubbed a hand across his face. "Hua…" He didn't know what to say next. She'd tried to kill herself to save them all? She sat in a cell awaiting her sentence? "She gave up." That was what it all came down to. The fierce warrior who'd faced the Kou with him had stopped fighting.

Nainai's hands shook as she wrung them together again. "My Hua is the strongest person I have ever known."

He nodded. Before he'd watched the knife plunge into her

stomach, he'd have said the same thing. "The Nagi... it has her. I don't know how to bring her back." He hunched forward, burying his face in his hands as the dam broke and emotions poured over him. "She..."

A hand rubbed his back, and he looked up to find Nainai beside him. "It's not over, Jian."

"How do you know?"

"The moment Ru told me he'd seen you, I knew Hua was here, that you'd found her. I also knew if anyone could help her, it was you."

He shook his head. "No, I can't. I've tried."

"Master Delun would not have aided you if he did not believe Hua could be helped."

His eyes snapped to hers. "How did you know about Master Delun?" He'd told Ru about the dragon, but not the dragon's name.

She wrapped an arm around his shoulders in the kind of familial embrace he'd rarely received in his life. There was comfort in the act. "There are many things you do not know about the Minglans of Zhouchang, secrets we hold that cannot yet be uncovered. Jian, do you trust me?"

He answered without hesitation. "Yes."

"Then please, take me to Hua, to the Nagi."

Jian stood, realizing she had as much right to see Hua as him. But before he could agree, the door burst open and Luca rushed in. "The Kou are coming."

CHAPTER 29

Jian

Jian stormed out of the room, needing to find Bo. Luca and Nainai walked behind him.

"I rode out to speak with my father today, and a messenger arrived at our door looking for a fresh horse to get to the palace. He'd been riding through the night from the Liudong Valley. The Kou have slipped past our forces in Kanyuan and march toward the capital."

"Jian." Nainai stepped up to walk with him. "It is more imperative than ever that I speak with my granddaughter."

Jian looked from Nainai to Luca, torn as to which direction was best. "I won't let you go to her alone."

She lifted a brow. "I can handle Hua and that beast inside her."

Luca glanced down the hall where two of the consorts peeked their heads out of a door. "We need to find Bo."

With a sigh, Jian snagged the arm of a passing guard. "Take this woman to the cells. Do not leave her alone in there. Do you understand?"

The guard nodded.

"Thank you, Jian." Nainai followed the guard toward the opposite end of the hall.

Empress Yanyu stepped out of a door to the right, a scowl on her face. "You two should not be in this wing of the palace."

"Where is Bo?" Jian had no time for her hatred.

"The emperor is in his quarters."

Jian brushed past her, and Luca ran to catch up.

"How long until the Kou reach Dasha do you think?" Jian tried to calculate it in his head.

"For a full army?" Luca thought for a moment. "It's a four-day march from the Liudong Valley."

"And for a single rider?"

"Two."

So, the Kou were most likely two days behind the messenger, two days from overtaking this city. Again.

He pushed open Bo's door without knocking to find the emperor sprawled on his floor in a fit of laughter as Chichi and Ru both tackled him. Duyi watched on with a grin on his face. It was a moment that didn't belong on a day like this, a day when the world they'd created started caving in.

Jian ignored the ache in his side from the wound. There'd be a lot more pain before this was done.

Duyi noticed Jian and Luca first, his smile sliding from his face. "Bo." He nudged his brother with his foot.

Bo looked up, his smile widening when he saw them. It only lasted a moment, a fraction of a moment, before he sat up and took them in more fully from their dour expressions to the tense set of their shoulders.

Even Chichi seemed to sense something was not right. He sat back on his haunches.

Jian cleared his throat. "We must speak with you. It's urgent."

Bo got to his feet, smoothing out his robe. Yanyu would have been aghast to see him on the floor wrinkling his clothing. "Duyi, will you watch Ru?"

Duyi shook his head. "Whatever it is, I want to know. I'm old enough."

Bo put a hand on his shoulder. "Yes, didi. You're right." He walked into the hall and knocked on another door. A woman Jian recognized as Holea answered. She was one of Bo's consorts, but Jian barely knew any of them.

Holea bowed as Bo spoke softly to her. When she rose, she nodded, not speaking a word. Bo turned to Ru. "Holea will look after you." He leaned down and dropped his voice. "Make sure Chichi behaves himself."

Ru nodded. "If I'm good, will I get to see Hua?"

Bo's tormented eyes met Jian's, their pain calling to each other. "I don't know, Ru."

Ru sniffed before squaring his shoulders. "If you can't save her, I will."

Jian rested a hand on the kid's head and ushered him

toward Holea. For once, the Nagi wasn't the biggest problem on Jian's mind.

Once Holea took Ru and Chichi into her room, Bo took off in the direction of his meeting room. The throne room in Piao was nothing more than a symbol. The real work took place at the far end of the palace where his advisors could come and go without using the main entrance in view of the public.

"Tell me." Bo gestured for Luca and Jian to follow him.

"The Kou will be here in two days." Luca didn't hold back.

Bo's steps faltered before he picked up speed. "Explain."

Luca told him of the messenger searching for a fresh horse, and Bo shook his head. "Can his account be trusted?"

"He looked like he'd been through battle. There are four villages in the Liudong Valley, and he says each was attacked. The Kou are burning everything in their wake. Crops. Homes. It is the only thing slowing them down."

Jian pictured General Altan riding at the head of his army, having managed to get through one of the mountain passes, avoiding Kanyuan and the army stationed there. "We didn't think they'd get through the snow this time of year."

"We were wrong," Bo snapped. Jian's congenial brother was gone, leaving a determined emperor in his wake. He pushed through the door into the meeting room to find his advisors waiting.

"Your Majesty." A man Jian didn't know crossed the room. "We've just received a messenger from General Yang. The Kou have slipped past them, and our army is currently chasing them across the Liudong Valley."

Bo looked to Jian. "Well, that answers that question. Our army is coming."

Jian should have felt relief at that, he should have felt something. Instead, he snapped into commander mode. No emotion. No fear. Only orders.

"Our first priority is to protect the people." He stepped up to a round table and put his palms against the wood. "Those outside the city walls must be brought into Dasha for protection."

Luca stood at his side. "My father and General Gen Minglan are already riding to nearby farms east of the city. We must send riders to the west and the south."

Jian looked to the man on his left. "You. Go."

The advisor's jaw dropped open. "Your Majesty, I cannot take orders from a disgraced commander."

Bo didn't even look at him. "You will do as my brother says. Go prepare the riders."

The advisor speared them with one more look before turning on his heel and storming away.

Bo glanced at each of his advisors in turn. "I am putting Commander Jian Li in charge of this city's defenses. You will obey his commands as if they came from me. We must send scouts north of the city to bring us news of the Kou army."

A guard snapped to attention and bowed. "I will see to it, your Majesty."

"Good. We will gather here again at dusk once we know what we face." Bo turned and left them all staring after him.

Jian ran to catch up with him. "You can't put me in charge of the city's defenses."

Bo didn't stop as he pushed his way into the courtyard separating the main palace from the temple at the back. "I seem to remember being the emperor. I can do as I please."

"Bo."

He kept walking as if he couldn't hear the way Jian's voice cracked on his name. Putting a hand on the ornate golden doors, Bo pushed them open.

"Please."

Bo froze with his hand still on the door. He stared down the aisle between golden statues to the gauzy curtain he liked to disappear behind. When Bo set foot in his temple, he wasn't the emperor anymore, not in his mind. He'd admitted that to Jian once. He became another servant of Buddha, another person stuck in Samsura.

His shoulders hunched forward for just a moment before he straightened and entered the sacred space, his steps echoing off the red marble floor. The only other sound was the faint trickling of a fountain inside the door.

Jian wanted to follow him, to continue this conversation and lay out all the reasons he should not be the commander once more, but he let Bo have the last few moments of peace any of them might see.

As he turned to walk away, every doubt he'd had rose to the surface of his mind.

He'd failed his men in the Shan mountain passes.

And again when the Kou attacked their camp.

He'd failed his people, his warriors, but also a girl who sat in a cell beneath this very palace. His feet took him there before he realized where he was headed. How was Piao supposed to survive the Kou and the Nagi?

The only way to remain standing once the dust of battle settled was to choose which threat to face and which to embrace. The Kou wanted Piao's fertile land, its trading routes, its access to the sea.

And the Nagi? Piao's destruction.

Yet, the Nagi had something General Altan did not. Hua. She was the conscience, the heart. And he had to believe that influence was stronger than any need for revenge.

He nodded to the guards as he passed them but stopped when voices reached him. Nainai sat in Hua's cell, only feet from the dangerous beast her granddaughter had become. But when Jian registered their words, he couldn't force himself to move.

"I sensed the history in your family." The Nagi's voice was low, hushed.

Nainai didn't respond right away. "The history in me, you mean."

From the shadows, Jian saw the Nagi nod. A conversation he'd had with Nainai in what seemed like another lifetime came back to him. *"I am the reason the Nagi chose Hua."*

He hadn't understood it then. *This family is strong, Jian.*

She hadn't only meant they were strong enough to recover from the battle and destruction of their home. She'd meant something else.

The Nagi continued. "When?"

"I was fifteen the first time I felt a presence within me." She smiled as if remembering a fond memory.

Jian's eyes widened. For hundreds of years, Piao thought the Nagi were gone, that dragons were a fabled creature, part myth and part history.

"Jian." The Nagi spoke into the darkness. "I can feel you watching us. Come."

Jian couldn't have resisted if he tried. He approached the bars and wrapped long fingers around them, his eyes finding Nainai. "You… you're Nagi?"

Sadness entered her gaze, and she shook her head. "No. As a young girl, I had a Nagi in me, but it left me long ago."

"It... left?" He looked from Nainai to the Nagi, hope sparking in his chest.

"Each Nagi comes to our world with a mission." Nainai shrugged. "Once it is completed, they have no reason to stay."

He swallowed. "And what was the mission of yours?"

"There was a young man who needed my help. I found him dying along the roadside and took him home for my mama, the village healer, to save. You see, he had a role to play in the future of the empire. Everything has a purpose, Jian. Every action, every event. They call to us from a higher power, leading us onto the path we must endure. The Nagi who came to me was only a small piece of a much greater plan for the future of Piao and its protection."

A growl rumbled in the Nagi's throat. "Our purpose is no longer to protect Piao. They have betrayed our kind."

Nainai reached out, boldly taking the Nagi's hand. "Dear, you are wrong. The Nagi have never had the hearts of men. Your soul comes from Buddha himself; your mission is his. You are beyond vengeance." She smoothed out her wool robe and stood.

Jian gestured to one of the guards, and he approached to open the cell. As she passed him, Nainai gripped his arm. "You must rest, Jian. The Nagi tells me you suffered an injury, and I'm afraid you will need your strength in the days to come." She patted his arm and moved past him to let a guard escort her from the damp cells.

Jian couldn't leave, not yet. He stepped into the cell and slid the bars closed behind him.

The Nagi didn't move, she didn't look at him. "I will have my revenge, Jian Li." Her words were weak.

Jian sat on the cool stone, his eyes focusing on the area of the ground where he'd seen the light fade from Hua's eyes. She hadn't trusted the Nagi to be anything other than evil, an assassin. But Nainai believed the Nagi could be more. She hadn't said those words, but the meaning was there.

"How does she do it?" he asked, his eyes not leaving the ground as memories of wooden buckets and bloody water tried to steal the air from his lungs.

The Nagi didn't ask what he meant. Somehow, she knew. "This body is not mine. I can control it and control the mind, but shifting into my true form has little to do with the mind. And this heart…" She put a hand over her chest. "It still belongs to her. I caught her by surprise in Kanyuan, and she opened her heart to me. And again in the mountains when she let herself fall away, surrendering complete control, thinking it was the right thing to do. But now, as long as Hua remains a presence inside me, her heart will not bend to my will."

Her heart. Jian closed his eyes, hearing Hua telling him she could keep herself from loving him. She'd taken the words back, but they'd never go away. Instead of being a spear of pain sharper than any wound, they now bolstered his hope, his faith. If Hua could control her heart, she'd never be lost.

"Would you have left her?" he asked. "After killing the emperor when your mission was complete."

"If that was my true mission."

Nainai didn't believe it was. "Do you have doubts?"

It was the most honest conversation he'd ever had with

the Nagi, but it was time he understood her. As the Kou rode toward Dasha, their greatest enemy remained right here in this cell.

The Nagi sat back on the cot and pushed Hua's long, normally beautiful hair out of her face. Now, the stringy clumps shone with grease. "Hua wanted revenge."

As had he. They'd both wanted to chase after Altan in a single-minded pursuit. "But not because of Piao. She wanted to protect her empire."

"An empire that terrified her." The Nagi sighed. "You will never understand what it is to live with such fear, Jian. The moment I entered her mind, I felt it. I was here long before she knew, long before she ever came to Dasha. That is what my people have suffered, unimaginable terror. Of discovery. Of death. They cannot change their heritage, yet your people would hunt them for it."

Tears gathered in Jian's eyes but not only for Hua. He'd seen the dragon festivals as a child, where the emperor held executions as part of the festivities. He'd heard stories of the emperor's soldiers roaming the countryside in search of the blooded. Neighbors turning on neighbors. Friends turning on friends. And it had been happening for centuries.

But there was a difference between hearing stories and facing the truths in front of him. His heart ached for Hua, for her family, for Piao.

"You're right," he whispered. "I cannot understand. I have been an outcast most of my life, but even that does not compare. This empire has destroyed the faith between its citizens and the Nagi. We do not deserve mercy."

"And yet, you will ask it of me."

Jian touched the cold stone that had once held a pool of

Hua's blood. "I do not. She does. Hua Minglan, the girl you say has lived in fear, tried sacrificing her life for this empire." She was unlike anyone he'd ever met. The horror of that moment would always be with him, but so would the honor. She'd tried to save his brother any way she could. The terror the Nagi spoke of must have been strong in her as she rode toward the palace.

"I've said it before, but Bo Xu Wei is not like his predecessors. Hua recognized this. She barely knew him yet tried to give up everything for the belief that Piao needed him." He couldn't sit there any longer staring into Hua's eyes and only seeing the Nagi, not when the Kou were coming, not when Bo needed him too.

If the Nagi refused to see her ties to Piao mattered still, there was nothing more he could do. She didn't speak as he rose to his feet or opened the door. A guard stepped forward to lock the bars in place as Jian trudged down the dark hall, the remaining pieces of his heart scattered in his path.

Because as he left the Nagi behind, he surrendered Hua to the beast, losing faith that she'd return to him.

And all he could do was march through the palace that was not his home, the place that once held so much pain for him, so much ridicule.

Because it was time to prepare for war.

CHAPTER 30

The Nagi

The constant drip drove the Nagi insane. She didn't know where the sound came from, but somewhere in that damp cell was her torment.

Drip.

Drip.

Drip.

When she first came into the world, the Nagi felt very much alone. She didn't feel another Nagi's presence until after she shifted for the first time.

She hadn't been able to control the emotions as they'd

twisted with Hua's own anger, her desperation. They'd amplified each other's need for revenge, making Hua leave her home behind in search of it. Others saw her actions as protecting her father, but the Nagi knew it was more than that. She may not have been able to control Hua's heart, but she saw into it.

Drip.

Drip.

Ripping herself from the cot, the Nagi slammed her shoulder into the wall, reveling in the pain snaking down her arm.

Drip.

Drip.

Drip.

Too much information.

Too many emotions.

Hua's Nainai had looked into the Nagi's eyes like she truly saw her, her fears. The Nagi were not supposed to live on this earth. They came for a short time and then left, but only once they did what they had to do.

Nainai Minglan saved a young boy who had a role to play. Small. Simple. Yet the act most likely had a profound impact on the future of the world.

And the death of the emperor of Piao? What kind of impact would that have? If Jian spoke true, if Piao finally had an emperor that would protect the dragon blooded… what would it do to take that away?

The Nagi gripped the sides of her head, knowing full well the action didn't belong to her.

"You are beginning to see." Hua's voice was weak inside her mind.

"Why did you do it, Hua?" The Nagi's breathing turned ragged. "Why did you try to sacrifice us for one man?"

"My sister believed in him."

And that was enough for Hua? Nagi did not have families, but they were tied to their descendants. Grief washed over her for a sister she never knew. "Luna."

"The only thing that matters in this life is my family." Hua assaulted the Nagi with thoughts of her parents, her nainai, Ru. The little boy's eyes held a light that had not yet been snuffed out by the fear of his own blood and what others would do if they learned about it.

"Ru is good."

A smile came unbidden to the Nagi's face. Hua's smile.

"And yet, we are locked away in a cell."

"That is not their fault. You won't beat them, Nagi. Do you want to know why?"

The Nagi didn't respond.

Hua's voice grew stronger. *"Because they have more than vengeance to fight for."*

"There is nothing more than vengeance."

"There is Piao."

CHAPTER 31

Jian

There was little sleep in the palace as they waited for their scouts to return, for them to bring the news most already knew.

Soon, a battle would come to Dasha.

Throughout the night, citizens from the farming settlements surrounding the city arrived, and Bo forced his advisors to open the barracks to them. Some took advantage of the hospitality. Others stayed in shops and homes opened to them by the Dasha citizens.

The trickle of people entering the gates had slowed by the

time Hua and Luca's parents arrived at the palace. Once again, Bo defied his advisors by letting them enter.

Jian approached the Minglans and bowed, shame racing through him. He'd been unable to keep his promise to them, unable to protect Hua. Gen Minglan stared at him for a long moment before pulling him into a hug.

Luca's baba, Liu Kai, put a hand on Jian's shoulder as he pulled back from Gen. They were the only two men who'd ever acted fatherly to him, something he'd forever be grateful for. He turned to Fa Minglan next and bowed but stumbled back as Song threw herself into his arms with a sob.

Bo approached slowly, cautiously, and Jian took note of the guilt in his gaze. Their eldest daughter died in his charge, and now their youngest sat in a cell beneath his palace.

Gen and Fa shared a look as Bo bowed to them.

Jian couldn't remember the last time Bo bowed to anyone. As the emperor, it was his right to stand tall. But now, he didn't rise.

No one spoke through the somber moment until a sharp bark drew their attention to Chichi who came running through the entryway, slamming into Bo and knocking him from his feet.

"Chichi." Gen jumped forward, horror flashing across his face. He reached for the dog but stopped at the sight before him.

Bo hugged Chichi to him, burying his face in the dog's brindled fur. His back shook with silent sobs.

Jian had seen many men break before. He'd seen them fall in battle and mourn their comrades. But this moment didn't belong to Bo alone. They'd both failed the Minglans.

Jian flicked a hand to a guard. "Show these people to their rooms in the guest wing."

Fa gripped his arm as she passed. Gen crouched down in front of Bo, giving him an assessing look. "Your Majesty, we do not blame you." With that, he stood and followed his wife, leaving Jian alone with his brother.

Bo looked up at him, still not releasing Chichi. "I'm going to lose my empire. People are dead, Jian, and more will soon follow."

Reaching down, Jian gripped Bo's arm in a way his advisors would protest. He pulled his brother to his feet. "Your empire looks to you for strength."

With that, he turned and started toward the back hallway, expecting Bo to follow. Guards nodded to him as he passed. There would be no sleep for them tonight.

Chichi ran at his heels, constant commotion in a seemingly lifeless palace. All joy had been sucked from these rooms the moment they learned of the impending battle.

Jian entered the study he knew so well to find Luca standing at the large window, his hands clasped behind his back. "There was a time, Jian, I thought I'd never fight beside you again." His words cut off when Bo slipped in.

"We all thought you were dead, Jian." Bo slumped onto the bench near the window. "Yet, you were carried from battle by a dragon, the same dragon that now sits a floor below us. This world wasn't supposed to exist, not anymore."

Luca took a seat beside Bo, bumping their shoulders together. "Has there been any word from the scouts?"

Bo nodded. "I was searching for Jian when your parents arrived. General Altan will reach the city tomorrow morning."

Jian pushed out a breath and leaned against the window frame. "I can't be your commander, Bo."

Bo's dark brows drew together. "We've been over this. You will always be my commander. Commander Yang will not be here in time with his army. We are all we have, all Piao has. The time for your useless self-sacrifice is gone. In one day, we will ride to face a Kou army with only the palace guards at our backs. I will not let you relinquish your duty."

The word duty stuck in Jian's mind, a path he couldn't break free of. His eyes met Luca's and then Bo's. They were the only people he'd ever relied on until her, until Hua.

"We cannot let the Kou reach the city." He straightened, the title of commander settling on his shoulder like a mantle calling to him. He'd made mistakes, many of his men died, but Piao remained under Bo's control, and he'd protect it until his last breath. "The northern fields."

Luca's eyes sparked, and his lips curved up. "You want to make a stand."

"It's the only way." He paced in front of the window. "If they breach the gate, this city will fall." To the north of Piao lay winter wheat fields. They had yet to be harvested, reaching waist high in their golden sway.

Bo rubbed his jaw. "We have almost a hundred guards in the city. How will they fare against a thousand Kou?"

"Guards aren't all we have." Since the Kou first started encroaching on the borders, Piao had been calling every man from their fields on a voluntary basis.

"Most of the young, fighting men are already with the army." Luca's voice held a note of understanding.

Jian nodded. "The young men, yes." He thought of Gen Minglan and Liu Kai, both generals in the civil wars of

Piao in the past, both men who'd ride to face any threat. How many other seasoned warriors lived in the capitol Piao?

Bo didn't speak for a long moment. He sat completely still as if behind his veil in the temple, deep in thought.

Jian stopped pacing and stared at his brother. "You are the emperor."

"Yes, but I have named you the leader in this. In matters of war, you make the decisions."

Jian didn't hesitate. "We will ask the people of Dasha to protect their city. And they will come for you, brother."

Bo shook his head. "They will come for Piao."

Bo had never believed anyone should show loyalty to him only because of the palace he called home. Instead, the people's loyalty, their honor should rest with the empire. No matter who they called emperor, no matter who they fought for, this was their home.

They'd suffered through the cruel reign of Bo's father, and still Piao was theirs. Now, Bo wished to lead the Wei dynasty in a new direction, one full of honor, one full of hope. They had to defeat their enemies to build a better world than the one they'd inherited.

General Altan could not be allowed to ascend the steps of the palace.

Lost in his own thoughts, Jian wandered toward the desk at the far end of the room. Battle plans rolled through his head, bolstering his weary mind. His gaze settled on a painting hanging along the wall. As kids, it was one of the reasons Jian and Bo loved this room so much. They'd called it the dragon room in hushed whispers as they stared into the all-seeing eyes depicted in the painting. A serpent-like dragon appeared from behind beautiful puffy white clouds, looking as if it belonged among them.

Since the last known dragons had walked the earth, their image had become nothing more than a symbol belonging to the emperors, used to show their strength, their power, their role in the protection of Piao.

It was why the dragon blooded were feared and hunted. Their connection to the flying serpents threatened the power of the emperor.

"We used to spend hours staring at this." Bo's voice was low, and Jian didn't know when he'd stepped up beside him.

"Your father tried to keep us away."

Bo laughed. "He tried to keep us from a lot of things. It wasn't until he decided I had the mandate to rule that he told me why."

Jian stayed silent, waiting for his brother to explain.

"This dragon was painted to represent truth."

Jian recalled some lessons he'd been forced into at the temple when he was a kid. When a dragon appeared from the clouds, it meant that the truth was difficult to see.

Bo went on. "My father's greatest enemy was truth."

There were different kinds of truths. The facts that were obvious and the ones a person avoided. What were they avoiding? The Kou would descend on Dasha, and there was a very good chance every one of them would die trying to protect the city.

So, what weren't they seeing?

"We can't do this alone, Jian." Bo looked from Jian to Luca who'd joined them at Jian's other side. The three of them had always been together in everything. They were a team, but they weren't enough.

"What are you saying?"

"The truth we are refusing to see is the dragon herself."

Jian took a step back. "No."

"Jian." Bo sighed.

Luca shook his head. "You can't possibly be considering this, Bo." At least Luca was on his side.

Bo rubbed a hand across his tired eyes. "I am trying to keep an enemy from destroying my empire."

"So, you would make a deal with another enemy?"

Jian flinched at Luca's use of the word.

Bo turned to Luca. "We are out of options."

"She tried to kill you."

"No," Jian cut in. "The Nagi tried to kill him. Not Hua. She is still in there, and she'd rather die than let the Nagi destroy anyone else. We cannot let her free."

"And what if the Kou take the palace?" Bo let out an exasperated grunt. "We let a Nagi fall into their hands? That wouldn't only destroy Piao, it could doom the rest of the world." His eyes met Jian's. "And what of Hua? She would be trapped here with Batukhan Altan."

Jian tore his eyes from his brother and the painting as pain churned through him. He couldn't decipher the fear from the never-ending sadness. He closed his eyes, thinking of every conversation he'd had with the Nagi. He didn't trust it. He never would.

But what if this was the mission? What if the Nagi was supposed to help Piao before she left? Was this the way to save Hua?

And was it worth risking Piao to save her?

Yes.

He hated his traitorous answer, but it was all he had.

"I will bring her to you." He walked to the door, ignoring Bo's words of thanks and Luca's protests. In that moment, he'd chosen a path, and he wouldn't be able to find his way back from it.

He just hoped he hadn't chosen wrong.

CHAPTER 32

Hua

Hua didn't know how the Nagi could stay awake for so long. She'd waited for her opportunity to wrest control back, but it hadn't come. So, she slept, fading to the back of the Nagi's mind, storing up her strength.

The last few days had been one nightmare after another, but it was the secrets that stayed with her. She'd listened to Nainai's conversation with the Nagi, absorbing every truth that now made so much sense. The cryptic conversations they'd had about dragons before Hua left her home now held more meaning. The tattoo her Nainai drew on her arm before the ink faded into her skin. Had the tattoo held meaning other than a confirmation that Hua held a Nagi inside her? Was her nainai only testing her?

How had Nainai never told her family?

And who was this mysterious boy she'd had to rescue?

Each Nagi had a mission to complete before they could leave, a mission that would help Piao work toward peace.

She refused to believe her Nagi's true mission was to kill the emperor, the first emperor in many years who deserved the trust of his people. The persecution of the blooded was in the past now. If Bo Xu Wei died, would his successor be as merciful?

Bo had no children and had not named an heir. Hua pictured Prince Dequan with his hard eyes and unforgiving countenance. Would he become emperor?

These thoughts plagued her sleep, but the fear was not for her. She'd already given up on ever having her life back, on surviving these trials. She worried for Piao, for her family. For Jian.

The clanging of the cell bars jolted her awake as the Nagi slid her eyes open to find Jian standing with four guards at his back. His jaw tightened as he looked at her.

Hua's heart ached, wanting to reach for him, to take the pain from his eyes.

"Hello, Commander." The Nagi cocked her head.

Light flickered at Jian's back from the torch one of the guards carried. It cast him in an ethereal glow. "The emperor would like to speak with you."

"I'm right here."

His eyes hardened. "The emperor does not come down here. You will come with us."

"Don't hurt them, please," Hua whispered in her mind. Without shifting, the Nagi was still stronger than any man, but not five.

The Nagi ignored Hua and got to her feet. "I will speak with your emperor."

Jian turned and marched down the dark hall. Two guards grabbed the Nagi's arms and pushed her forward while the other two followed.

They made their way up through the sleeping palace, past closed doors behind which people rested for battle.

A sharp yip drew the Nagi's attention and Hua cried out, the sound not leaving her lips. *"Chichi."*

The dog ran toward them, barking vigorously. He growled when he reached them, his back arching as he stared at her.

One of the guards kicked him away, and Hua wanted to lunge at him, to tell him to leave her dog alone.

If Chichi was in the palace, Ru must have been too. Did he come with Nainai? And where were her parents? Were they all under the same roof?

The guard kicked the dog again.

Jian stormed back to them, shoving the guard. "Do not touch this dog."

"Dogs don't belong in the palace," the guard grumbled.

Jian pointed down at Chichi. "This one does." He jabbed his finger toward a closed door. "Bring the Nagi in there." As they passed, the Nagi's eyes tracked Jian, and Hua watched him bend down to lift the too-large dog into his arms. Chichi quieted like he trusted Jian.

Jian followed them into a library and set Chichi down as he nudged the door shut with his foot. Shelves of ancient-looking books lined one wall, stretching all the way to a desk at the other end.

A guard shoved the Nagi forward, and Hua focused on the two men standing near the window. Luca refused to meet the Nagi's gaze, but the emperor lifted his chin and stared.

"Guards," the emperor said. "You may wait outside the door."

"Bo." Luca shut up when the emperor sent him a scathing look.

"Out."

The guards looked at the Nagi, indecision warring in their eyes.

Jian nodded to them. "We will call for you if we have a need."

That seemed to reassure them, and they left their emperor with the Nagi—who wanted to kill him—and only two men for protection.

The emperor's gaze softened, and he gestured to the bench seat near the window. "Please, sit down."

To Hua's surprise, as soon as the Nagi obeyed, the emperor sat beside her. "The last time we were together, things did not go exactly as planned."

Luca snorted.

"General Kai," the emperor barked.

The use of his title made Luca snap to attention.

"Do you need to wait outside this room?"

"No, your Majesty. I will not leave you."

"Then forgive me if I tell you to keep your words and insubordinate noises to yourself."

Hua caught sight of an amused smile forming on Jian's lips before it was gone just as quickly.

Luca took a seat, not saying another word.

"I wish to begin anew," the emperor started. "A fresh start."

The Nagi didn't speak for a long moment. "And what of my people? Did they ever receive a fresh start?"

The emperor hung his head in remorse. "When I think of what the dragon blooded have endured in this empire, I am ashamed. For hundreds of years, they've lived in fear. I know I cannot erase that history."

"Someone needs to pay for what Piao has done."

"Vengeance is a vicious cycle. It prevents healing."

"And why should Piao be allowed to heal?" The Nagi's voice cracked on the last word.

"It is not only Piao that must heal. The dragon blooded are a part of this empire, and they must be allowed to move on from their past."

"If it's truly the past."

A beat of silence passed between them before the emperor rose. Jian and Luca sucked in simultaneous breaths when the emperor dropped to a knee in front of the Nagi and lowered his head.

"I pledge myself to your people, to protect them and help them move into the future as an integral part of this empire."

The Nagi stared at him. "You need something from me."

The emperor lifted his head, his young face twisting in sadness. Yet, he did not rise. "The Kou army will be here tomorrow. Our own forces are too far behind them to prevent the attack on Dasha. If we do not defeat them, Piao will be lost."

Hua's mind couldn't quite grasp what he was saying. For so long, she'd focused on defeating the Nagi and regaining herself. But this all started when she left to face the Kou. Images of fire and death entered her mind, but she didn't know if the thoughts were hers or the Nagi's.

The Kou were going to destroy them.

The Nagi nodded in understanding. *"They wish me to fight for them,"* she said to Hua.

Hua wanted to tell them what a bad idea this was. The Nagi couldn't be trusted not to destroy both sides of the war like she did in Kanyuan.

"Piao is not my home." The Nagi cocked her head. "I owe it no allegiance."

The emperor sat back on his heels, his robe fanning out over his knees. "The Nagi of old were loyal servants of Piao, meant to keep us safe."

"How can you think your mission is to kill this man?" Hua's voice echoed through the spaces of her mind, twisting with the Nagi's thoughts. If the Nagi was ever going to leave, she needed to fulfill her purpose, a purpose connected to protecting Piao.

The emperor met the Nagi's eyes. "Jian, Luca, leave us."

"No." Luca crossed his arms.

Jian mirrored his stance, not issuing a word.

The emperor rose to his feet to face the two men. "I am the emperor. Do not make me command you, not you two. Trust me in this. Please. For your love of me, I need you to go."

Jian's shoulders dropped. "We will be right outside that door should you need us." He looked to the Nagi, but Hua got the feeling he looked only at her. "Protect him." Those words weren't for the Nagi. Hua used them to strengthen herself. She couldn't let the Nagi hurt the emperor, not again.

Luca hesitated once Jian left, and the emperor walked to him, putting a hand on both of his arms. "Please. Trust me."

Luca sucked in a breath, his hand rising to trace the line of the emperor's jaw. It dropped, and he tore himself away.

The slamming of the door echoed through the room, reminding Hua it was now only her, the Nagi, and the emperor.

The emperor leaned against the window-frame, his gaze drifting to the dormant fountain in the courtyard. "I will do anything to protect Piao." He paused. "Even if it means sacrificing myself."

"You will die by no one's hand but my own."

The emperor turned to the Nagi, a new fire in his eyes. "That is what I'm counting on. If the Kou take Dasha, they will control all of Piao. I cannot allow that. If I die, someone else will become emperor, but if I let Piao fall, I will have ended a dynasty that has lasted hundreds of years."

Hua saw where he was going with this as the coming words sliced through her heart prematurely.

"What are you saying?" the Nagi asked.

The emperor dropped down onto the seat and hesitated before reaching over to take the Nagi's hand again. The sensation wound through Hua. She wasn't sure how she could feel it, but it only made what was coming worse.

"If you believe your purpose is to kill me to avenge your people, I will not stop you."

"No," Hua cried.

The Nagi ignored her as she stared down at the emperor's hand in hers.

The emperor continued after a beat of silence. "This is the moment I decide what kind of emperor to be. My advisors will not want me to release you. My own brother has advised me against it. And Luca... he will not understand. But I do not matter, my reign does not matter. The people do. And the people need the Nagi to protect them in a way I cannot."

He closed his eyes. "When the battle is done and Piao is safe, you may complete your mission and send me into the next life."

Tears built in the Nagi's eyes, but they did not belong to her as Hua tried desperately to rise, to speak the words the Nagi would not. This was not the way. He couldn't sacrifice himself.

"And yet, it was okay for you?" The Nagi's tone held condemnation.

"He is the emperor. I am only Hua."

The Nagi sighed inwardly. *"I must complete this mission, Hua. One way or another. You were willing to face execution to save an emperor you did not know, to save the people from me. It was a noble deed. Does the emperor not have a right to nobility as well?"*

Hua tried to tell herself that was different, that her sacrifice was warranted and his was unnecessary. But the Kou were almost at their gates, and she'd seen how vicious they could be.

The Nagi removed her hand from the emperor's and stood to look out across the courtyard, where the entrance to the temple shone like a golden beacon of righteousness.

The emperor got to his feet and walked toward a painting behind the desk. "Sometimes the truth is difficult to see." He looked back over his shoulder. "And sometimes, it is all one can face."

"I will help you," the Nagi finally said. "We will defeat your enemy because you speak true. The Nagi have a loyalty to Piao no matter what the emperors or the armies have done." She paused. "I do not need revenge on the people. I feel… remorse for what happened in Kanyuan. That will not happen to Dasha. I do not need to destroy the empire to fulfill my mission. Once the battle is over, what is left will be between you and me. But you must make me a promise. I am entrusting my people to you with this vow. Your successor will not return to the ways of old. They will be safe."

Acceptance shone in the emperor's gaze, not unlike what Hua had felt upon making the decision to turn herself in, to face her own death. She realized then how alike she and the emperor were. Maybe that was why Luna had put her faith in them both. She hadn't known the fate of Piao would one day lie at their feet, but maybe she'd known they'd do the right thing if it did.

The Nagi and the emperor remained locked in their gaze, an agreement passing between them.

The emperor nodded. "I have chosen who will rule once I am gone, and you can trust in his heart."

"I will not leave until I see it is so."

When the battle was won, they would face each other once more, the tentative alliance nothing more than blood on their daos.

CHAPTER 33

Jian

Bo wouldn't talk to him. After Jian and Luca waited for him outside the study, their hands on their daos ready to charge back into the room, Bo walked right past them, stopping in front of one of the guards.

"Hua Minglan is to be taken to a comfortable room," he'd said. "Wake some servants to attend her."

For a few brief moments, Jian wondered if Hua had come back to them, but the look in her eyes spoke true. The Nagi still had control and had struck an accord with the emperor.

When Bo walked away, Jian and Luca tried to follow him,

but two guards stood in their way, instructed by the emperor to not let anyone pass.

Jian knew where he went, where he always went to still the turmoil inside him. But the temple would provide none of the answers he wanted.

And now, after a few hours' rest, Jian stood at the top of the palace steps, looking out into the city square as the guard fanned out, winding through the streets to call on the few men who hadn't joined the army months ago. Most of them were older, but they had experience that could not be taught.

Piao had been through many wars, and each time, the people came. Fighting for their homes was important to them.

"This city does not know what is coming for it." Prince Duyi stepped up beside Jian, a wisdom in his words that belied his young age.

"No, my prince. I am very much afraid it does not."

Duyi crossed his arms over the embroidered forest green robe. "Commander, you are my brother's brother. That makes you family. I am not a prince to you."

Jian smiled at the defiance in his tone. "Then I am not a commander to you. Though, your mama will not like it."

Duyi pushed out a breath. "Mama likes few things."

Empress Yanyu had made herself scarce along with the three remaining consorts in the days since Jian returned. She'd never had a taste for war, despite urging her sons to fight for their right to rule the empire.

The elder princes held estates throughout Piao, but not one of the four men had sent their forces to fight the Kou. Prince Dequan gave them sanctuary in his home, but if the fight hadn't come so close to his lands, he wouldn't have involved himself.

"I want to fight." Duyi's words were quiet, like he feared the way they'd shake the earth.

How could the youngest prince who was raised by the same woman differ from his own brothers? Jian looked to him out of the corner of his eye, taking note of the stubborn tilt of his chin, the courage flashing in his eyes that spoke of Bo's influence on the young man rather than his mama's.

"You are too important to the empire." Jian put a hand on his shoulder. "But your bravery is admirable." He turned to walk back inside and out of the cold.

Duyi's voice called him back. "And if there is no empire? What then? It won't matter if I'm a prince when Batukhan Altan sits in our brother's place." Duyi was the first member of the royal family other than Bo himself to acknowledge Jian's relationship to the emperor. *Our brother.* He turned back to face the young man, wondering how he'd grown so much in such a short time.

Where was the little boy who hid behind his mama, who let her speak for him in all things?

"The empress will never allow it."

Duyi stepped toward him, the sun flashing in his eyes. "My mama is not the commander."

It was Jian's job to keep the royal family safe, to make sure they didn't walk too close to the flames. Bo. Duyi. Even the old empress herself. They did not belong on a battlefield bloodying their blades.

But as he stared into the eyes of the prince, he saw a boy who wanted nothing more than to fight alongside his people.

He saw himself. Jian and Luca had been Duyi's age when they joined the army.

"Duyi," a voice snapped behind him as Empress Yanyu stepped around a column and into view. "Come inside. Now. You do not belong among soldiers." Her eyes swept the square where men had started to gather around the palace guards handing out weapons.

Duyi sighed and looked to Jian once more. "You can't stop me."

"I know."

"Duyi." Yanyu grabbed his arm, yanking him behind her as her eyes fixed on Jian. "Stay away from my son."

Duyi's shoulders hunched as he followed her through the doors.

Jian looked to the guards by the door and shrugged, not ready to go back into the stifling palace where Bo's insipid advisors continuously argued over a plan that had already been set in motion. Where Bo avoided his gaze, and the Nagi was free of her cell, roaming the halls in Hua's body.

He descended the steps slowly, shielding his eyes from the light glaring off the smooth marble. The closer he got to the square, the louder the day became. Guards and would-be soldiers walked by in a hurry with only one day to prepare for a battle for the city.

He lifted his eyes to the northern gates, the arches rising over the flat roofs in the distance. How long would they stand if the battle was lost?

"Commander," a melodic voice called to him.

He turned to find Lihua, one of Bo's consorts walking toward him, a stream of armed eunuchs and servants in her wake. A bright smile graced her painted face, pink lips stretching wide.

He bowed as she neared but didn't speak.

"This is exciting, is it not?" She gestured to the bustle of preparation around them.

"Necessary, consort, not exciting." He'd once found the thought of battle an adrenaline pumping journey as well, but now, he knew better. There was nothing exciting in war, only too much death.

Her smile fell. "Yes, of course. I just meant that so many have come for the fight."

"Dasha is a proud city." He didn't tell her it still wouldn't be nearly enough, or that every man in this square might die. When they rode through the gates in the early morning, they'd have a few hundred men to meet over a thousand Kou.

Her smile returned. "Yes. We are." Her gaze drifted toward the armed men rushing by, and he would have sworn a wistful sigh left her lips. "Well, I shouldn't keep you from your duties." She looked to where Alix and Holea were aiding the guards in recording names of the men who'd come. If nothing else, they'd be remembered. "It feels good to be of some use." She sent him one final smile before leaving to join the other consorts.

Jian had never considered how difficult it must be to join Bo's harem. He loved them as he loved everyone in his service, but he'd never have romantic feelings for them. They were nothing more than an ornamental hope that the emperor would produce an heir—or many.

Their quiet nature had always struck Jian as a bit eerie, but they were chosen for what they weren't, not what they were. The council selected girls from prominent families who would cause no trouble. They were calm, safe.

Except Luna.

Jian remembered the day Bo first saw her. They'd travelled to one of the prince's estates by way of Zhouchang. She'd been in town with her mother and smiled at them with no recognition in her eyes.

He hadn't fallen in love with her exactly, but he'd wanted her in his life, to make it brighter. It had taken weeks to convince the council, but they eventually decided General Gen Minglan deserved the honor of having his daughter chosen.

No one expected that choice to get her killed.

Commotion at the edge of the square snapped him from the memory. People ran toward the gate. Jian sprinted after them as fast as he could. It was too early for the Kou to have arrived, but still, fear shot through him. Dasha wasn't ready.

He darted through the streets until he caught sight of the giant black gates swinging open. Guards rushed forward as a handful of bedraggled men rode through. A familiar face caught his eye, and he ran toward the horse Zhao Shi nudged forward, a body draped over the back of the saddle.

"Zhao," Jian called.

Relief flashed across Zhao's face when he caught sight of Jian. "Commander Yang needs a healer."

Jian drew closer and recognized the commander despite the blood sprayed across his face. "Follow me." Jian turned and started running, listening to the clop of hooves to make sure Zhao was still with him. He raced through the square, his muscles tightening in exhaustion. But he didn't stop until he reached his destination. Unlike the last time he'd come to the healer's shop, the door stood open. A stream of visitors waited to see the healer.

Zhao pulled the horse to a stop next to Jian and slid down before the two men lifted Commander Yang's limp body and pushed through the crowd.

At the back of the shop, an older man waited for his next patron. "Sir," Jian called. "We need help."

The healer rushed toward them. "Put him here." He pointed to an empty cot.

They set the commander down and backed up.

"I am Healer Liqin." The man didn't look up. "What happened?"

Zhao rubbed the back of his neck. "Our camp was attacked." He looked to Jian. "We thought we were behind them, that we couldn't catch up before they reached Dasha, but they attacked on all sides. We weren't ready."

"Zhao, what are you saying?"

His tortured eyes met Jian's. "The army isn't coming. It has been destroyed."

Every last bit of faith Jian had faded away just as he feared Piao would in the coming hours. The Piao army wasn't going to save them. He'd counted on his men only needing to hold off the Kou for hours before relief arrived.

Now…

Healer Liqin straightened. "What happened to this man? I cannot heal the army, but I might be able to help him."

Zhao nodded and rocked back on his heels, his tarnished armor jangling together. "Trampled by a horse. He saved a lot of the men, but then…" He held his hands up.

The healer nodded. "I do not see any flesh wounds. I will do what I can. You two leave. There is no time for hovering."

Jian clapped a hand on Zhao's shoulder and ushered him back into the cool air. He looked to the brilliant blue sky, wondering how such a day could come before the end. "We are alone." As soon as he said the words, he felt them. Dasha stood as a final resistance to Altan, a final stand. Once it fell, all of Piao was doomed.

He couldn't look into the faces of the men arming themselves for a hopeless battle, so he kept his eyes on the ground, wondering if it would swallow him whole.

It took him a moment to gather his courage to ask the next question. "Where are the others? Chen… Yan… Qara…"

"Alive."

The tension in Jian's chest eased.

"We left a camp of injured in the valley with enough men to care for them along with Qara and a few other healers. The rest of us rode hard for Dasha. We had to ride through the night and skirt around the Kou army. They suffered many losses in the battle, but it will not slow them."

"I know."

"If the Kou defeat Dasha, they will return to the valley and kill everyone in that camp."

"I know."

Zhao's shoulders sagged, and Jian needed to take him somewhere quiet to rest. The guards took care of the other men he'd ridden with, but Jian needed Zhao to inform Bo of everything that had happened. "I'm taking you to the palace."

Zhao froze, his eyes widening. "No."

"The emperor must speak to you."

He shook his head. "Our time in the army together has made you forget how I got there, Commander."

Right. Zhao had been a prisoner. He sighed, a crease forming in his brow. "Do you think that matters anymore?"

"Do you wish to know why the emperor imprisoned me?"

"No. You are no longer the man you were before. We are soldiers. That is all. And as soldiers, we fight together." Jian started up the steps, looking back over his shoulder to make sure Zhao was still there.

Reluctantly, the big man followed him, sweeping one hand over his top knot to fix it in place. He ran his other hand down the filthy armor, but Bo wouldn't care about Zhao's appearance, only his information.

A guard opened the door, and they strode in through the gleaming marble entryway.

Empress Yanyu walked toward them with a scowl. "First, we allow a dog into this palace and now a common soldier is dirtying the floors with his boots." She looked closer at Zhao. "I know you."

Zhao ducked his head and bowed stiffly. "Empress."

Jian looked to one of the servants who'd followed her. "Find the emperor and General Kai, and bring them to the study."

Yanyu's cheeks reddened. "You do not summon the emperor."

Jian stared at the woman who had always enjoyed making people feel small, seeing her own insecurities flash across her face. Her husband was dead, and as soon as Bo had an empress, she would cease to have a role at all. Most in the palace still called her Empress out of respect, but if it weren't for her youngest son's favor with Bo, she'd have been sent away as soon as her husband died. Whatever power she'd once held was now gone. Without a word, he walked past her.

A greater battle than he'd ever imagined was coming to Dasha, and it was time he stopped believing the lies about himself.

Jian was the commander. His past mistakes held no more power over him.

All that mattered was what he did next.

CHAPTER 34

Hua

The first thing Hua wanted to do when she opened her eyes—her, not the Nagi—was find Jian. The deal the Nagi made with the emperor swirled in her mind, but she understood him on another level.

He thought Piao was worth his sacrifice, just as she had.

What right did she have to take that away from him?

She lifted her hand, flexing her fingers. The Nagi slept, gathering her strength for the coming battle, allowing Hua these last moments.

Moonlight streamed through the painted window,

casting prisms of color across the floor. She sat up and slid her legs over the side of the bed. When her feet hit the cold marble floor, the sensation flooded her. Such a simple act, yet she felt it, reveling in the sensation. The Nagi hadn't slept in days, leaving Hua as thoughts scattering across her mind.

She reached for a lantern and lit it before pulling on a cloak over her robe. More than anything, she needed to see the stars, to know they would continue shining long after the battle hours from now.

Slipping her feet into soft slippers, she left her room to creep through the eerily silent palace. On the eve of battle, everything was prepared, everyone had been armed and now rested for what was to come. Only a few guards and servants wandered the halls. She nodded to each she passed before pushing out into the courtyard between the main palace and the temple.

The dormant fountain reminded her of what Piao might become, an empire of failed potential, a place of dying dreams.

She sat on the edge of the fountain and lifted her eyes to the stars. The dragon spread across the black sky, obscuring the other constellations from view. Was that a sign?

"You once thought the stars held all the answers." The sound of Nainai's voice was like a salve in an open wound, both soothing and painful.

"I was naïve." She lowered her gaze to the woman who'd reached her side, the one who'd hidden so many things from her.

"Not naïve, child." Nainai brushed a hand over Hua's head. "The stars themselves hold no answers for us. But in searching them for truths, we find answers within ourselves. In being still and reading the skies, we search inward."

Hua's eyes burned with tears. It was the kind of thing Nainai would have said as they sat on the roof of their home outside Zhouchang. That time seemed like another life. "Oh, Hua." She sat next to her.

Hua leaned into her, soaking in the familiar comfort. She hiccupped back a sob. "Before Luna was chosen as consort, could you ever imagine us here in this world of royalty and wars?"

Nainai smoothed the hair back from Hua's face. "Our family was always meant to play a part in the fate of the world. That is why a Nagi chose me when I was a girl. It is why you have been chosen now."

Hua pulled away. "Your Nagi only needed to save a boy. I don't want to kill the emperor, Nainai."

She pressed a kiss to Hua's forehead. "I know, child."

A door opened behind them, and Hua turned to see the emperor slipping into the temple.

Nainai smiled sadly. "Your family needs you, my girl. They need to know you are not yet lost. But that young man also has need of you. Go. And then find us."

Once her Nainai left, Hua stared at the temple doors, knowing she would not be welcome inside. The only conversation she'd had with the emperor ended in the Nagi taking control and trying to kill him.

But she found herself walking toward the ornate carved gold and pushing on the handle. Living in a remote part of the empire, she'd never entered a temple, and the silence was as loud as any crack of thunder. She inched forward to where a sheer veil separated the emperor from her.

"I can feel you watching me." The emperor's voice held no annoyance or anger, only an immense weariness. "What need has a Nagi for the temple?"

Hua pushed aside the curtain and stepped through. "None, I suppose." Fighting in the army surrounded by crude men made her immune to the intimidation many of them tried to portray. But Bo Xu Wei was not that man. She'd once thought he had a joy about him, but that joy had been snuffed out, just like hers.

She kneeled at his side, not saying a word. This all started for her with the death of Luna, with meeting the emperor. And now it would finish with him too.

"Will the Nagi have control during the battle tomorrow?" He leaned forward as if to touch a bronze statue but pulled his hand back.

"I will surrender to her, yes." She'd never willingly given over control, but Piao didn't need Hua Minglan. It needed the dragon.

"You should be resting."

Hua ignored that. "I understand you, your Majesty."

He snapped his eyes to hers, the flickering of candlelight reflecting off his irises. "I guess you do."

"You refused to kill me."

He sat back on his heels. "Do you wish I had?"

"I don't know."

He considered that for a moment. "Do you love my brother?"

It wasn't the kind of conversation she'd ever thought to have with the emperor, but it was here nonetheless. "I'm not sure that matters anymore."

"I suppose you're right."

"Do you love Luca?" Insinuating such a thing was dangerous, but against all better judgement, she trusted the emperor.

"I'm not sure that matters either." He sighed. "My decision will hurt them both."

"Just as I knew mine would."

He offered her a weak smile. They were in this together. She tried not to think about the fact that he wanted her hands to be the ones that killed him, that he allowed the deal in exchange for the Nagi's help. She would do what she could to prevent it, but she was helpless under the Nagi's control.

Yet, there was one thing she could control. It was why the Nagi couldn't shift, why Hua wouldn't fade away. She put a hand over her heart. "For what it's worth, your Majesty, maybe it does matter. Maybe it's all that matters."

He reached over and took her hand, giving it a squeeze. "I wish that were true."

Hua lifted her hand to a closed door but didn't knock. How was she supposed to face her family after everything she'd done, all the blood she'd spilled?

She knew it hadn't been her, that she hadn't consciously chosen to end lives and destroy others, but she'd still felt the actions and would forever live with the scars on her soul.

Searching her mind, she could barely sense the Nagi as she slept. Maybe that was for the best. This was something she had to do alone.

But did she have the strength?

Beyond that door, her family would be preparing to send

her father into battle, a fate she'd tried to spare him when she stole away in the night to join the army.

Beyond that door, they were together as they had been since she left, trying to heal from everything she'd put them through.

Beyond that door, she wasn't sure she belonged anymore.

Laughter filtered through the solid wood, and for a moment, she was an older sister wondering why Ru was awake at this hour. He'd need his rest to get through the coming day. Most of the people in this palace would not be riding into battle, but they'd face a battle of their own as they waited to see who would return from the soon-to-be bloody field. Would it be victorious Piao warriors? Their sons and fathers? Or the Kou coming to claim the city?

The last time she'd faced her parents as herself—Hua, not the Nagi—was the night before she defied them and left for the war. And now, she'd leave them once again come morning.

As if it had a will of its own, her hand rapped against the smooth oak. Her heartbeat pounded in her temples as she waited. All sound coming from the room cut off as the door opened, and her father froze, his eyes widening.

Tears gathered in Hua's eyes. "Baba."

"Hua?" he whispered, searching her eyes. "My dear." He reached for her with tentative movements, slow at first. The moment his fingertips grazed her cheek she fell into his arms.

"I'm so sorry, Baba." And she was. Sorry for everything. Leaving. Letting the Nagi destroy Kanyuan. Killing an entire unit of sleeping men right in front of him. And then abandoning them once again.

Her baba saw the evil in her, the wrong her hands could do, but when his arms molded around her, they held on tighter, his entire body shaking.

"It's you. It's you." He whispered the words over and over as if reassuring himself.

"Hua?" Her mama rushed toward them, and Hua released her father to repeat the collapse into her mama's arms.

But it was the next voice that broke her, the next reunion she'd seen in her dreams. Little arms wrapped around her legs, holding on tighter than either of Hua's parents had.

Hua smiled through the tears, releasing her mama to bend down and fold Ru into a tight hug. Unlike their parents, he didn't cry. Instead, he whispered into her hair. "I was strong for you, Hua. I knew you'd come back to us."

She leaned away from her brother to look into his eyes, eyes that had seen too much for his young age. "You were, didi. You were strong. Thank you." She pulled him back to her chest, wishing she never had to let go, wishing she could tell him she didn't have to leave him again, that this wasn't the last time she'd hold him in her arms.

She hadn't realized it as she stood outside their door, but this was both reunion and farewell. If she survived the battle, the Nagi planned to kill the emperor, and Hua would suffer the consequences. The Nagi would leave once she completed the mission, but Hua… the empire would punish her.

Nainai walked toward them with Chichi at her heels. She smiled in understanding as if she'd read Hua's mind. She knew what the cost of this life was, a life of being chosen for a purpose out of her control.

As her family led her farther into the room, she caught sight of unfamiliar armor sitting in the corner by a silver table, a reminder of both past and future. Hua had taken her father's armor, so now, he'd ride to battle wearing scales that were not his.

Just like her.

Because Hua knew, if she was truly going to help Piao, she'd have to let the Nagi shift into her true form.

Hua listened to the soft snores of her family. The room held two beds and a settee. Her parents slept across the room in an elegant four-poster bed while her Nainai took the smaller one. Hua, not wanting to leave her family for her own room, had curled up on the settee after spending half the night sitting with her family in front of the hearth just like they would have at home.

She shifted onto her side, pulling Ru's little body with her. Her brother had insisted on staying with her, and she could never say no to him. Chichi curled up on the settee at their feet. It wasn't comfortable physically, but mentally, it was everything.

Ru eased the tension in her mind, letting her live in the moment.

"You shouldn't be here." The Nagi's voice returned in her mind.

"There's nowhere else I should be."

"You do not lack intelligence, Hua Minglan. Do not act like it."

There was one farewell she hadn't been able to face, one man she tried to avoid thinking about. Even if the Nagi performed the act, once the emperor died, Jian would never forgive her.

"How can I look him in the eyes?" she whispered.

The Nagi didn't respond for a long moment. *"How can you not?"*

Since when was the Nagi a romantic? Hua wanted to hate the beast inside her, she wanted to hold on to the anger and fight with everything she had. But tonight was not a night for anger, not when she held her little brother, not when Jian was somewhere in this palace preparing to ride to war in only a few hours.

Nothing was certain. There was a good chance they'd all die trying to protect Dasha.

And she had to look into his eyes one final time. She needed him to see her, not the Nagi. Releasing Ru, Hua climbed over him to kneel on the floor at his side. She pressed a kiss to his forehead. "I will protect you, didi." She'd give everything she had left to keep the Kou out of the city, even her life.

Chichi lifted his head to stare at her.

"Take care of him." She rubbed the dog's head, letting her eyes drift to the rest of her family. "One day, I hope you'll all be able to forgive me."

Her mama stirred but didn't wake. Her baba remained still, his body storing up energy for what was to come. She'd see him on the battlefield.

But Nainai... her eyes slid open, and her understanding gaze rested on Hua. Hua bowed her head, and Nainai nodded, telling her it was okay to go, giving her permission to do whatever was required of her for Piao.

Hua rushed from the room, tears burning her eyes. She wiped them away and straightened her shoulders. This was not a time to cry, to wallow in everything she'd lost.

The Nagi gave her strength from within so she could walk away from her family—again.

At this late hour, she didn't expect Jian to be awake. The Nagi directed her to his room as if she could sense him. Not wanting to wake him, Hua tried the door, finding it unlocked. She pushed it open, revealing a room awash in starlight. Her eyes skittered past the large bed covered in furs. They didn't stop on the ornate marble hearth or intricately woven rugs.

Because standing at the window with moonlight setting his skin aglow was Jian Li, the commander she'd befriended, the friend she'd fallen in love with.

And the last person on earth she had the strength to say goodbye to.

He wore only a pair of silk pants, his robe discarded over the end of the bed. The muscles in his back tightened as he turned, his eyes drinking her in.

He was beautiful, but the way he looked at her made her believe she could be too. That was the power of Jian Li. It had nothing to do with his sheer strength or skill in battle. He saw past the lies, past the Nagi, to her, Hua Minglan.

His arms had held her after she'd tried to kill the Nagi by taking her own life. He'd spent months searching for her in desolate mountain ranges across enemy territory.

He'd saved her family.

And when he looked at her, she saw every reason.

"I love you." The words felt right on her tongue. This time, she didn't fight the feeling, there wasn't a weapon she was trying to get from him or any other goal.

The words cracked the stillness between them, and Hua pushed the door shut as Jian marched toward her, intent in his every step. In this moment, there was no Nagi standing between them and he wasn't the commander.

Their bodies collided like they were drawn together by some invisible force, their lips warring for supremacy. If there was one thing they did well, it was battle.

Jian backed her up, pressing her against the door as the last few months fell away, and they were two people falling in love for the first time without the constraints of war or tradition. All that mattered was the fire burning through their veins.

Closer, she needed him closer.

One arm slid up around his neck while the other wound around his back, careful to avoid his tender side. She pulled him against her as she poured every bit of fear and desperation into their connection. His hands tangled in her hair, holding her in place like he thought he'd lose her the moment he let go.

"I'm sorry," she whispered against his lips.

"Shhh," he responded.

Hua shook her head, pushing him back for some space. She'd never forget the sight of watching him scrub her blood from the floor of her prison cell. "Jian."

He dipped his head to meet her eyes, the faint light making them shine. "It really is you. I was sure I'd imagined it."

"The Nagi is resting for tomorrow."

He backed up, running a hand through his hair. "You will give back control?"

"I have too." It was the Nagi's deal with the emperor. And it was also the only chance they had against the Kou.

"Did you mean it?" His voice cracked. "That you… were your words just a night before battle confession?"

She stepped forward and put a hand on his chest. "I would love you no matter what tomorrow meant."

That seemed to be all the confirmation he needed, because he pulled her against him, walking back toward the bed.

"Jian," she whispered.

"I just want to hold you. Can you give me that?" He sat on the edge of the bed. "In a few hours, we will ride to a battle we cannot win. But for now, it's just you and me and dreams of a future we could have had."

She cupped his cheek, letting her thumb trace the curve of his lips. Bending down, she fit their mouths together like they'd always been meant to connect. Her kiss was slow as she burned this moment into her memory.

"Our plight seems hopeless now, Jian," she whispered against his lips. "But that does not mean we give up hope."

CHAPTER 35

Jian

Jian knew the moment Hua left in the early morning. It wasn't a physical absence right at first, but her breathing changed, her touch grew cold.

After only a few moments, the Nagi slipped from his embrace and left without a backward glance.

He'd refused to say goodbye to Hua when they were together. Goodbyes before a battle would bring bad luck, but it was more than that. He couldn't imagine never seeing the fierce look in her eyes or the stubborn tilt of her chin again.

But Hua wouldn't be on that battlefield with him. The Nagi, even after everything, would fight for Piao.

Jian sat on the edge of his bed and hung his head. He didn't know what Bo had said to the Nagi or how the Nagi had convinced his brother she would obey Piao on the battlefield. Jian couldn't shake images of Kanyuan or the thought they could be going down the same path.

The difference was Hua.

Somehow, she had kept the Nagi from shifting since flying from Lóng Bǎolěi. Somehow, she'd managed to maintain that bit of control.

He stood and pulled on his robe before starting to don his armor piece by piece. It was a mesmerizing dance, one he'd performed many times before. As each piece of armor slid into place, encasing him in steel scales, his mind cleared.

Whatever this battle meant, however the odds were against them, he was ready to fight for Piao one final time.

Pushing his dao into his scabbard, he stared out the window once more, watching as the moonlight sparkled through the square, hiding the city from the coming trauma.

Closing his eyes for a brief moment, he sighed. This was what he'd trained for his entire life. He reached the door in three strides and walked out into the bustling palace.

The sun would not rise for a couple hours yet, but the palace prepared for war. Servants rushed to feed the guard before their departure. Guardsmen finished sharpening their weapons and checking their armor.

They issued short bows to Jian as he passed. On this day, the palace would not see him as the bastard son of a treasonous consort. No, today, he was the commander who would lead them all to war.

He reached the entryway where two of the consorts fussed over Duyi in his unblemished armor. Jian stared at him for a moment, wanting to tell him to go back to bed, to stay behind where he'd be safe.

But even Dasha wasn't safe anymore.

"Bo won't like it." Luca's voice came from behind Jian. He looked toward the prince.

"He will understand." As Jian said the words, his eyes found Bo striding from one of the hallways, a robe covering his chain mail and a helmet under one arm.

He gave them a grim smile when he stopped walking.

"Absolutely not." Luca shook his head.

Jian only closed his eyes, wishing none of them were in this situation.

"I will fight for my empire." Bo shrugged as if the emperor hadn't just proclaimed he was riding to war.

"Bo." Luca put a hand on his shoulder. "You are the emperor. We cannot risk it."

Something Jian couldn't decipher flashed in Bo's eyes, some knowledge he hadn't shared.

Bo pushed Luca's hand away. "We are asking the men of Dasha—most who are past their fighting ages—to go to battle against the Kou to save this city. They are leaving their homes, their families. Yet, you did not ask it of me." Hurt flashed across his face as he turned to Jian. "I need to stand with my people, Jian. They need to see that their emperor will fight for them as they fight for him."

This wasn't a battle for the warriors of Piao. Most of them died days ago in the Liudong Valley. Now, was a time for the remaining people to protect their way of life, to protect each other. Jian met Luca's gaze, trying to convey that to him. Finally, Luca stepped back, the fight leaving him.

Jian bowed to Bo. "I will be honored to have you fight at my side, brother, but I hope you will consider riding with the guards and not the foot soldiers." For their battle plan, Jian had no need of a horse. He'd hide in the fields with the men of Dasha along with the Nagi, Gen Minglan, and many others.

Bo nodded. "I have already told someone to ready my horse."

A thought struck Jian. There was only one horse he trusted to take care of his brother. He waved to a guard. "The horse I arrived on. Her name is Heima. She will carry the emperor today."

The guard nodded and hurried away to ready Heima.

A second guard approached with Zhao following close behind. After bowing to the emperor, the guard spoke. "This man says he had permission to enter the palace."

Bo didn't speak, but Luca raised an eyebrow. "Zhao Shi?" He waved the guard away. "Jian told me you were in the city."

Zhao had refused to sleep at the palace, camping in the square with the other soldiers instead so he could be closer to Commander Yang. "Yes, General." His lips twitched. "I am glad to see you alive."

Jian cleared his throat. "Any news on Commander Yang?"

Zhao nodded. "Healer Liqin expects him to make a full recovery, given time."

Some good news at least.

Bo froze, spotting something over Jian's shoulder. He knew what it was. Dropping his voice, he stepped closer to his brother. "If you have the right to fight, so does he."

"Duyi is a child."

Jian shook his head. "Not anymore. Village boys train for war at his age. You must let him go."

Bo sighed and ran a hand over his head. "I know."

Zhao nodded to them both, not meeting the emperor's eyes. "The men have gathered in the square. We are ready."

Jian scanned the crowded entryway, wondering if it would belong to them when this was over. "Luca, gather the guard and have them join the men outside. Bo, go tell Duyi that he has to at least tell the empress he is leaving." Yanyu was nowhere to be found, and that could only mean she didn't know. "And he too must ride with the guard."

Despite being the emperor, Bo obeyed Jian's command. Today wasn't about royal status. When they left for battle, Jian was the highest authority.

"Lihua." Zhao's words were no more than a whisper as his eyes tracked the young consort.

Jian remembered the stories he'd heard about why Zhao had been sent to war. He was a young guard who fell in love with a consort and faced prison or war. Turning to regard the young woman, Jian stilled. She entered the room wearing lightweight armor that molded onto her frame as if it had been made for her.

Her long dark hair was swept up into a high tail. Two daos hung at her waist.

After spending months training Hua, Jian no longer wondered if women belonged in battle. Lihua was important to the empire as a consort, but this was an important moment for Piao. Just like Bo. Just like Duyi. If she thought her place was in this war, he had no right to tell her otherwise.

And yet, Zhao looked like he'd seen a spirit.

Lihua took no notice of them as she sent a scathing look to the eunuchs who tried to follow her out the doors and down the steps to join the makeshift army.

"Are you okay?" Jian asked.

Zhao shook himself. "I… Yes. I will not commit treason against the emperor again."

That wasn't what Jian meant. He knew more than anyone what it felt like to love someone he had no future with. Clapping Zhao on the back, he pushed open the doors to find their small army—if one could call it that—gathered at the bottom of the steps.

It was all Piao had to stand between victory and destruction.

Jian's eyes caught on Hua as she wound through the crowd, but it wasn't her. He steeled himself as the remaining guards ran down the steps. At the front stood Luca, staring up at Jian with more faith than Jian had in himself. Zhao stood beside him, his face a cold mask.

Even Lihua joined the men rather than standing at the top of the steps.

Commotion sounded behind Jian, and he turned to see Bo arguing with Yanyu as Duyi stood silently by.

"Enough," Jian commanded, his eyes hard. "Empress, we must prepare."

All fight left her, and her shoulders sagged as a sob left her lips. Jian had never seen her as anything other than cruel, but in that moment, she was just a mother afraid for her son.

Jian gestured for Bo and Duyi to stand with him, but Bo shook his head. The entire collection of men watched the emperor and the prince descend the steps to stand on even ground with the army. In this, they were together.

This was the moment when the battle could be won.

A rallying cry.

A spark of hope.

Even in the dark of the pre-dawn morning, there was light. It lived in the people before him, come from their homes to protect the empire. It lived in the emperor willing to lay down his life, the warriors who'd already died in this fight.

And it lived in the Nagi who stood on their side, at least for today.

Jian drew himself up to his full height. "The Kou destroyed our army." Gasps rang out as the news wound through the crowd and back to those who'd come to see the warriors off. "No one is coming to help us." He stepped forward and down the first marble step. "I have seen these warriors. They are vicious and will fight without mercy. We will be outnumbered, out-skilled, but there is something they do not have."

He took another step down.

"Something to fight for. They would take our fields, our homes, our empire for their own ambition. But they do not know us. They do not know you have come from your farms and your shops for love, not duty. You do not owe us this fight, yet you are here to protect everything you hold dear. Make no mistake, they will try to take it."

He stopped halfway down the steps. "Will we let them?"

The sound started low before more joined in, shouting "no" and issuing their own battle cries.

"I am honored to fight with you by my side. If this is the end," Jian yelled. "Let's take them with us."

The cheer grew, and Jian stared at the bravery of the ordinary citizens of Piao. Most of the men had fought their wars years ago, yet they'd come. He let the sounds wash over him, bolstering his own strength.

The crowd parted as he walked through them, leading them toward the northern gate to the fields beyond where they would make their stand.

CHAPTER 36

The Nagi

The Nagi didn't know what she had expected of Jian's plan, but this certainly wasn't it.

She crouched down, hidden in the wheat fields north of the city. Behind them, along the road winding through the fields, sat what remained of Piao's trained army, the palace guard. They perched high above their war horses, encased in steel armor that shone as the dawn broke across the horizon, throwing blood red streaks of haze across the sky.

It was fitting on a day like this.

Even with her help, the Nagi didn't believe Piao would

emerge victorious, not unless Hua loosened the reins, letting the Nagi control her heart as well as her mind.

Only then would she be able to shift into her true form. A dragon.

"Instead, I'm hiding in a wheat field with a dao as my weapon." She shook her head, flexing her fingers around the hilt. Steel was not the weapon of the Nagi. Fire. She needed fire.

"I will not risk everything." Hua's voice grew stronger.

"You do not trust me."

The Nagi would have sworn Hua laughed. *"After everything? No."*

"I will succeed in my mission, Hua. The dynasty will pay for what they've done. I have no more need for destruction."

"You never had any need for it, and yet destruction is what we got."

With a growl, the Nagi sank lower, letting the swaying wheat bend around her. The foot soldiers of Piao, no more than too-old warriors, remained still, waiting for the enemy to arrive. Jian crouched up ahead, determined to fight on the front line and leaving Luca to command the guard at their backs.

Hua's friend, Zhao, bent next to her, darting glances at her every chance he got. But Hua wasn't there, and only the Nagi looked back.

"What?" the Nagi hissed.

Zhao shrugged, his gaze turned to the consort who'd chosen to fight with them. "I am honored to fight at Hua Minglan's side once more."

A pang shot through the Nagi, but it wasn't her own. She swallowed, shoving Hua's thoughts away. She didn't respond, soaking in the stillness before battle, the calm before the chaos.

Horses thundered down the road, and the Nagi heard them before anyone else, but the sounds didn't come from an army. She guessed twenty or so men tried to outpace something, driving their horses at full gallop.

Shouts erupted through the field, and Jian lifted a hand in signal to the guards. They drew their bows, but no arrows loosed as one of the riders waved his arms, yelling to Jian.

Zhao cursed. "Chen." He pushed through the wheat to run toward the road. Jian yelled to him as he sprinted after him.

The Nagi straightened, moving closer.

Two of Hua's fellow soldiers led the tired looking force. Chen and Yan.

Chen yelled something to Jian no one could make out.

Yan's voice cut through the field. "We were trying to make it here before the attack."

"The Kou are coming." Chen's body jerked as soon as the words were out, and he slid sideways, tumbling from his horse, an arrow in his back.

Jian only stared for a moment before yelling to the riders to join the guard. He crouched low in the wheat, his voice the only thing telling of his presence. "Warriors, stay down. Do not reveal yourself."

The Nagi crept through the wheat until she reached Jian's side. The movement didn't belong to her, but she let Hua be the guide, and Hua wanted to fight with Jian.

"Low," Jian whispered. "Stay low."

The thunderous sound of hooves beating into the ground sounded like a storm trying to break over them.

And the Nagi saw him.

General Batukhan Altan rode atop a giant black stallion, his eyes cutting through the field as if he could see through the wheat to what lay in wait.

The Nagi had no vendetta against Altan, yet hatred burned through her. Hua's hatred. Piao's hatred. For just a moment, the Nagi felt as though the entire consciousness of Piao raced through her, making her heart skip a beat.

The Nagi readied her dao as she waited for the enemy to reach them, waited for them to slow. But they didn't. The Kou raced for the guards on their horses like prey calling to its predator. Wheat bent under the force of a thousand horses, trampled into the ground that had given it life.

The Nagi spared one glance for the guards, knowing the emperor and prince were hidden among them, ready to face the enemy with a bravery she hadn't expected.

"Wait," Jian commanded as the enemy neared. "Wait." He looked back over his shoulder at the gathered warriors. "If you should fall, I will see you in the next life."

And then he struck. He lunged forward, driving his dao up into the leg of the first man, knocking him from his horse while flipping his knife in his hand and sending it end over end into another.

With a battle cry, the rest of the hidden men sprang their trap, jumping to their feet to meet the nomadic warriors who were bigger, stronger, and more skilled. Piao fighters did not train for war their entire lives. They came from their fields and homes when the need arose.

Death was not their medium.

But on this day, they became death.

The Nagi whirled around to find Zhao at her back,

protecting her vulnerabilities as he fought with strength and power.

Nagi were solitary creatures, but there, on that battlefield as she sliced through another Kou warrior, she learned what it meant to not be alone.

Jian cut a path to her, his face pained every time he had to harm a horse instead of its rider. Together with Zhao, they formed three sides of a triangle, shifting to help each other remain standing, remain in this life.

Heat burned down the Nagi's arms as she called on her strength while the Kou streamed through the fields in a never-ending flow.

Bodies littered the ground, blood spattering over the once-golden wheat. Horses ran free, sprinting away from the ensuing battle and chaos.

"We have to keep going," Jian yelled to no one in particular as he looked to the army that was bigger than any they'd expected.

A Kou warrior ran for them, his dao aimed for Jian. Without thinking, the Nagi jumped in front of him, batting the dao away and spearing the enemy with her own.

The palace guard thundered into the battle, their horses crashing into those of the Kou. It provided a momentary distraction from what the Nagi already knew.

This battle had been doomed from the start.

"Hua," Jian yelled, his pleading eyes meeting the Nagi's.

"You have to keep him safe," Hua begged. *"Please."*

Jian ducked another attack before ramming the blunt edge of his dao into a Kou warrior, driving him down to his knees. "Hua." His turned to face the Nagi as Zhao covered his back. "We can't do this without you."

"No," Hua whispered in her mind. *"I can't do it."*

"You have to let go." He reached out, his thumb brushing the Nagi's—Hua's—cheek.

"I can't."

Jian couldn't hear Hua's words, but whatever he saw in her eyes made him press his lips to hers as the battle raged on around them. The Nagi felt the kiss in every cell, but not for the action itself. As Jian backed away to face another attacker, Hua's remaining control slipped away, sending energy through the Nagi, a burning, breathing energy.

"Don't hurt him." Hua's voice grew weak. *"I need you to promise..."*

And then she was gone. The Nagi searched her mind for her constant companion, finding only emptiness where Hua's presence had been.

There was no time to worry over her as the Nagi focused inward, letting heat sear through the heart that now fully belonged to her.

A scream rose up from the depths of her soul as muscles tore and stretched. Jian and Zhao fought with renewed vigor as the Nagi sucked in flaming hot breath, letting her body return to her true form.

In the place Hua Minglan once stood, a beast rose from the ashes of her soul, ready to fight.

The flap of giant wings ripped through the air as the dragon rose above the fray, surveying the army that had come to tear Piao apart.

Flashes of another battle came back to her, one where she had wanted to hurt Piao, to take her revenge.

But that was before.

Before she saw the lengths a single girl would go to for Piao's salvation.

Before she felt the connection between two people who gave up their own ideas of revenge.

Now, the fire building in her throat had a new purpose, protect the empire. There would be time for revenge when the battle was won.

Her scaled body twisted through the sky over the Kou army before barreling down on them, cutting through their ranks with a swath of fire. The screams of burning men echoed in the Nagi's mind as she turned to carve another path through, trying to avoid burning the horses if she could. There was a kinship between all beasts of burden.

That was what a Nagi was after all.

A vessel for the humans.

For centuries they protected Piao, and she had thought it was time for that tradition to end. But the Nagi would no longer punish the people of Piao for the deeds of a few men. People like Hua and Jian, Luca and Zhao.

Their hearts deserved to be preserved.

The Nagi spiraled through the sky like a winged serpent finally set free. The Kou foot soldiers scrambled out of the way of their burning comrades, causing the lines to break as they sprinted toward the fight.

And still, the Kou pushed the Piao warriors closer and closer to the northern gates of the city.

The Nagi circled above, catching sight of the vast Kou army below.

Something had to be done.

One man on the ground caught her eye. Bo Xu Wei, emperor of Piao, fought a man twice his size as another ran for them.

It happened in slow motion. Others saw them. Luca. Prince Duyi. They tried to fight their way to the man they loved above all else, but they wouldn't make it in time.

If the emperor died, the Nagi's mission would be complete, and he'd spare Hua the struggles of taking the man's life with her hands.

But rational thought flew from the Nagi's mind as she remembered the measured tone of the emperor offering his life if the Nagi helped Piao.

"Hua, I need you." But the Nagi hadn't ever needed anyone. *"Tell me the right path."*

She didn't respond.

Without thinking, the Nagi soared through the skies as the Kou warrior drove the emperor to his knees and prepared to strike one final time.

Gathering flames in her throat, the Nagi released them in a desperate burst, drawing a circle around the emperor before reaching out and pulling the burning Kou warrior into her grasp. The emperor lifted his chin, meeting the Nagi in an unflinching stare before the Nagi rose higher and higher, spiraling toward the clouds.

"You saved him." Relief washed through the Nagi as Hua's voice returned.

But that relief didn't last long as her muscles weakened, and she dropped the Kou warrior. The man sailed through the air, but by the time he hit the ground, he was already dead.

Energy receded from every cell, every scale of the dragon's form as pain seared through her, and she flipped through the air.

"What's happening?" She searched inward, needing Hua to give her the answers. Was she somehow taking control?

Those thoughts grew faint, and she couldn't hold them in her mind as the world went hazy, like a fog encompassing the earth.

She couldn't stop her descent as her wings drew in, folding back into her skin.

By the time the Nagi hit the earth, no scales covered her skin.

The last thought she had before retreating into darkness was that she had been wrong.

So very wrong.

CHAPTER 37

Hua

Heat.

That was the first thing Hua felt as the fire encroached upon her when she opened her eyes. The battle raged on around her, but a ring of fire protected her and one other from any who'd do them harm.

She blew out a breath as a shiver traveled up her spine. She thought she'd lost, that she'd finally faded from the Nagi's mind when she gave over that final control.

"Nagi!" someone yelled, but the clash of daos and the popping of the fire drowned out the rest of his words.

Flames licked her arm, and a searing pain traveled along her skin. Her eyes widened, and she sat up, pulling her arm in. The flames burned her. The pain was real.

"Nagi!" The other person trapped in the ring of flames scrambled toward her, and she met the emperor's panicked gaze. He tore off the robe covering his chain mail and jerked his arm toward her. It was only then Hua realized no clothes covered her body.

She yanked the robe over her head, thankful it fell almost to her ankles. But her armor... she didn't have any armor. Or weapons.

And they were locked in the flames. She reached out again before jerking her hand back as the fire scorched the air.

"It burned," she said.

The emperor took her hand, examining the red blister forming.

A smile curved her lips, and she repeated herself. "It burned."

An arrow sailed through the air, and she dove, tackling the emperor to the ground as it flew through the space they'd occupied moments before.

Hua searched her mind for another presence and only found herself.

"We have to get out of here." The emperor rolled to his feet. "You trapped us."

Hua shook her head, lifting her eyes to the smoky sky. "She saved you." She remembered it all. The Nagi saved the emperor, but now the beast was gone. "She completed her mission." The Nagi's mission had never been to kill the emperor, only save him.

Hua searched the ground near them. Just outside the fire, a Kou warrior lay dead, her eyes staring up at the sky. Reaching her arm through the flames, Hua gritted her teeth against the white hot pain. "Help!"

Together with the emperor, she dragged the warrior through the fire before kneeling to remove her leather armor.

"What are you doing?" The emperor tried to pull her back.

Hua slid a helmet onto her head, her eyes focused on the battle ensuing without her. "Piao is my home. It is time Hua Minglan joined this fight."

As a gust of wind blew through the fields, lowering the flames, Hua took a running start, leaping into the air to sail over the ring of fire.

As she landed on the other side and waited for the emperor to join her, she realized she was a prisoner to fire no more.

Because her mind and her heart were her own.

Hua jumped into the fight, joining Prince Duyi in keeping two Kou warriors at bay.

The Kou overwhelmed the Piao forces, and soon they'd breach the gates of the city.

Hua thought of her parents, Nainai… Ru, and it reinvigorated her. Wearing a dead enemy's armor and carrying weapons that were not her own, she fought with a renewed sense of everything she had to lose.

Everything she refused to give up.

For so long, her actions had not been her own. She'd done things she'd never forget, but she was in control now.

If she had to face her death, at least the end would belong only to her.

Duyi grinned as they fought, enjoying the fight in a way Hua didn't understand. She didn't want to kill the Kou warriors. She didn't want their families to mourn their deaths.

But she'd do anything to protect the people she cared about.

Yan and Zhao bulled through the Kou to get to her.

"It's you." Yan grinned as he twisted out of the way of an attack.

"How did you know?" Hua ducked low, cutting at a woman's legs.

Zhao knocked his man away, and for a moment, it was just the three of them feeling the absence of Chen. But there'd be time for mourning once this was through.

Yan finally answered her question. "Because no one fights like Hua Minglan. Not even a Nagi."

She didn't have a chance to think about what he said because Jian's voice cut through the fight. "They've reached the gates."

Her relief at knowing he was still alive was quickly replaced with fear. She scanned the remaining Piao forces as more and more Kou warriors pushed into the fray.

"Keep fighting!" she screamed to the surrounding soldiers. "Do not let them defeat you."

Jian's eyes snapped to her, and everything after that happened in slow motion. A Kou warrior took advantage of his momentary distraction, running for him. Jian didn't see him in time, but the prince did. Duyi jumped in front of Jian, blocking the first arc of the dao. The man's knife flashed as sunlight glinted off the blade before he swiped it at Duyi's stomach.

For a moment, as the prince stumbled back, Hua's heart rose into her throat. She couldn't breathe again until he righted himself.

Jian whirled around, killing the Kou man effortlessly before pushing Duyi behind him. The emperor sprinted through the battle to join them, and the hopelessness of this fight sank into Hua.

They could not defeat the Kou, not when the true Piao army lay dead in the Liudong Valley.

But then she saw the one thing she needed for her faith to return. Her father. He fought with a fierceness she'd never known he possessed. Even with his bad leg, he didn't stop. He couldn't.

Because if they did, everything would truly be lost.

Hua sucked in a breath as she joined her father and Luca, forming a barrier with them. Her father looked into her eyes for a brief moment before nodding in acknowledgement of her return, of her status as a warrior, worthy to stand and fight for her home.

They advanced on a cluster of Kou together, her father on her right, Jian and Luca on her left. The emperor joined them to form their final stand. If this was the end, they'd fight with everything they had.

Hua thought she imagined the sound at first, a horn ripping through the air. But then it sounded again, and she knew. Piao was about to lose the city.

They were about to lose everything.

Lifting her eyes to the horizon, she caught sight of a single rider sitting atop a lonely hill.

But then, even louder than the horn.

The flap of giant wings.

Rising over the stranger was a black dragon, so large his shadow blocked the sun when it fell over Hua.

Reinforcements had indeed come.

For Piao.

CHAPTER 38

Jian

Chaos.

It was Piao's best friend.

The Kou warriors they'd been fighting stared to the skies as the beast circled overhead, joined by the remaining Piao warriors who didn't yet know this dragon was on their side.

Jian met Hua's eyes, seeing the emotions swirling in his chest mirrored back at him.

His lips tipped into a grin as he lifted his voice. "Hold the lines." His smile widened. "It's on our side."

A single rider thundered toward them, cutting his way

through the Kou in his path. Jian raised his dao in greeting, because Master Delun hadn't come alone. Khenbish fought with a ferocity rarely seen. But he didn't only come for the people of Piao. Jian spared a quick thought for the camp of Kou in the mountains.

They too wanted to save their empire from Batukhan Altan.

This Kou warrior was on their side, and he was a sight to behold.

Jian turned to jump into the fight once more, searching for Altan himself.

He had yet to see the general as he'd fought to stay alive, but as he turned toward Khenbish once more, he caught sight of the man who'd haunted his waking hours. There was a time Jian wanted nothing more than revenge on the general sitting atop his horse at the edge of the battle.

And now? He couldn't make himself move from Hua's side, not when he finally saw life in her eyes, not when she'd come back to him. In armor that wasn't her own and clothing belonging to his brother, her appearance told little of the true story of Hua Minglan.

Hair hung in her face as she turned to battle a Kou woman. Speckles of blood dotted her pale skin, and he couldn't help glancing over his shoulder as her skill took over, her drive.

She was a true warrior.

Heat blasted through the air as Master Delun unleashed his fire, separating the larger part of Altan's army from the remaining bedraggled Piao men.

A cheer wound through the warriors as elation replaced the fear in their eyes.

Jian whipped his head around as Master Delun swooped low.

"The Nagi have finally come to protect Piao." Gen Minglan wiped sweat from his brow.

Jian couldn't take his eyes from the beast the stories said was always meant to protect Piao. Just like the Nagi inside Hua he'd fought to defeat.

An arrow sailed through the fight, and Jian's eyes tracked it for what seemed like a moment stretched into eternity as it carved a path through his heart right toward Hua. He didn't move fast enough, knowing it couldn't hurt her, not while the Nagi lived inside her.

So, why did her cry echo in his mind? Why did she stumble forward, her face twisting in agony? Why was there an arrow shaft protruding from her arm?

"Hua." His eyes widened as he reached for her, catching her against him. Blood seeped out past the arrowhead.

Her father and Luca created a protective circled around them, soon joined by Yan and Zhao, their daos ready to keep Hua safe at all costs.

"Jian." She lifted her blood-spattered face, meeting his gaze.

In that moment, he knew. The arrow. The burn snaking down her arm. The clarity in her eyes.

Hua was back, fully and completely.

And now he might lose her again.

"Jian." A voice roared over the din of battle as General Altan charged through the fire atop his muscled steed.

Jian looked from the fading light in Hua's eyes to the man he'd once sought despite the consequences. This was the moment he'd waited years for, the fight he'd wanted.

"Fight me!" Altan yelled, sliding down from his horse, his boots pounding into the earth.

Jian looked behind him where Altan's forces had started retreating across the fields, horses and footman stampeding through the high wheat as fire rained down on them.

"It's okay, Jian," Hua whispered. "You need to fight him. It is the only thing that will bring you peace."

Jian's jaw clenched as the desire for revenge he'd once had came back in full force.

Hua went limp in his arms, and he realized the act of killing Batukhan Altan held no promise of peace. "I need to save her." He was the commander in this fight, but none of this would have any meaning without Hua. Piao would have fallen if not for her, and he'd be dead on this field.

"Luca." He looked to his friend. "I need a horse."

Luca pointed his dao at Altan. "He has one." Almost as one, their friends approached Altan, their weapons ready.

"Are you a coward, Jian?" Altan yelled. "Sending your men to fight me?"

Jian gathered Hua into his arms, ignoring the psychotic yells of the man who'd controlled so much of his life.

Before he could reach the horse, large scaled black feet slammed into the ground and serpent-eyes settled on Jian, communicating without words.

Knowing it was the only way to get Hua into the city quickly enough, Jian nodded, trusting Hua to the beast before him. Master Delun wrapped long claws around Hua's body, taking her from Jian before lifting into the air.

Jian settled his gaze on General Altan. Around them, the battle had waned with Altan's remaining forces either dead or fleeing from Dasha altogether. Master Delun had made masterful work of defeating them.

"Don't kill him." Jian couldn't believe the words coming from his own voice. "Batukhan Altan, you are now a prisoner of Piao."

It wasn't until he stood face to face with the man who'd altered the course of his life he realized Altan wasn't his to kill. This was the end to someone else's story, not Jian's.

He turned away, his eyes locking with those of a familiar horse. Most of the horses had either fled from the dragons or were dead, but not Heima. She'd been the only horse Jian trusted to carry Piao's future, to protect his brother.

Panic gripped his chest as he realized he hadn't seen Bo or Duyi in too long. As Luca disarmed and arrested Altan, Jian ran through the remains of battle, staring into the faces of Piao men who'd died protecting their homes.

"Bo!" he yelled.

He slammed into someone who'd been running in the other direction, sending him stumbling back over a body. Duyi's eyes lifted to Jian's. "I can't find him." His breath came fast. "Bo and I were fighting side by side and then..."

"Bo," Jian yelled again.

With Duyi by his side, he stumbled on tired legs through the smoky remains of fire and death.

When he caught sight of Bo's prone form, his heart stopped beating in his chest. Duyi dropped by their brother's side, checking for injury.

Jian watched with bated breath until a cough racked Bo's body, and his eyes slid open. He continued coughing as Duyi threw himself over him. "You're alive."

"Yes," Bo wheezed. "Took a heavy hit, though."

Jian finally breathed again, but his heart didn't mend. It wouldn't until he made it to the city. A nose nudged his shoulder, and he reached up to wipe soot from Heima's mane. "One last desperate ride, girl?" He met Bo's gaze once more. "Are you okay?"

Bo nodded.

Jian pulled himself onto Heima and nudged her around. He didn't need to direct her or dig in his heels to send her into a gallop. It was like Heima could sense Hua, and it wasn't the first time he'd gotten that impression.

The northern gates opened as they neared, and Heima thundered through the streets of Dasha until they caught sight of Master Delun in his human form pacing outside the healer's shop. Jian pulled Heima to a stop and jumped down.

"How is she?"

Master Delun stopped his pacing to face Jian. "I do not know."

Jian ran by him, forcing his way into the healer's shop and past the sleeping Commander Yang. Healer Liqin bent over the cot where Hua lay on her stomach. He'd removed her armor and cut away part of her shirt. A flush crept up Jian's neck, but he was too worried to look away. "Will she live?"

Healer Liqin carefully removed the arrow without looking at Jian. Blood seeped from the wound as he applied herbs to it.

Hua's eyes fluttered open, and she turned her head, pain clouding her gaze. Her lips formed his name, but no sound escaped.

Jian rushed toward the bed, but a cutting look from the healer kept him back. "She will be fine." He worked to bandage her shoulder, his fingers grazing over her skin with a delicate touch.

And that was how Jian's life started again, with those words.

Healer Liqin asked questions about the battle and said something about leaving to treat the wounded beyond the gate, but all Jian could hear was the sound of Hua's breathing, telling him she was still there.

Finally, the healer stepped away. "I am needed on the battlefield with the city's other healers."

"Take my horse." Jian didn't take his eyes from Hua. "Heima will get you there faster than any other."

Healer Liqin issued a thanks before leaving.

The door burst open, and Master Delun ran in. "She'll live?"

Jian only nodded as he knelt on the floor and brushed the hair out of her face.

"Dear girl." Master Delun met her gaze. "Your Nagi is gone, isn't it?"

Hua managed a nod, confirming Jian's suspicions. Without the Nagi, arrows and fire could harm this beautiful woman.

Sadness swept across Master Delun's face, a sadness Jian didn't understand. With a simple nod, he turned and left them alone.

Jian didn't have a thought to spare for the old man as he pressed his forehead to Hua's. "You aren't allowed to leave me. Not again, Hua. It's you and me now, and I never have to see something else control you again."

A tear tracked down her cheek, streaking through the

blood, reminding them of what this day held. "Jian," she whispered. "So much bad."

"What?"

"I did…" She closed her eyes. "So much."

He shook his head. "It wasn't you, do you hear me?"

"But I—"

"No. Hua." He took her hand in his. "These hands are clean of all evil. You are good, Hua. You protected all of us."

A small smile curved her lips. "I love—"

He didn't hear the rest of those words because her eyes slid closed. Panic gripped him for a moment before he realized she'd only fallen asleep, that she would wake again to give him one of those rare, heartbreaking smiles.

"It's over, Hua," he whispered, sitting back on his heels. "We did it."

CHAPTER 39

Hua

The days following the battle were a whirlwind of activity. Jian had Hua moved to the palace into a room more lavish than she'd ever seen before. The city mourned the lost even as it celebrated the fact Piao was still standing and the return of a dragon to protect them.

Hua's mother and Nainai were constant companions while she remained in bed recovering from her injury. Every time Jian came by, they refused to leave her alone with him. Suddenly, after everything, their sense of propriety had returned.

Hua had lived in an army camp full of men, she'd fought in numerous battles and had lived with a Nagi inside her, but spending time with an unmarried man was somehow not right.

She'd have fought them on it if she wasn't so relieved to be with them all. When Ru wasn't following Jian or Bo around, he came in and jumped on Hua's bed, jostling her and sending pain right through her shoulder. But she didn't mind if it meant she got to see him every day.

A new dawn had risen in Piao, one with the Kou as allies instead of enemies. She'd gathered bits of what was happening. A man named Khenbish had arrived with Master Delun. He led a group of Kou in the mountains who'd been fighting against Altan's rise to power for many years. There hadn't been time for their army to come, but he flew with the dragon. These Kou now controlled Koulland and believed in more than fighting their neighbors to the south.

Peace was not something Piao had experienced in a long time, and it was only possible because of two Nagi.

Hua pressed a hand to her heart. *"Thank you."*

There was no response, but she hadn't expected one. The Nagi was truly gone.

"Hua." The door to her room burst open, and Ru ran in. "More people are arriving."

"What do you mean, Ru?" She pushed herself up, ignoring the pain in her shoulder.

"The shopkeepers sent wagons days ago to the Liudong Valley. The people of Dasha brought the injured here."

Hua couldn't lay in bed another day. She swung her legs over the side, needing to see for herself. The Kou decimated Commander Yang's forces before marching on Dasha. She'd assumed the Piao soldiers who'd arrived with Chen and Yan were all that was left. "Show me where they are." She looked to the settee where her mother had fallen asleep, knowing she wouldn't approve.

Ru only grinned.

When they stepped into the hall, Chichi ran for them, but Ru stepped between her and the dog, quelling the excitement.

They wound through the busy palace. Hua didn't recognize anyone they passed until they reached the entryway where Yan and Zhao rushed through the door. She followed them out, and they smiled when they saw her, but there was something missing.

Chen.

Their fourth. Without him, they weren't complete.

A lot of people had been lost in the battle, but that one stung the most.

People crowded the steps to watch the train of wagons enter the square. Even Empress Yanyu and the consorts joined them. Hua watched Zhao's gaze travel to the consorts and the one who was missing.

Lihua had been injured in the fight. She'd live, but she'd never be free of the scars marring her once-beautiful face. No one had seen her publicly since.

When the emperor stepped from the palace to stand among the columns, a hush overtook them.

The wagons circled before finally coming to a stop. Healer Liqin and his counterparts ran forward to care for the wounded soldiers.

Hua barely saw them because her gaze fixed on a familiar

woman. The emperor was the first to move, ushering his people down the steps to help the injured.

Hua waited for Qara to see her, to tell her what would happen now that she was just Hua Minglan again, no greater purpose.

But Qara approached Master Delun instead, and the two of them walked across the square. Hua ran after them. Neither seemed surprised when she fell in step beside them.

"When a Nagi fulfills their mission, it is a time to rejoice." Qara's voice was soft. She made no mention of either battle they'd been through or the days since. "But two… that was surely a sight to see."

"Two?" Hua couldn't breathe as her eyes flicked from Master Delun to Qara.

Master Delun smiled sadly. "My Nagi was with me for many decades. It seems it was waiting for the moment it could come to Piao's rescue."

"Not just any moment." Qara met his gaze. "That specific one. A Nagi's fate is written before it is born. If you'd come to Piao's aid in any other fight, it would not have fulfilled the mission." She turned to Hua. "And yours, Hua, was meant to save the emperor. Bo Xu Wei is the only man who can bring Piao into a peaceful future. I have only ever known of one other Nagi to walk this earth in the last one hundred years. It was put here to save a young boy, a task that could set that boy on the path that lead to this future."

Master Delun was quiet for a moment. "Me. It was me. I was taken in by a girl before the Nagi came to me. She saved my life and then disappeared. I searched for her for years after that."

Hua couldn't comprehend everything they were saying. She'd heard the story of the Nagi saving the boy before.

Qara went on. "And in saving you, she made sure you were around to welcome in a Nagi, guide Hua when she came to you, and finally complete your mission by coming to Piao's aid."

"And I wouldn't have been in Dasha to save the emperor if Master Delun's Nagi hadn't convinced mine it could take complete control." It all made so much sense now. She gripped Master Delun's arm. "You must come with me. I need you to meet someone."

Master Delun didn't question her. Instead, he followed her with trust as they left Qara to aid the healers. Hua's eyes found the person she needed, the one who'd been through more than her family had ever known.

Hua always felt a connection to her Nainai, and she knew why now. They shared a sacred bond, an experience no others could claim—except the man at her side.

"Nainai," she called. "I need you."

Nainai smiled upon seeing her, but then froze. "Niu?" She put a hand to her chest. "It's been many years, but I would recognize those eyes anywhere."

"Jie." His eyes widened as he looked from Hua to her nainai. "I..."

"She saved your life, didn't she?" Hua wanted more than anything for her suspicions to ring true.

Master Delun swallowed and nodded. "Before the Nagi, my name was Niu Delun, and I was a simple boy. Jie found me after I'd been beaten and left alongside the road. I thought I was going to die."

And with that simple act, Hua's nainai saved Piao with just a small kindness.

Hua left them to their reunion as her shoulder started to ache. She'd left the herbs that helped the pain in her room, but she wasn't ready to go back to the solitude yet, not when the activity in the city was so different from days ago.

Gone was the gloom of impending battle. Now, a different future lay before them.

She just wished others were here to see it. Before she knew where she was going, she'd found her way to the pillars she'd hidden behind with Luna in the moments before her sister's death. Tears gathered in her eyes, and she didn't hold them back as she slid down a pillar to lean against it.

"You would not believe what has happened since you entered your next life, Luna." She looked toward the sky. "I know you can't hear me because you are probably living another grand adventure, one I'll join you on someday, but I wish you could see us now." The killings of dragon blooded by the emperor had stopped the moment Bo Xu Wei came to power, but Hua knew it would take longer for the people to accept. They'd hear what happened this day and fear a return of dragons once more.

Changing the hearts and minds of men and woman wouldn't happen overnight. The dragon blooded would remain hidden from their neighbors to avoid persecution.

The people's fears of what happened in Kanyuan would override what happened here in Dasha.

Hua sighed and leaned her head back against the pillar. "I'll protect them, Luna. For you."

"I talk to her too." A voice intruded on the moment, and

Hua shifted her eyes to the emperor of Piao who stood nearby with his eyes downcast.

She didn't know what to say to him. The Nagi saved him in battle, but she couldn't forget the deal he'd made with both her and the Nagi.

He'd been willing to let her kill him.

As if he was thinking the same thing, he dropped to one knee and bowed his head. "You saved my empire."

Hua stared at him, an emperor on his knees. Again.

"We had a deal. I willingly give my life to you."

Hua's heart leapt into her throat, and she didn't speak for a long moment before getting to her feet. "You told the Nagi you'd let her kill you in exchange for her aid, but your Majesty, she saved you instead. The Nagi is gone."

His eyes snapped to hers. "Gone?"

"Her mission was never to destroy the empire, but to save it, to save you. The deal you made was never her purpose."

"Deal?" A new voice entered the conversation, and Hua stepped back as Jian appeared, a scowl marring his features.

Bo sighed and got to his feet, exhaustion more than relief flashing across his face. "Jian—"

"What deal?" Jian growled.

Hua wrung her hands together as the ache in her shoulder intensified. "I was supposed to kill the emperor."

CHAPTER 40

Jian

"No." Jian turned on his heel and walked away from the two people he loved most in this world.

The two people who'd kept a painful secret from him.

If the Nagi hadn't left, she would have killed Bo. And the worst part? Bo would have let her.

He glanced toward the healers taking care of the injured with the aid of shopkeepers, tired soldiers, and even the consorts. Dasha had come together in this time of need, but all Jian could think of was the night before the battle with

Hua. Why hadn't she told him of the plan the Nagi and Bo had devised?

He rubbed a hand along the back of his neck, forgetting entirely why he'd followed Bo toward the pillars after speaking to Khenbish. Hua's family had been keeping her mostly in confinement as she healed, and he'd needed to see her, to hear her voice.

To know it truly was her.

And now… Footsteps sounded against the stone as he reached the bottom of the marble steps. "Wait!" He turned to find Hua running after him, pain flashing across her face with each step.

"Slow down. You'll only injure yourself further."

"I don't care." She stopped in front of him, panting. "You don't get to just walk away from me."

"I need time, Hua."

"Well, I'm not going to give it to you. Your brother and the Nagi made a deal. If the Nagi helped Piao in the battle, the emperor would not stop her from killing him. That was the only thing that could bring the Nagi onto Piao's side when all she wanted was revenge."

"And you? Why didn't you tell me?"

An apology shone in her eyes. "I promised your brother I wouldn't. I'm sorry, Jian, but this wasn't your decision to make. Just like it wasn't your choice when I tried to sacrifice myself. You may be a commander once more, but you do not get to control us." Her chest heaved with the words.

"I—"

"No." She stepped closer. "I'm not done. I have spent the last few days in bed with nothing but time to contemplate how close we came to losing everything. And I won't do this again."

"Do what?"

"Sacrifice everything. We don't need to. Jian, I lied to you."

His brow scrunched.

"I can't keep myself from loving you." A tear escaped her eye. "I have done so much evil. Destroyed cities. Killed sleeping allies. Lied to everyone."

He tried to speak, to tell her once again none of that was her, but she put a hand up.

"I know it wasn't me, but I still felt every action. I felt the satisfaction the Nagi derived from them, the cold calculation in her mind. I don't want to be cold. I don't want those memories to overwhelm the good. I—"

He slammed his lips into hers, cutting off her final words and stealing the breath from her lungs. With her injured shoulder, she could only slide one arm around him, but it was enough to know this was right, true. Everything they'd fought for, every struggle they'd faced had been for this moment.

The moment they got everything they'd dreamed of.

Commander Yang was able to leave the healer a few days later with the help of some of his soldiers. Yan rarely left his side, and Jian wondered if he needed to keep himself busy after Chen's death. He wished he could take the pain from Dasha and wipe the city clean of blood, but too many people had been lost.

After avoiding Bo for too long, Jian sought him out in the palace courtyard where he sat side by side with Luca.

Luca grinned when he caught sight of Jian, but Bo's reaction was more reserved.

Jian sat on the bench beside the two men who'd once been Jian's only family.

After a few moments of silence, Bo sighed. "I know you don't understand."

That was the thing. Jian *did* understand, but it didn't make it easier. "I love you, Bo. I just need you to know that. And Piao needs you now more than ever."

Bo was quiet for a long moment. "I've always loved you, brother."

Even when the rest of the palace had nothing but scorn for the bastard son of a consort, Bo had loved him. Just like Luca.

Luca bumped Jian's shoulder. "So, my betrothal is broken, isn't it?"

A smile slid across Jian's lips. "I sure hope so."

Luca laughed. "It was an interesting conversation with my father when he asked why he saw Hua kissing you. Then Song told him you deserved Hua more than I did. I always knew she liked you better than me."

Jian smiled at the thought of Luca's family. They'd returned to their home, thankful Song's husband was among the injured who arrived from the Liudong Valley. "You didn't want to marry Hua, anyway."

"No. But I would have. And I think we'd have been content."

"Is content all that matters?" Jian fixed both men with a stare. "Shouldn't we strive for happy? For fulfilled?"

Luca laughed. "For most in Piao, that is just a dream."

But did it have to be? "A new age has come to Piao." Jian stood. "Maybe it's time for a new way of life." He stood and put a hand on each of their shoulders. "Wherever I go, you two will forever be my family."

Bo looked up at him with glassy eyes. "That means you're not staying, doesn't it? You won't continue to command my army?"

Jian shook his head as he saw a new future before him. "I think I'm due for a quiet life now."

His brother nodded. "Be happy, Jian."

"You too, Bo." He met Bo's eyes, trying to communicate with just a look, before tearing himself away from his two brothers and walking from the courtyard without looking back.

Jian pulled Hua in close to his side as they stood in the crowded square waiting to hear the emperor speak. Gen and Fa Minglan readied Heima, hitching her to the small wagon Bo had given them for the journey.

Nainai put a hand on Hua's shoulder as Ru bent to wrap his arms around Chichi. In a few moments, they'd leave Dasha behind, but not before hearing Bo's victory address.

Jian could imagine what he'd say. They'd won. Dasha had pulled together.

The empire would support the families of the lost.

But as Bo walked to the top of the steps, Jian knew this was a moment Piao would never forget.

"People of Piao." Bo raised his arms, starting with all the

things Jian had known he'd say. Finally, he looked to the future. "The path before Piao is one of peace, and if we are to hold it in our grasps, we must change the way we live our lives. Someone I love very much told me we can't live to be content. It is time all of those in Piao strive for more, and that starts with me. Which is why I have chosen today to name my heir."

A gasp wound through the crowd. Bo had no children.

He continued. "It has become obvious to me who has the mandate of heaven to rule after me and to carry on the Wei dynasty. This boy fought beside us all in the recent battle, he has shown himself to have unmatched bravery and kindness, a combination that cannot be ignored."

Bo gestured to a surprised looking Duyi. "Join me, didi." Duyi walked forward with tentative steps, and Bo grasped his hand. "I cannot have children, but my brother will carry on once I am gone."

Jian stilled. Bo couldn't have children? The crowd shouted questions, but Bo only nodded to Duyi. In his next breath, he brought the traditions of Piao tumbling to the ground. "I will no longer keep consorts in this palace. The three honorable ladies who have served me will be taken care of, but I have no more need of such a practice."

The consorts, unlike Duyi, looked like they'd been told in advance. Smiles graced each of their faces. Lihua, making her first appearance with a scar stretching across her cheek, rushed down the steps, pushing through the crowd. She flung herself into the arms of a shocked Zhao.

Bo was still talking, and Jian looked back to him, his heart pounding in his chest as Bo changed Piao forever.

"I have chosen to marry."

The words shocked Jian more than any other until he saw Luca go completely still in his place behind Bo.

Bo didn't seem to notice as he pushed on, but Jian saw where this was going. Bo said he couldn't have kids. He chose someone else to carry on the dynasty and disbanded the harem.

A smile overtook Jian's face as Hua gasped. "Is he…"

Bo turned to Luca finally. "I guess I should make sure it's okay with him."

Luca's face paled. Jian had watched his brother and his best friend dance around their feelings for each other most of their lives. Neither of them had understood what it meant, only that acting on those feelings wasn't a possibility for them.

Until now.

In the aftermath of a great victory, Piao would give Bo whatever he wanted.

And what he wanted was Luca.

Luca didn't react at first, but slowly, tentatively, he nodded. Joy lit up Bo from the inside out, and he pressed a kiss to the stunned Luca as the crowd murmured in surprise before erupting into cheers.

Master Delun stepped up beside Nainai and kissed her cheek. Their reunion had obviously gone well. "It seems everything is as it needs to be."

Jian bent to skim Hua's ear with his lips. "Yes. It is."

CHAPTER 41

Hua

Hua had never taken the chance to marvel at the beauty of the landscape she'd seen her entire life. On the outskirts of Zhouchang, the fields rolled as far as anyone could see with creek beds crisscrossing from the hills to the trees.

She lifted her face to the sun warming the morning, thankful to be past the winter chills. Soon, it would be time to plant the crops, but until then, the Minglans focused on rebuilding their lives. When they'd returned from Dasha a few months before, the only structure still intact on their land was the barn.

In the back of her mind, she remembered the fire that took her family's home. She remembered the flames waking her as they licked along her skin, the heat soaking into her every pour. But that time was still hazy to her, as though it had happened to someone else.

She supposed it had.

"Where are you?" she whispered, knowing the Nagi wouldn't be able to hear her. No one in Piao—not even Qara—had known where the Nagi went when they left. It was another great mystery of life.

"What are you searching for?" Jian wrapped his arms around her from behind.

Hua smiled, but she didn't shift her eyes from the hills before her as she stood along the tree line. "Nothing."

He pressed a kiss to the side of her head. "That's not a nothing face."

She turned in his arms, and he didn't release his hold on her. "I don't need to search for anything. Not anymore."

When she'd left home the first time, there were grand adventures awaiting her, answers she needed to find. But now, as she looked into the eyes of the only answer she'd ever needed, she knew the adventures that mattered now were right here.

He fit his smile to hers, kissing her slowly like they had all the time in the world. She supposed they did. "There has been news from Dasha."

She pulled back in surprise. They hadn't heard from the emperor or Luca since returning to Zhouchang. The two men had an entire empire to convince of the changes coming to Piao. Hua and Jian were the two people they'd never needed to persuade.

"Good news, I hope."

He shrugged. "I didn't want to open the message without you."

Her arms slid up around his neck to pull his face back down to her for a kiss.

"Hua Minglan!" Fa Minglan's sharp voice cut through their happy moment as she charged toward them.

Hua pulled away from Jian to face her mama. She opened her mouth to speak but her mama cut her off.

"Where have you been all morning? While your father works, you two wander off." Her cutting glare snapped to Jian. "Do you wish to be lazy?"

"No, ma'am." Jian suppressed a grin—poorly.

"Do you wish to cause dishonor to my daughter?"

His face sobered. "Of course not."

She nodded. "Then if you two insist on going off on your own, you will marry."

Hua's jaw fell open. Marry? It wasn't the first time her mama told her she had to wed, and she wanted Jian to be hers forever, but that wasn't the issue. "Mama, when we marry, it will be our decision, not based on antiquated proprieties. You worry about us being alone together now, but you do realize I lived in a camp with only men, right?"

Her mama's face paled.

Hua walked past her with a laugh. "I think I can handle kissing the man I love." She held out a hand for Jian to join her, and he jogged forward, wrapping his fingers around hers, unable to even look at her mama.

Mama followed at a distance, her arms crossed over her chest in disapproval.

Jian leaned in, his breath warming Hua's ear. "You said when."

"What?"

"I never thought I'd ever get married, Hua. I was the bastard son of an executed consort, so I became what everyone expected of me. Bitter. Strong, but bitter. I gave my life to the army, searching for something to give it worth."

"Did you find it?"

He nodded. "The day Huan Minglan walked into my camp." He sighed. "I don't want to be that man anymore."

Hua wrapped an arm around his waist. "You can't change where you come from, Jian. But I don't believe for one moment you've ever truly been that man."

"Then who am I?"

They reached the clearing where her baba and Jian had been rebuilding the house with the help of some villagers. She caught sight of Nainai in the half-planted gardens. Ru and Chichi ran through the yard, Ru's peals of laughter bringing a sense of joy to the scene.

Baba poked his head out of one of the windows and smiled when he saw them. Mama passed them to reach the gardens.

Hua released Jian and gestured to the setting before them. It was a scene Luna would have loved, so Hua would love it for her. "You're one of us."

Jian's eyes glassed over as he smiled.

"You have a family now, Jian." It was something she knew he'd always dreamed of, the fantasies of an unwanted boy, a soldier who spent his life in army camps or on the move. "You have a home."

A giant bird flew overhead, its flap of wings a reminder of the dragons that brought them here, that gave them peace.

Hua ruffled Ru's hair as she passed him to enter the house. It wouldn't be finished for quite some time, but it was livable. In time, they'd build a second home for Hua and Jian. Because whatever he thought of himself, they were always meant to be husband and wife.

She stopped when she caught sight of the elderly man sitting at the simple wooden table, a teacup before him. In the next chair was a child Hua never thought she'd see again.

Boqin looked at her, his face brightening.

"Master Delun." Hua bowed as the old man's eyes found her. "I did not know you were here."

Jian walked in behind her. "Didn't I say that? Master Delun intercepted the Dasha messenger on the road and offered to bring the message himself."

Hua glared at him, annoyed he kept such a thing from her. Master Delun was the only person other than Nainai who could possibly understand the ache in her chest, the emptiness that had once been filled by another presence, her reasons for continuing to talk to the Nagi.

"Dearest Hua." Master Delun stood and bowed his head. He picked up a scroll from the table and held it out to her.

Hua untied the twine holding it together and let her eyes scan the page. A gasp escaped her as her fingers trembled.

"What is it?" Jian took the scroll from her, and she saw the moment he finished reading because the paper tumbled from his hands, floating to the ground. No one moved to pick it up.

"He's dead," Jian whispered, dropping into Master Delun's vacated seat.

It was over, truly over. General Batukhan Altan had been executed weeks before. The man both Hua and Jian had sought revenge on, the one drawing them into the fight was gone, and neither of them had been there. Their revenge was taken by the executioner's hands.

Hua pushed out a breath and put a hand on Jian's shoulder. "He's gone." She closed her eyes, issuing a prayer to the heavens.

That wasn't all the message said. The emperor left Altan's fate up to his sister. Qara chose this path, his execution, a path that could finally let Piao heal.

Hua looked to Master Delun. "Your people will rejoice. Batukhan Altan is dead."

Sadness entered his gaze. "Death is never something to rejoice. But they are not my people. I do not wish to lead them. The Kou now have a new future in front of them, and I have never been one of them. Now that I am alone in my mind, my place is in Piao." He put a hand on the young boy's shoulder. "Our place." His eyes searched the room.

"Are you looking for something?" Hua turned to see what he could be viewing. Through the window, she saw her nainai gently tending to flowers. She hummed as she worked, the sound twisting through the air. Understanding clicked in Hua. "You have come for her."

The girl who'd saved him all those years ago, the one who'd disappeared.

Hua laughed. "Go to her."

Master Delun gave her a shy smile before walking out the door, Boqin following behind. It seemed the Minglan land would soon be welcoming more residents, more members into the family.

Once alone again, Hua leaned down and wrapped her arms around Jian. "Did his death bring you peace?" They both knew who she was talking about.

Jian was silent for a moment. "There is no peace in revenge."

"But there is in love."

He looked back at her over his shoulder. "Yes. In love, there is everything."

Master Delun didn't leave. Instead, he and Boqin became part of the family. The living quarters were crowded until they could build another house on the land, but none of them minded. After being separated for so long, they enjoyed the closeness.

Days of hard work, work that had a purpose.

Dinners around the simple table filled with laughter.

Games played by candlelight.

It wasn't until a few weeks later that another visitor arrived at their door. She was young, probably around Hua's age, and a bruise stretched down the side of her face.

Hua ushered the stranger inside. The girl walked with a limp. Something awful had obviously happened to her.

"What is your name?"

"Chun Huang." She hung her head, unable to look Hua in the eyes.

Hua busied herself with the kettle, pouring two cups of tea. "What happened to you, Chun?"

It took a long moment for the girl to answer. "I'm from a

village a day's ride from here. They..." She sucked in a rattling breath. "They found out what I am."

"And what are you?"

The girl finally met Hua's eyes. "I am of the dragon blood."

Something inside Hua deflated. "But the emperor has stopped persecution of the blooded."

She shook her head. "He has stopped the crown's persecution of us, but in the villages, it is still very much a way of life."

"That is why you've come here." Hua handed her the tea. "You came for me?"

Chun nodded as tears came to her eyes. "They killed my brother. I did not know where else to go. And I am not the only one. There are stories traveling through the villages of the blooded fighting for their lives."

How could Hua have assumed peace would be so easy to achieve? A decree from the emperor couldn't erase centuries of fear ingrained in the people. Chun shook with sobs, and Hua listened to her talk about the attack and all the other horrible things she'd seen.

These people were Hua's.

And even two Nagi saving Piao didn't change their hearts.

She didn't know how long she sat with her visitor before the girl curled up on the settee and fell fast asleep.

A new fire burned within Hua, one that was entirely her own. She walked outside, ignoring Baba's call of greeting to her as she marched to where Master Delun helped Jian begin the foundation for a second home.

Heat blazed along her skin, having nothing to do with a

Nagi inside. She was angry. This empire was still hunting the blooded, and they had no one to protect them. Except her.

"I want to fight for them." As soon as the words were out, she couldn't call them back.

Both Master Delun and Jian stopped working to look at her.

"The blooded are still being persecuted." She pointed back to the house. "There is a girl asleep inside right now who lost her brother because of this. And she came here believing I could help her."

"Hua—" Jian started.

Hua cut him off. "I have to do this. I'm supposed to protect them. I know it. This is my purpose. You can't tell me otherwise."

Master Delun nodded, pride glowing on his face. "You are their hope, Hua Minglan."

Jian lifted a brow. "I was only going to tell you to take Heima with you. She could use some excitement."

The emptiness Hua had felt since the Nagi left filled, a purpose once again settling on her shoulders.

This was why the Nagi chose her.

Because Hua Minglan was meant to protect Piao in any way she could.

Right now, that started with the blooded.

And Jian believed in her, in her need to do this. She matched his smile, knowing this was only the beginning.

ABOUT M. LYNN

M. Lynn is a USA Today bestselling author of love. Yes, love. Whether it be YA romance (Under Michelle MacQueen), NA romance, or fantasy romance, she loves to make readers swoon.

The great loves of her life to this point are two tiny blond creatures who call her "aunt" and proclaim her books to be "boring books" for their lack of pictures. Yet, somehow, she still manages to love them more than chocolate.

When she's not sharing her inexhaustible wisdom with her niece and nephew, Michelle is usually lounging in her ridiculously large bean bag chair creating worlds and characters that remind her to smile every day - even when a feisty five-year-old is telling her just how much she doesn't know.

See more from Michelle MacQueen and sign up to receive updates and deals!

www.michellelynnauthor.com

ALSO BY M. LYNN

Queens of the Fae

Fae's Deception

Fae's Defiance

Fae's Destruction

Fae's Prisoner

Fae's Power

Fae's Promise

The Hidden Warrior

Dragon Rising

Dragon Rebellion

Fantasy and Fairytales

Golden Curse

Golden Chains

Golden Crown

Glass Kingdom

Glass Princess

Noble Thief

Cursed Beauty

Legacy of Light

A War For Magic

A War For Truth

A War For Love

www.ingramcontent.com/pod-product-compliance
Lightning Source LLC
Chambersburg PA
CBHW030526310726
48979CB00010B/1811/J

9781970052732